Lu.

BETH TROY

This book was published in 2017 by Kingsbury Publishing., LLC
29 N. Beech Street, Oxford, OH 45056, USA
www.kingsburypublishing.com

Cover Design: Emily Perry

Author Photograph: Jeane Johnson

ISBN-13: 978-1548131463
ISBN-10: 1548131466

For the girls who are looking but still haven't found—this one's for you

CHAPTER 1

All the stories have been written, including mine.

This thought crowded out all others as a delivery truck pulled in front of me, curbing my speed to 40 miles per hour. I hadn't driven this road in awhile, but I remembered it enough to know that when this truck turned another would take its place. Plus, I knew where the road ended.

So I settled in, my back to the seat, my head to the headrest—slowly, gingerly, like a whisper, so the car wouldn't know. It was an '85 Cutlass that had defied life expectancy, but not without fallout. I no longer had a driver's side window. The car swallowed it whole when I'd stopped for gas at two in the morning. I was nervous the driver's seat was next.

"Twenty minutes," I reassured the car with a pat to the dashboard. "Enjoy the view."

The coral sunrise stretched over acres of crowded cornfields. The two-lane road meandered around them like a river, as if its engineers had prioritized scenic enjoyment over travel efficiency. It was easier to get lost on these roads than to get somewhere. I knew this from experience, thanks to the Sunday family drives of my childhood. I was a bit more expectant then, with my nose to the glass and my imagination wondering where Dad would land us that day.

There was no glass to press my nose to now, and the thick heat of morning promised a hot July day that would continue the good work the humidity and wind began on my hair. I didn't need to

1

look in the mirror to know it was a balloon. To know my eyes were red.

I looked to the horizon instead. There's great hope where the road meets the sky—maybe even an answer. But this road led to home. Just home. I thought I'd finished writing that story years ago, but then yesterday's story happened—the one about the boy who cheats and the girl who leaves. You could dress it up and call it a journey. But there was nothing new in the story about the girl who went home because she had nowhere else to go.

I turned onto the narrow gravel driveway leading to mine—an old, green, shingled house in a quiet neighborhood where everyone was still tucked in bed.

Everyone but my family. I wasn't surprised the front doorknob turned as I reached for it.

"Trying to sneak in, Lu?" Grandma Pat asked, blocking me from moving past the vestibule with her tiny frame and fiery red hair. When I was little, I thought her curls were on fire. It still seemed unwise to jostle them, and I stayed put.

She thrust a cinnamon roll toward me. "Eat. You look half-starved."

I wasn't starved or even hungry, but I have a reserved chamber in my stomach for Grandma's cinnamon rolls. I took a bite as I looked over Grandma to see Mom and Nana Bea standing behind her. Dad, my only ally, maneuvered through the women and squeezed my shoulder before heading out the front door without a word, presumably to unpack my car.

I was about to tell him not to bother when a petulant, "Well?" from my mother turned my open mouth in her direction, which is when I remembered it still held a half-eaten cinnamon roll. I stalled to finish my chew.

"You've been waiting for me?"

"What did you expect after your voice mail?" Mom asked.

"I told you not to worry."

"Right," Mom said. "Not worry while you drove all night from New York. Do you have any idea what happens to girls on the road at night?"

"They get tired."

"They get sold into white slavery, is what," Nana Bea corrected. I raised my eyebrows.

"I heard it on the news the other day," she said with a nod.

"What do you have to say for yourself?" Mom demanded.

"That next time I won't leave a voice mail first."

Mom's eyes widened as she pressed her lips together in a straight line. She had a lot to say about my response, but Grandma Pat snuck in with her thoughts.

"Or next time, you could leave a bit more information in the voice mail. 'John cheated on me and I'm coming home' isn't a lot to go on," she said. "I'm going to need more details, honey. I want to know what the other girl looks like."

"No. Louisa has said plenty already," Nana Bea disagreed. "In my day you didn't mention such things."

"What did you do?" I asked, curious.

"You either stayed put and didn't say anything, or you came back and didn't say anything."

I could think of three women who could use a little more of that principle right now, and thankfully, Dad made it happen when he came back through the front door. He was carrying a Crock-Pot—a 1970s pea-green model without the removable bowl. Mom had given it to me—among other random household items—when I'd first moved to New York.

"I found only this in your car, kiddo," Dad said, waving the old cord around in a lazy circle while everyone looked to me for an explanation.

But it wasn't a story that needed telling now.

"How about I take that," I said, tucking the Crock-Pot against my chest and balancing the cinnamon roll on top of it, like I'd brought home the Crock-Pot for this express purpose. To hold cinnamon rolls.

"I think I'll head upstairs now," I said, using my cinnamon roll holder to push through the crowd, beginning with Grandma Pat, who gave me a tight hug before stepping aside.

"I never liked that boy."

"John wasn't really ours to like or not to like," Mom inserted after also giving me a quick hug and moving out of the way so that I could finally exit the vestibule. "Still, I wasn't a fan."

"I didn't care for him, either, but it's all in the past. We need to focus on what to do now," Nana Bea said before inclining her cheek for a kiss, which I dutifully planted.

"Me, not we," I clarified.

But they didn't hear or didn't care and continued to brainstorm my future dating life as I trudged the two flights of stairs to my attic bedroom.

My room looked exactly as I'd left it, but smaller—the walls narrower, the pitched ceiling lower—but isn't that always the way? You go away, return, and wonder if these old spaces can still accommodate you. How was I to arrange myself in this place—so much of it familiar, down to the pale pink of the walls and the placement of the wrought-iron bed to the right of the door.

Nothing here changed, but I had. I'd visited since I'd moved out after college, but never to stay. I was wary of even sitting on the bed and creating an impression in a place I didn't want to be. So I stood at the door instead, surveying the space and wondering what I'd need to do to make it my new home. The air was hot and still; a window air conditioner would solve that. Throwing out everything else would help me breathe in other ways.

I set the cinnamon roll and Crock-Pot on the dresser with a wild idea of purging everything right now, but then I saw a photo of John and me wedged into the upper right corner of the mirror. It was from the first time I'd brought him home to meet the family, and we'd just finished playing a game of cornhole. The picture captures me in my element: my yard, my cornhole boards, my family, my mastery of the game. John? Not so much. He's the pressed khakis to my cut-offs.

Had we always contrasted like this? Maybe, but I was only one night and five states away from his cheating confession and not ready to answer that question. I couldn't prevent my visceral reaction at seeing him, though. My eyes locked to the picture of his blue ones, and I traced the outline of his face. I didn't feel the same as my family. I liked this man very much.

I shook my head and put the picture in my back pocket. I was too unnerved to stay in the room. I walked down the stairs, out the front door, and around to the backyard to haul out the cornhole boards from under the deck. Like any girl would.

I paced them apart and went through my standard pregame routine of breathing out the distractions and breathing in the game, as if this morning's Game of Me would decide them all.

I stepped forward and launched a bag into the air. It sank in the hole. It was like riding a bike. Like a dork riding a bike, which was confirmed by the look my best friend, Gracie, gave me when she stepped through the back screen door of her house. We'd known each other since we were four.

"Who plays cornhole at five on a Sunday morning? I thought you'd be curled up in your bed, crying your eyes out."

"Whatever happened to 'Good morning' around here? Or 'Welcome home'?"

"We're only that polite to strangers."

"But I'm fragile, dammit."

She crossed our backyards and wrapped me in a tight hug.

"I know you are," she whispered, and I exhaled for what felt like the first time since I'd left New York.

"Now put down the bag and come to my house," Gracie said. "I made you a cup of coffee from that snooty French press you got me last Christmas."

"Freshly ground beans, right?"

"Oh for the love. Come here, right now," she shouted before throwing the bag out of my hand and manhandling me all the way to her house.

"Shouldn't I tell my family where I'm going?"

"Where else would you be, Lu?"

Gracie situated me at the table with her right hand while her left poured coffee. I took a sip, the bitter taste waking me up like nothing else could.

"Very tasty. Now did you use filtered water or tap?"

Gracie rolled her eyes and sat across from me with a cup of her own. "What happened?"

"John cheated."

"Then it was good you left."

"Yes, but I've looked at my cell a thousand times to see whether he called."

"You're going to have to cut back eventually."

"And the only thing I brought from New York was a Crock-Pot."

That admission warranted a surprised look.

"Toothbrush?"

"No."

"Clothes?"

"No."

"Why?"

"Packing a suitcase cut into the drama of my exit. And when your boyfriend tells you he's cheated, drama is all you've got."

There was a lot more to say, but not now. I pushed away my coffee to make space for an arm pillow, exhausted by everything that had happened. But when I closed my eyes, I could see John coming into our apartment and telling me things I never wanted to hear. For a man who normally spoke little, John's narrative had seemed without end, but I stopped listening after he said her name. *Avery.*

What the hell kind of name is that? As soon as he said it, I'd slid off the couch and assumed the classic picture of relationship roadkill with my arms wrapped tightly around my knees, as if this defensive posture could stop his confession from shattering my world. But I couldn't stop him from talking anymore than I could rewind time to stop him from looking at another woman.

I needed sleep, but not if it came with this memory. I was about to open my eyes and push through the day when I felt Gracie wrap a quilt around my shoulders. She held me for a long time, her head on mine, and soon I matched my breathing to her steadier pace. Her kiss on my head and words of "I'm glad you're home. I missed you" were the last I heard before I caught my dreams.

CHAPTER 2

When Billy Sweeney broke up with me after two dates to the mini golf course in seventh grade, I woke the next morning to a vase of wildflowers from my mom and a card from my dad.

Apparently, the morning after a twenty-eight-year-old breakup is celebrated with a Cheerio to the head and a whispered, "Lu-ser," repeating like the beep, beep of an alarm, courtesy of my older brother, Ted, also known as Gracie's husband. Such was the risk of falling asleep at her kitchen table. Well, Ted plus their three little girls— Caroline, Abigail, and Holly—who seemed to think Aunt Lu's return to Dunlap's Creek was exciting enough to shout about at seven o'clock.

My first day home was anything but exciting. I took advantage of my family's church habit to sneak back to my room so I could spend the rest of the day feeling sorry for myself. I assumed the next day would run similarly, though hopefully with a later waking hour.

But Monday began with opera loud enough to wake up a girl's broken heart two stories up. This was unwelcome but not unexpected. Grandma Pat is one-hundred percent Polish and cooks like one, but always to Italian opera. I constructed a pillow fortress as a buffer around my head and was falling back asleep when someone knocked on the door. I peeked at the clock. 7:07 a.m.

"Sorry to disturb you, kiddo." It was Dad. "I wanted to let you know I'm taking your car into the shop on my way to work. It's leaking oil."

"That's its superpower," I muttered.

"What?"

"Don't take it in. I'll be downstairs in a minute."

"What?"

"One minute."

"I can't hear you."

"I will be down in a minute!"

Seven minutes later I shuffled into the kitchen, and Mom looked up from her newspaper.

"Dad is waiting for you outside," she yelled over the music. I glanced at Grandma's boom box and then Grandma, who was humming along as she stood by a large stockpot to watch water boil.

"Did you make coffee?" I asked Mom.

She nodded toward the Mr. Coffee. I headed to the driveway. Dad was crouching next to the Cutlass and removing a sheet pan from underneath its oil faucet.

"I wish you would have told me the car was leaking oil."

"That's not exactly news, Dad."

"I'm going to take it in."

"Don't do that. I don't have any money."

"I'll take care of it."

"It's not worth it. I'm not spending another cent on this car. Plus, I have a solution."

I popped the trunk to reveal a cache of Castrol.

"You could sell those to pay for fixing your car."

"The car doesn't want to be fixed. I guarantee you: Fix this leak, and she will burp oil from somewhere else."

"Well, use this pan when the car is parked in the driveway, okay?" he requested, placing the sheet pan back under the front of the car.

"Where are you headed?" I asked as he hauled his toolbox to his pick-up truck.

"We're building the new church outside of town."

I hadn't been back to my family's church since I'd left college, so this was news to me, as was that Dad was working on a project of this scale. His line had always been renovations and additions more than the ground-up stuff.

"That's a pretty big contract. How'd you land it?"

"Cheap labor." At that, Ted walked out his front door.

"Now I understand the cheap labor," I said, loud enough for my brother to hear.

"Morning, Lu-ser."

"Don't you think it's time to put aside that name?"

"Sure, when you stop living up to it," he said, messing my hair before putting his toolbox in the back of the truck. "Ready, Dad?"

Dad nodded before turning to me.

"How about you come to work with us today? We could wait until you get some coffee in a thermos and head over together."

A day of miscellaneous construction tasks sounded nice. I'd done it often as a little girl, hammering for a token two minutes before wandering off to daydream. I should join them. But, I had day full of moping ahead of me, so I was all booked up.

I waved bye, walked back to the kitchen, and searched the cupboards. "Where's that French press I got for you guys two years ago?" I yelled to Mom over the music.

"In the bottom left cupboard next to the fridge, behind the fondue pot."

I found it, pointedly blew off the dust from its box, and picked at the tamper-proof tape.

"I didn't know how to use it," she explained.

"It's not rocket science, Mom. You grind the beans coarsely, steep them in hot water for four minutes, and press."

"Well, now that you're home, you can teach me."

I was ten minutes into that tutorial when Nana Bea walked in.

"Can someone please turn that racket off?"

"The pierogies need the encouragement that opera provides," Grandma Pat responded.

"Aren't pierogies a Polish thing? You should play polka," I said.

"Dough is universal."

Ah. Pierogies without borders. I poured myself some coffee and took a seat at the table at the same time as Nana Bea.

"Louisa, could you please pour me some coffee and turn that music off?"

I did as requested and resumed my seat, closing my eyes to inhale the rich smell of coffee and exhale all the women surrounding me.

"If you're going to sit there, you might as well pinch pierogies," Grandma Pat said before I swallowed the first sip. She plopped a

9

cutting board of circular dough to my right, a bowl of mashed potatoes to my left, and an empty plate to my center.

"When did I graduate to the pinching stage?" I asked. Grandma had never let me assemble an entire pierogie before. This must be her way of saying she felt sorry for me.

"I'm desperate. I have a huge order for the Knights of Columbus party on Friday night—you should come, there might be some single men there—and I'm behind on my inventory for the farmer's market," she said.

I placed some potato in the center of the circular dough.

"How much are you charging for a dozen now?" I asked.

"$10."

"$10?"

"That's right, but I won't be able to charge that much if you skimp on the filling. It's a heaping tablespoon, Lu!"

I added a touch more and looked at the dough skeptically. I didn't see how it could possibly wrap around the filling without breaking.

It didn't.

"The dough broke," I announced, holding up my massacred pierogie.

Grandma deftly repaired the holey dough, pinched the ends together, and placed the finished product on the empty plate—a process that went faster than my second swig of coffee.

"Keep trying," she ordered and returned to the stove.

"And what is it that you're doing so importantly over there?" I asked as I dutifully filled my next pierogie.

"I'm waiting for the water to reach a soft boil."

"You might want to turn the heat off because I've botched my second attempt."

"That's enough out of you. I am not going to have you wreck my livelihood. I need you to help me at the shop this week."

I shook my head over the contradiction. Her fabric store, Penny Thrift, was her main source of income, though pierogies at $10/dozen were no joke.

"Even you can dust shelves," she said to clear up the confusion.

"I already told you, Patricia. I need Louisa to help me this week," Nana Bea said. "I'm thinking about moving."

Nana had moved to our home fifteen years ago. Grandpa had died of a heart attack, and the morning after his burial, she was here for breakfast. She didn't bring anything other than a wedding portrait in a silver picture frame and a suitcase of clothes that she swapped out every week when she journeyed to her big house across town to pick up the mail. But she never admitted to the arrangement, and we all played along.

"Where are you thinking about moving?" I asked.

"I haven't decided yet."

"Well, I hate to break it to both of you ladies, but I'm not slave labor."

They looked at me. How could I put it more plainly?

"I need money." I led a thrifty life, but even my frugality got me only so far on an hourly income in a big city. I had exactly $1,837 in my bank account.

"Lu is right," Mom said from across the table. I'd expected a familial lecture about respecting my elders, not support.

I smiled at her in gratitude; she looked confused by my appreciation.

"How else are you going to pay us rent?" she asked.

"What?"

"You're an adult," she explained. It would all have sounded so very logical if it weren't so mean.

"Do they pay rent?" I asked, jerking my thumb at Grandma Pat and Nana Bea.

"Your parents still owe me back pay for moving in to raise you kids," Grandma Pat said.

"And I don't live here," Nana Bea said.

"How much are you charging?" I asked.

"$200 a month."

"Will I be signing a lease?"

"Don't be so dramatic, Lu. This is more than fair. It's not due until the end of the month, and it includes groceries and utilities. If you don't like it, you can live with Gracie."

"She'd make me babysit."

"Oh, that reminds me," Mom said. "Gracie called and asked if you could babysit this Friday."

"It's only"—I paused to squint at the clock—"7:44! Doesn't anybody ease into Monday mornings around here?"

They all looked at me like I was nuts.

"Doesn't anybody care that I am less than forty-eight hours from relationship fallout?"

11

"What's that?" Grandma Pat asked.

"The time period after a relationship ends in which you tiptoe around the dumped party and help her get back on her feet."

"That's what we're doing," Grandma Pat said.

"Starting with my house," Nana Bea followed.

"No, starting with *The Daily Press*," Mom corrected.

"What?"

"I made a call," she said, practically bursting with excitement.

"You didn't ..."

"I did! RJ said to stop by at nine-thirty."

Whenever people in New York asked me where I was from, I'd say the Midwest and leave it at that. This area of the country is a blur to them anyway, and it's not like Dunlap's Creek sports anything significant enough to put itself on the national scene. It's an hour away from the largest city, with enough cornfields and two-lane byways in between to keep it from being a suburb. It's not as small as the many one-stop towns that surround it, but it's small enough to risk running into familiar faces if I chose to look up from my feet, which I didn't on my walk to meet RJ.

The Daily Press is a biweekly that prints world news at the back of the classifieds. I'd worked here as an unpaid intern in high school and underpaid intern in college because it was the only paper in town. I was happy to leave it behind after graduation when I landed a job at a features desk for a legitimate daily in a city far, far away from Dunlap's Creek. John and I moved to New York after he graduated from law school. He'd successfully moved up the firm ranks, but my midwestern journalism experience didn't translate. After a year of searching for jobs, I gave up to work at Starbucks.

My failure didn't change my dislike of *The Press*. I'm sure RJ knows this, but he has a bit of a crush on my mother. They grew up together.

"How's your mother?" he asked as soon as I jingled into the office. No joke, there's a bell above the door.

"Still married."

"I wouldn't offer you a job if she hadn't asked," he pointed out.

"Are you offering me a job?"

"At least temporarily. There's always more to cover than writers

12

on hand. We'll see how you do."

I looked around the teeny office crammed with rusty metal desks and gigantic desktop computers that had been staged for the dumpster back in my previous iteration here. "What's your going rate?"

"Dollar a line."

"It was a $1.50 the last time I worked here."

"Times are hard."

"Do you want to see any of the clips I wrote after I left?"

"I thought you worked as a coffee shop girl."

"Barista," I corrected. "I worked at a daily for three years before I moved to New York."

"Uh-huh."

"It had a circulation of 200,000. I was a staff writer on the features desk. I had my own desk."

"You won't here. You can use the green desk by the window, but don't mess it up with anything personal since you'll share it with other freelancers. Mailboxes are by the back door, and for now, take whatever interests you from the Miscellaneous slot. You'll get your own slot if it works out."

Something to work toward.

"Where is everyone?" The office was silent except for the whirring of the various fans that tried to compensate for the poor air conditioning.

"Covering their beats."

Demanding, those small-town beats. I made my way to the cubbies and moved my pointer finger to "Miscellaneous." It contained two assignments: community cookbooks and nuptials.

"Community cookbooks?" I asked RJ.

"All the women's organizations in town seem to be publishing cookbooks this summer to raise money for their charities. It's straightforward: a fifty-word description of each, the price and where to purchase it."

I skimmed the list and realized that I knew most of the ladies, including Grandma Pat, the cookbook contact for my family's church, and Nana Bea, the contact for her country club. I pointed out this potential conflict of interest.

"You're not selling the cookbooks, you're describing them."

The man had not a clue. Ten women's clubs, all selling cookbooks with essentially the same recipes for essentially the same price—and my grandmas on rival sides? I might get kicked out of the house.

"Any obits? I'd prefer that to nuptials," I said.

"I thought you'd like that assignment, given your demographic."

"My demographic?"

"Youngish and female. Someone in your crowd is always getting married."

There were so many problems to tackle in that statement, but I addressed the least offensive.

"I don't have a crowd. I have one girlfriend, and she was married years ago with a crepe-papered reception in the church basement. We sipped on punch made from ginger ale and sherbet. Hardly, *Knot* worthy."

RJ ignored me.

"In addition to writing the standard announcements, we now include a wedding feature in the first Sunday edition, which means you'll attend one wedding per month. The stories should include some background about the bride and groom— how they met, fell in love, got engaged—and then all the news about the wedding itself."

"Like whether someone objects during the ceremony?"

"That would be great, but it never happens."

I couldn't afford to say no, but I didn't want to do this. The pomp and crowds of weddings was not my scene under normal circumstances, and given what happened with John, covering it felt extra mean. RJ didn't know any of this, but he could see the hesitation on my face.

"It's a big feature—around one-thousand words. It's a lot of money."

"A dollar a line?"

"Two hundred dollars total."

"How does that compute?"

"The perks—you get to eat wedding cake and do the chicken dance. Plus, a lot of people will read it, unlike the rest of what we print."

RJ gestured toward old editions stacked in teetering piles along the back wall. "Look through some old papers for examples. Wedding/engagement announcements are due Wednesdays and run Thursdays, and wedding features are due by ten o'clock on

Saturday evening and run Sundays."

He returned to his work, and I took some newspapers to my desk. I eased into a chair, wondering whether the seat, stitched with duct tape to repair gashes in the vinyl, would give way. But it only gave a squeaky sigh. Or maybe that was me.

I spent the next few minutes breathing in and out while I carefully positioned the papers in parallel lines across the desk. How long had it been since I wrote anything? I was nervous. I looked over at RJ. He was pounding away at his computer, filling up blank space with words like it was nothing.

The phone on my desk rang. RJ looked up. "Did I mention you double as receptionist when you're in the office?"

I rolled my eyes, but picked up anyway.

"*The Daily Press*, Lu Sokolowski speaking."

"Hi, honey."

"Hi, Mom."

"How's work?" she asked.

I looked down at my blank legal pad. "Slow."

"Could you pick up some milk on your way home?"

"Sure."

I hung up and opened a paper to a wedding feature, but immediately closed it. I couldn't handle canned shots of lovebirds right now. Engagement and wedding announcements might be more innocuous, so I looked at my assignment sheet for that instead. The gig was simple: Copyedit the received announcements and fit the info to our template.

I could do this, and I set to work with the top announcement in the stack: an Ellen Smith to marry a James Jameson. What were his parents thinking?

Three forms, thirty dollars, and thirty minutes later, the phone on my desk rang again.

"*The Daily Press*, Lu Sokolowski speaking."

"Good morning, Louisa. I'm calling to remind you to pick me up at four," Nana Bea said.

"Can't you pick me up?" I asked. "I walked to work."

"I cannot."

"Fine, I'll see you at four."

Another thirty minutes passed before the phone rang a third time.

"*The Daily Press*, Lu Sokolowski speaking."

"Working hard, Lu?" Grandma Pat asked.

"When my family isn't calling me."

"What assignments did they give you?"

I told her about the weddings. She offered to be my date. I said no.

"Why are you calling?"

"To let you know you're off the hook for helping me at the store tonight."

"That's nice."

"And to talk with you about our church cookbook. My sources tell me that you are doing the write-ups this year."

"Your sources?"

"I can't reveal them."

"I can't show favoritism."

"You won't need to. My recipe for banana bread is better than anything the Baptists put in their cookbook. And Fanny Jones stole my casserole recipe. She calls it Fanny's Favorite, but it's Pat's Favorite."

"Fanny's Favorite has better alliteration."

"What's that?"

"Nothing."

"Are you taking this down?" she asked.

I said no and hung up.

The day passed in blissful quiet after that, and I typed up announcements and gathered cookbook stats. It felt nice to get into the groove of something, and when I glanced at my watch, I realized I was late for picking up Nana Bea.

"Why am I here again?" I yelled to her from the mountain of linens she'd had me individually pluck from their shelves and unfurl to her scrutinizing gaze, only to eventually confer them all to a "keep" pile.

"Put them all back, Louisa."

"What?"

"Put them back, please."

I scrambled over the top of Mt. Linen to face her directly.

"I'm sorry, Nana. I mistakenly heard you tell me to put back the linens that you asked me to empty from this closet.

"That is because I was operating under a misapprehension."

"A misapprehension of what?"

16

"That any of these linens needed to go."

I picked up the nearest handkerchief. "What about this one?"

"Your great-grandmother Marjorie embroidered that!"

Stitching in the shape of a bird and flower caught my eye. So she had.

"And this one?" I asked, grabbing handkerchief number two of 489.

"No."

"Why not?"

"I might need it. Put everything back please—refolded and in its proper place."

All this refolding according to the proper seams returned us home after seven o'clock—after dinner and without the milk I'd promised to pick up.

"I'm sorry, Mom, but I've had some things to do today, including unpacking and repacking one of your mother's linen closets."

"I asked you to do one thing."

"Add it to the pile!" I said in my outdoor voice, as I turned to dramatically exit the kitchen for my room.

"What about dinner?" she asked.

"I'm not hungry."

"What about hot chocolate?" another voice asked. It was Gracie, on the other side of the screen door and holding two steaming mugs.

"Will you be my mommy?" I whispered as we crossed the deck to sit on the steps. I took a mug from her and inhaled the earthy scent of the cocoa. A little stress went away. I took a small sip and a little more stress went away as the bitter chocolate ran down my throat. No matter the July heat, I'd drink Gracie's cocoa any day.

"You make one very fine cup of hot chocolate," I commended. "Tell me about your day." I loved hearing about Gracie's world, as much for the stories as the way she told them. She kept to the facts.

"It started at four-thirty when Abigail woke me up to let me know that she didn't feel well. Then, she puked. After we washed everything and settled her back in bed, Holly woke up and said, 'Poop.' And even though I don't think she's ready, she wants to use the toilet like her big sisters. So, I set her on the toilet, and she sat there.

I accidentally fell asleep on the bathroom floor, and when I woke back up, the sun was out. 'Did you poop?' I asked. She nodded, but the toilet was empty. I put her in a diaper, and guess what she did a minute later?"

"Pooped."

"See, you could be a mom. Now, let's hear about your day."

I relayed it all—the opera, the oil leak(s), the pierogies, the rent, the RJ, the assignments, the trip to Nana's Magical World of Closets. I tried to describe everything with tone of irony, but I think I ended up sounding like Eeyore.

"Coming back was a bad idea."

"Not to me. And don't worry about the family. They want to help. They'll calm down soon enough."

"Or not. Would you rather have your day or mine?" I asked.

"Mine." No hesitation.

"Yours started at four-thirty with projectile puking."

"True, but I always wanted to be a wife and mom. I don't love days like this, but I don't really mind them—especially now when Ted's putting the kids to bed, and I'm one yard away. I'll be ready for tomorrow."

I tossed back the last sip of my hot chocolate and handed her my empty cup. "Thank you for this."

"Don't forget, you're babysitting for me on Friday," Gracie said as she moved from the top step to the lawn. She paused midyard, looking at me. "What do you want?"

"Right now?" I hedged. "A good night's sleep."

She ignored me. "And what about tomorrow?"

John. I wanted to be with John. I wanted to live in New York. Tomorrow, I wanted to wake up to a life that worked out on some level, but I'd retreated from New York without anything to show for my time there. No man, no money, no real job.

But mostly, I wanted the man. Two days since I'd left. I had enough dignity not to contact him, but if he called me? I'd answer before the end of the first ring. I'd forgive before he apologized. I'd go back before he asked. It was hard enough to admit all of this in my mind. I certainly wasn't going to say any of it out loud.

"I have no idea what I want," I said and headed to my empty bed

CHAPTER 3

That Friday, I discovered what I didn't want.

It had been a long week. Time doesn't fly when one chooses to gaze catatonically out the front window, and though I'd logged more office hours than any other writer, my aversion to all things wedding prevented me from working on the one—the only—story I had due in the next forty-eight hours. There were a lot of pitches to choose from. The mile square of Dunlap's Creek radiates from the smaller town square with a church on each corner. Couple these old stone churches with the pastoral feel of town, and you've got a place people want to marry, even if they're not from here. Plus, it's the county seat. But by three o'clock on Friday afternoon, I still hadn't decided. Unless I could convince RJ to let me write a story about how scavenger hunt engagements are no longer original.

He wouldn't agree to that, so I resorted to the classic question: If someone held a gun to my head and said, "Write a wedding story for this Sunday's paper or die," what would I write about?

When I chose death over answering the question, I asked myself another: Is there a wedding story I would read?

And then I had it.

I crossed the town square to get it done with the one couple— Peter and Lisa—who showed up in jeans at the courthouse that day to get hitched. Courthouse weddings aren't a new thing, but in the past three years of *Daily* issues I'd skimmed, no writer had written about one. Their laid-back wedding vibe made for a story unexpected enough to give readers a double take. I wasn't sure whether RJ would go for it, but given my procrastination and disinterest in anything more typical, I decided it was better to ask forgiveness than permission.

High from my courthouse find, I didn't give much thought to why Nana Bea, Grandma Pat, Mom, and Gracie were clucking like a flock of angry chickens in the living room when I came home. They were huddled around something.

"What's that?" I asked, all innocence.

"What's what?" Mom asked back.

"What, what are you talking about?" Nana asked, looking around as if I'd inquired about an airborne pathogen.

"The cardboard boxes behind your feet."

Nana continued to squint at the air, but Grandma Pat practically jumped aside in anticipation as Mom moved forward to offer some preemptive assistance. But I didn't need to cross the room to see "New York, NY" written in large, bubbly script— definitely not John's handwriting.

Silence hit—the type of silence I'd been looking for since I arrived, but never found.

The four women looked at me to do something, so I did. I counted: one, two, three, four, five. Five boxes.

"She must be a good packer," I murmured as I walked toward the boxes, stopping a toe short of touching them. "How long have these been here?"

"Since noon," Mom said.

"Why didn't you call me?"

"What good would that have done?" Grandma asked. "You wouldn't have been able to tell us what's in them."

"Isn't it obvious? They're my clothes."

They looked skeptical. I snapped my fingers, and Grandma produced the X-Acto that she'd obviously been itching to use since the boxes arrival. I dissected the nearest offender, and sure enough, a confection of clothes, including my favorite jeans, popped out. I did the same to boxes two, three, four, and five, and out came more jeans, shoes, shirts, sweaters. Though I couldn't see it, I could smell my Starbucks uniform somewhere, too. I haphazardly skimmed my hands through all of them in search of a note. Nothing.

"Well, if that doesn't beat all ..." Mom started.

"Glad that's over with," Grandma Pat said.

"Someone should carry these upstairs," Nana Bea finished.

And with that, they turned to me. They all seemed so certain that these boxes brought closure, but they opened a lot of questions for me. I closed my eyes and shook my head, overcome by the distaste of all I didn't know—the events, conversations, motivations that led to my clothes being sent from my ex-boyfriend's apartment and addressed in a girlish scrawl. I'd thought about my clothes as I'd scavenged everyone's closets to cobble together outfits this week, but I hadn't thought about how I'd reclaim them. Yet here they were, at no expense or trouble to me, other than the mystery of it all.

There was so much I didn't know. But, I finally had the answer to Gracie's question about what I wanted, or at least, its opposite. I did not want this. The jilted feeling I'd carried inside all week was bad enough without the physical evidence. In my most decisive action of the week, I grabbed my phone from my back pocket. No calls or texts from John. No surprise there, but his silence made me angrier. The nasty text I'd been planning to send would no longer do. I thought about calling him, but what was the point if I couldn't finish the conversation with a slap to his beautiful face?

I did the next best thing. I walked to the garage, dropped the phone on the cement, and beat the life out of it with a hammer. It only took five hits; my dad had trained me well. And then I cleaned up my mess like my mother had taught me and returned to the living room. The women of my family were standing in the exact same place I'd left them. My eyes must have still looked a touch wild because they didn't say anything.

"Help me with these boxes?"

I bent over to pick up one. Everyone—minus Nana Bea—did the same, and we climbed the two flights to my room.

"Did you have a good day?" Mom asked as we set the boxes on my bedroom floor.

"I interviewed some nice people who got married after four years of dating."

My life was like ripping off consecutive Band-Aids. I was about to politely kick my family out of my room so that I could find some other relationship artifacts to smash, but then Gracie reminded me it was time to babysit.

The girls and I sat cross-legged on Gracie's bed as she pushed and shoved her way into a dress I'd nabbed from one of my boxes before heading over.

"Yellow is not my color," she said, doing a half turn in front of the full-length mirror.

"True, but most of your dresses are in the jumper category, and jumpers and dates are an oxymoron as ..." I blanked. The numbness from John's insensitivity had dulled my quick wit.

"Jumbo fried shrimp," Caroline, my eight-year-old niece, said. Score one for her. I bet she was never going to find herself on the other side of clothing boxes from her ex-boyfriend.

"Regardless, the color won't matter with such overfloweth," I said. Three pregnancies had added curves to Gracie's choice places.

"What does that mean?" my five-year-old niece Abigail asked.

"Never you mind," Gracie said, shooting dagger eyes at me. "Make yourself useful, Lu, and take the girls downstairs to feed them dinner."

We were halfway into our fluffernutters and Doritos when Gracie and Ted came downstairs. They looked good. Gracie could apply some deft makeup when she chose, and Ted was noticeably attractive. I think he recognized my reluctant approval because he winked at me.

I smiled. "Taking her out for all-you-can-eat at the Sirloin Stockade, followed by a pitcher of Bud at the bowling alley?"

"You've got it, Lu-ser. Don't call boys while we're gone," he said. "Oh wait, you'll have to glue your phone back together first."

"You told him!" I exploded at Gracie.

"I told you not to say anything!" Gracie shouted at Ted, who laughed harder when she smacked the back of his head. It was the start of another hot date.

If some babysitters feel at a loss for activities to occupy their charges, they've never hung with my nieces. Caroline was obsessed with Zumba, which meant the younger two were also obsessed. The girls spent the next two hours teaching me the new routines they'd learned at the community center, but it's physiologically impossible to move my hips like they can. The pictures they took of my attempts proved me right.

Zumba preceded sleepy time, and by eight o'clock I had two down with one to go. I offered to read Caroline a book before bed, but she countered with a mess of hot pink construction paper loosely bound with Scotch tape.

"Is this an in-house publication?" I asked.

"It's your plan."

"My plan?"

"For what to do now that you're back."

"It's so pink."

"Are you going to listen to my plan or not?"

"Will you go immediately to bed afterward?"

"Yes."

I turned to page one.

"First things first," Caroline said. "You have to move out of Grandma and Grandpa's house."

Isn't that the truth? "Where will I go?"

"Here," she said, pointing to a purple and turquoise house with a glitter roof.

"How am I going to pay for it?"

"Your husband will buy it for you."

Oh my. "What am I going to do in this house?"

"Bake cakes."

"This is a 1950s nightmare."

"You will sell the cakes, but not very many at first because they won't taste or look very good."

I could see that. The cakes on page four consisted of a lot of crayon scribbling, but no puffy paint or stickers to help them out.

"Time for bed."

"But, I'm not finished."

"You are until I get a rewrite."

"Will you read the rest?" she asked as she lay down. I smoothed her hair across her forehead, and smiled. Her hazel eyes looked so much like her mama's. "I'm glad you're back, Aunt Lu."

I kissed her cheek before turning off the light.

By eight-thirty, the house was still. I cleared the kitchen table to make way for some rough drafting. There's something about a large, clear surface that helps, even it was only to hold the ancient laptop I'd pilfered from *The Daily* and my interview notes. What a day. I'd thought the climax was Lisa and Peter, and then the cardboard boxes trumped them. I guess this would all work out in the end because according to Caroline, I would soon be living in new digs with a new man and making a mess of cakes.

As promised, I dutifully flipped through the story of my future life before setting it aside to focus on my present, which included a deadline and a paycheck. Maybe.

CHAPTER 4

Saturday morning was the second time that week I woke up with my head on Gracie's kitchen table. Remembering the unwelcome site of Ted that welcomed me last week, I carefully peaked out of my right eye. It was Ted again, but the quiet version this time.

"Is Gracie dead?"

"No."

"She finally left you?"

"No."

"I didn't accidentally kill the girls, did I?"

"I haven't checked."

Gracie walked into the room, the humming opposite of her husband.

"Morning, Lu! Would you like some coffee?" she asked gesturing to the French press.

"What's going on? Is it more boxes from New York? Did my old apartment arrive in front of Mom and Dad's on wheels?"

"No, nothing like that."

"So, what's with his silence and your humming?"

She leaned in close as she poured my coffee. "It's game day."

"Grace!" Ted admonished, sharply.

"What?"

"We don't talk about it."

Gracie turned toward me. "That's right. We don't talk about." And then she rolled her eyes.

They didn't need to because I'd finally caught on. The ballpark had been a fixture of my childhood, along with the football field, and basketball court, and whatever other sport Ted was inhaling and exhaling that season. Ted had gone on to play baseball in the minors before a chronic shoulder injury sent him back to Dunlap's Creek to marry Gracie, work with my dad, and make little girl babies.

Last year, he'd joined with a local league, and today's game wasn't the first, but it was a fundraiser at the new AAA stadium outside of town. The game was a big deal. Ted was pitching, and if I hadn't been so absorbed in my own drama, the girls and I would have tee-peed the house while I was babysitting last night.

"Cheer up sport, it's going to go fine," I said after a couple sips of coffee. I couldn't help but heckle him. "I'm sure your team will win the Super Bowl."

"You mean the World Series," he gasped before galloping to the bathroom.

"Well," I said loudly over Ted's lurching sounds, "I think I'm going to catch a little more shut eye before the game. It starts at one o'clock?"

When I woke up for the second time that day, it was hotty, hot, hot. Even the clothes boxes across my room were perspiring. I began to methodically refold and sort them in teetering piles on the floor, though the heat made me question whether clothes were necessary. Too bad it wasn't Nude Day at the ballpark.

Mom yelled, "Lunch!" and the clock blinked 12:15 p.m., ending any further deliberation, as well as the option of a shower to replace one sheen with another. I settled on a white tank and cut-offs, and after a quick lunch, we headed to the ballpark.

The line for tickets was longer than I'd expected. Clearly, I was alone in my baseball apathy. Dad paid for the whole family, leaving me with enough pennies to purchase a chocolate and vanilla swirl custard dipped in crunch coat. My skills of licking ice cream cones hadn't mastered beyond the primer level, and I took the farthest seat so that I'd drip on my family as little as possible. Hopefully I'd be finished by the time people filled the seats to my left.

As I popped the last of my cone in my mouth and ineffectively wiped the sticky mess on my thighs, the players ran onto the field. Gracie beamed next to me, and the girls kicked the back of the seats in front of them like crazy people.

The initial brouhaha died down as the players took their spots. I leaned in and watched Ted wind his right arm backwards and forwards, and do this little stomping dance with his feet. He tossed the ball from his right hand to his glove and then hot potatoed it back and forth a few times. He settled in, turned, and stared down the batter. He raised his left leg, reached back and catapulted the ball toward the batter. Strike one.

Now that I'd witnessed a good play, I could read for the rest of the game. I removed a book from my back pocket—my old copy of *Little Women* that I'd found in Caroline's room last night—and started reading. Gracie jabbed my right side with her elbow somewhere around the sixth chapter.

"Lu, they're doing the Kiss Cam," she whispered.

"That's nice," I said, not looking up from my book.

"Maybe you want to give the camera something to look at?"

I snapped my focus to one of the giant screens across the field. Sure enough, I saw my face squinting back at me. And a man sitting to my left.

Brown hair and green eyes. He looked familiar, but I couldn't put a name to the face. I thought about ignoring him and turning back to my book, but the camera wasn't moving. I had no idea what to do.

He did, though.

"It's nice to see you again, Louisa," he said, extending his hand in greeting to take my sticky one. And instead of giving me some much-needed information—like a name—he started talking over my head.

"Gracie, Mr. and Mrs. Sokolowski. It's nice to see all of you again."

He continued the pleasantries to my grandmas and nieces, who all seemed to know who this man was—a situation I'm normally fine with, minus one Kiss Cam. In the next 30 seconds it had zoomed to other couples, but returned to us twice. I knew this because I was staring stupidly at it while the stranger made small talk.

After it returned for a third round, I turned to him.

"Excuse me!" I interrupted, with more angst and volume than I intended.

He looked at me. I looked back at the Kiss Cam; he looked at the Kiss Cam. Now we were both staring at it and doing nothing, which was arguably worse than my squinting at it while he leaned over me to talk to my dad. I shooed the camera away, to no effect other than the laughter of the crowd.

I turned back to the man. Blunt and fast was the only way out.

"Kiss me."

"What?"

"The camera's not going anywhere, and I don't like being the main attraction," I said.

"Do you think I do, Louisa?"

"Lu," I corrected.

He looked at me. Then, he reached for my right hand, lifted it to his mouth, kissed it, and placed it back in my lap. I didn't talk to him for the rest of the game.

"Who was that?" I finally asked later that evening as Grandma Pat sautéed cabbage and noodles for dinner. My hand was still burning, but my family was remaining uncharacteristically quiet about the whole thing.

"That's Jackson, the new pastor of our church."

"The divorced pastor," Nana Bea clarified from her seat at the kitchen table.

"You remember him—the pastor's kid," Gracie said as she stacked plates to take to the dining room table. "He was in between our year and Ted's in school. Nice guy but uptight. He dated Kate Mullen."

I nodded at the faint memory, though the man who sat next to me today looked nothing like the skinny kid who always buttoned his shirts straight up to his neck. "Right. The promise rings."

"They got married and moved away ..." Gracie started.

"Which is where they should have stayed ..." Nana inserted.

"But now they're divorced, and he's back as an assistant pastor under his dad," Mom cut in as she returned from filling water glasses.

"I'm surprised the church allowed it." My tone landed snarkier than I intended.

"They shouldn't have," Nana Bea said. "And I'm not the only one who thinks so."

"Well, no one asked you or them," Grandma Pat responded.

"If it wasn't for that wussy hand kiss today, I'd say you should get with that boy."

"Jackson didn't have many options. Lu's face wasn't totally clear of ice cream," Gracie reasoned.

"Neither was my hand," I murmured before I could catch myself.

"Are you saying you wanted him to kiss you?" Nana Bea asked.

"No, I'm saying there was the same amount of ice cream residue on my hand as on my face."

"That's not what you said." Grandma Pat laughed.

"Over."

"What?"

"This conversation about my love life is over."

Grandma Pat raised an eyebrow. "What love life?"

And that's where we left it because in puffed Ted like a proud rooster, and we shifted our full attention to his play-by-play for the rest of dinner.

One round of dishes, several good nights, and two hours of writing later, I sent my final draft to RJ. I'd met my deadline, in time for him to fill the space but not enough time for him to find something else if he wasn't thrilled with my courthouse angle. I'd deal with that Monday.

But now, I drew my knees to my chest and rubbed my thumb over the top of my right hand as I turned to look at the Crock-Pot on my dresser, letting my mind wander to the exact place it shouldn't go.

I was twenty-two when I met John. I was covering a story that took me to a Christmas law firm party, and I dressed in red. Everyone else in the room looked like they'd come from a funeral. It was the first time I realized black came in shades.

Reporters, in general, seek to blend, and I always strived never to be noticed, on the clock or not. But from the looks of things, the bar had opened long before I'd arrived, and if I wanted any interview of substance, I needed to get to it right away.

As I was about to approach the nearest group, a hand touched my elbow. I turned and saw clear blue eyes looking straight into mine.

I wanted to be with him in that instant. It was a strange reaction—not for its intensity or immediacy. Never mind that I didn't know this man. It was strange because it happened at all. I'd

29

always prioritized work over relationships and never met anyone to persuade me to change that. And technically, I hadn't met this man yet. But I knew enough to free my elbow and step back. I was about to turn away when his words stopped me.

"May I get you something to drink?"

"No."

"Something to eat?"

"No."

"How about I stand here with you?"

"Yes," I blurted before I could stop myself.

"I'm John," he said, reaching out to shake my hand. It was warm; mine was freezing.

"Are you a law student?" he asked.

"No."

"A lawyer?"

"Obviously not," I said, gesturing to my outfit, "But if you are, you need to work on your powers of observation."

"I observed; I was just hoping."

"For what?"

"To see you on a regular basis instead of running into you at seedy places like firm parties."

"You don't even know me."

He hesitated. I still like to think that it was at this point, the banter stopped.

"But I feel like I do. Or I feel like I should, which is why I'm standing with you when I'm supposed to be making myself perfectly agreeable to the rest of the lawyers."

"You're a law student?"

"First year."

"Then you can help me. I need to interview students for an article."

"You're a writer?"

I nodded. "For the newspaper."

"Okay, as long as you don't interview me."

"Why?"

"I don't want to create an ethical dilemma for you when you go home with me tonight."

He smiled, but I was way out of my element.

I abdicated with open hands. "I don't know what to say to that."

"Nod your head."

I shook it instead.

"Okay, I will help you anyway, but you have to do two things for me."

"What?"

"First, it's easier to mingle with a drink in your hand. If you don't drink while on the clock, have the bartender fill a martini glass with water. No one will know the difference."

I moved toward the bar and did as John suggested.

"Second?"

"I'm going to need your name."

"Lu," I said.

Before meeting John, I'd intended on staying at the party for as short a time as possible. I stayed until midnight. His comfort radiated to me, and he took care of all the conversation while I took notes. John knew the right questions to ask, when to laugh, and how to keep the conversation flowing without forcing it. He was much more socially adept than I, and he could talk as easily with his peers as with the lawyers he was trying to impress.

As the evening continued, I focused more on him instead of the people I was supposed to be interviewing. I'd never met a man like him, though my experience with men was limited. My parents had discouraged dating, and I hadn't met any boys worth the rebellion. But, in this setting, in this place, something changed. I could barely stop looking at him. I normally didn't have a problem listening to the people I interviewed—I was a journalist because I enjoyed listening to people's stories—but John's presence created a kind of fog. I couldn't get past the sensation of him standing next to me, his right arm only inches away from my left. And I was surprised when he called it quits.

"It's time to leave," John said.

I looked around. The room was practically empty.

"Well, even lawyers have to sleep, I guess."

"They're not going to bed. They're heading to the bars."

I faced him. "Are you going with them?"

"I'll walk you home first. I'd invite you to go out with me, but I have a feeling it's not your scene."

"Why do you say that?"

"The way you're holding your glass."

I looked down and saw that my hands circled the upper rim of my wa-tini.

"There's a stem for a reason." He smiled.

Oh.

"And," he continued, "you never sipped from your glass."

"Maybe you should be a detective instead of a lawyer."

"Lawyers make more. So, I'm right about you not wanting to go out?"

He was. I thought about saying otherwise, but I was feeling uncomfortable enough in my newfound boy-crazy state without adding a lie.

"You're right," I admitted. "I don't drink, don't like bars, and don't really like socializing. I only live about ten minutes from here, so it won't be too much out of your way if you still want to walk me home."

We grabbed our coats, waved at the stragglers, and turned south from the office. The brisk air felt more like January, and I hoped it would knock me back to myself. We walked in an easy silence, and when we got to the building, we turned toward each other.

"Well, now I don't need to ask for your phone number since I know where you live."

"Come in daylight; it's safer."

"May I come tomorrow?"

"Yes."

Then he stepped forward and probably would have commenced with the world's most amazing kiss had I not blurted, "I've never kissed anyone before."

He stepped back, which is exactly where I didn't want him to go.

"Come back here, please," I said.

"I can't."

"What do you mean you can't? Move your feet two steps."

"I can't. I'm sorry."

We stood a breath apart. If he'd been kissing me, I'm sure I wouldn't have felt the snot freezing in my nose, but I did because he was standing there staring at me.

"So, let me get this straight," he began, sounding more like a lawyer and less like a dreamboat. "You've never kissed anyone."

"That's what I said, counselor."

"Anyone?"

"Not like I assume we were about to."

32

"How is that possible?"

"It's too complicated to explain in this weather, in this dress, and in these shoes. Call me, and we can talk about it over coffee sometime. Good night."

I grabbed my keys from my purse to unlock the door, head inside, and bemoan an aborted love life that I'd only now discovered I wanted. I was three locks into that plan when John said my name.

"Lu."

"Yes?"

"May I still see you tomorrow?"

I nodded without looking at him, walked inside and did what any lovelorn girl does: called my best friend. Caroline had just been born, so I knew Gracie was awake.

"How's the kid?" I asked when she picked up on the second ring.

"Finally fell asleep. What's up?"

"Well, I almost got kissed, but then I screwed it up by saying I'd never kissed anyone before."

"That's not good."

"Where was this advice before?"

"Well, I thought that was something everyone knew, like don't kiss with morning breath. Never kiss with morning breath. Write that down."

"I'm nowhere close to that stage." I sighed.

"So, are you going to tell me about it?" Gracie asked.

I did, and for the next hour, we combed through every detail of the evening to see whether John would return the next day. Gracie thought yes, but I wasn't so sure.

"It's best he doesn't since I can't kiss anyway."

"You'll figure it out."

"But that's the problem. Most people figure it out when they're pimply and prepubescent and their partner doesn't know any better. I'm twenty-two; a certain amount of proficiency is expected."

Silence.

"Gracie?"

"Sorry, I fell asleep. What were you saying?"

"That people need to know how to kiss before they're as old as me."

"Ted didn't figure out how to kiss until we were married."

Silence.

"Lu?"

"Talk about crossing a line."

"Quit."

"I'm going to go, but give that baby girl a kiss from Aunt Lu, okay?"

"Why don't you come here and give her a kiss yourself? Bring your man with you."

My man. I paced a lot that night. I knew I wasn't going to sleep because star-crossed lovers don't sleep; Shakespeare taught me that. Too bad The Bard hadn't written a kissing tutorial in iambic pentameter.

At seven o'clock, the sun rose, and I heard a knock. I didn't need to look through the peephole; I knew who it was. Tie askew, rumpled hair—he looked good. I moved closer, and John ran his right hand down my hair to the nape of my neck, looked at me for a moment, and then pulled me toward him and kissed me.

"Good morning," he said afterwards, leaning his forehead against mine.

"Coffee?"

He nodded, I shut the door, and we were inseparable from that moment on. Until now, of course.

CHAPTER 5

Lisa's wedding day didn't begin with a bridal brunch, but a six o'clock shuffle to her small kitchen for a bowl of Grape Nuts. Peter followed thirty minutes later to pour his cereal and take his seat across from her at their small round table for two. He smiled.

"How would you like to get married?" Peter asked.

"Sure, honey," Lisa responded, not looking up from the morning paper. She wasn't being callous; he'd asked this question before, and she'd given the same answer.

"Today?"

That caught her attention. "Today?"

"When?"

"After work."

"Well, I'd better go shower and get in there early if I'm going to leave early."

They cleaned up their dishes, showered, dressed, and left each other with a kiss and a promise to meet at the chapel—courthouse—at four-thirty ...

RJ read my story out loud as I came into the office on Monday—all 1,136 words of it. I knew he'd run it, but that didn't mean I still had a job.

"Should I pack now?" I asked after he finished.

"Oh, you think you're fired because at the last minute you submitted the opposite of the type of story I requested and then ignored my phone calls?"

"I smashed my phone with a hammer."

That tidbit threw him for a few seconds, but then he continued.

"I intended to fire you. You might be Mary's daughter, you might even be a decent writer, but your attitude stinks, Lu. You've made it clear you don't want to work here. And then you turn in this eleventh-hour piece you knew I wouldn't agree to. Feel free to interrupt if anything I'm saying is untrue."

I swallowed hard and nodded.

"But what you intended as spite has taken on a life of its own."

RJ rotated his monitor. I squinted at the screen and saw email after email with subjects titled "Wedding Feature" and "Not Going to the Chapel" and "Peter and Lisa." RJ hadn't set up an email for me for my trial run at The Daily, so responses to my stories went to him.

"Your story has touched a nerve. Women like weddings—bridal magazines are still going strong in this publishing market—but it appears they also like to read about the simple approach.

"You may have written this reluctantly, but you retell Lisa and Peter's day with warmth. And there's something else, too. Not sarcasm, not skepticism … I don't know how to describe it other than by saying it's a wedding story a man could read without first checking his balls at the door. People are responding.

"So, here it is. You may continue at The Daily as our wedding writer. It's not that you won't get other assignments," RJ said, preemptively holding up his hand to my objections. "But, subscribers and advertisers are hard to come by, and given the level of response we've received on your feature, maybe I can increase both if I focus you here. Two wedding features each month, wedding and engagement announcements every week and any other wedding news that comes our way. You'll also need to start promoting from a social media angle. Deal?"

Deal? I didn't want to write about weddings; I didn't know if I could handle it. The adrenaline of my leaving was gone. In letting my mind flashback to John, I'd opened the door to the good memories that drained me of everything but feeling sad and hurt. I wasn't sure I could write about happily ever after with objectivity. Weddings have enough drama without a crying journalist in the corner.

But I didn't have anything else.

"Deal," I mumbled.

"I'll set up your email so you can start responding to this. And I'll get you your own cubby," RJ said.

I'd arrived.

I spent the rest of the day looking for the next great wedding to cover. My readers had ideas—mainly their own weddings. My family also had ideas, with Nana leading the charge over monkey bread at breakfast the next morning.

"Robert Smith is marrying Stephanie Thompson this Saturday with a reception at her parents' estate. I think the governor is invited, and of course, I'll be attending," Nana said.

"How about Josh and Rachel?" Mom suggested, omitting their last names because I knew these people? "They're getting married in the fall. Such a cute couple."

I swallowed some sweet, sticky monkey bread and shook my head. No offense to Josh and Rachel, but I couldn't handle cute couples right now.

"How about a good elopement?" Grandma Pat posed. "I'll even go with you."

"Tough thing about those elopements, Grandma," I responded. "You rarely know when they're happening."

I licked my fingers clean of butter and cinnamon and pushed my chair back to exit the room before my family pitched more ideas. I climbed the stairs and moved through what would become my morning routine: shower, unpack a box until I found something to wear, and get dressed. The regimen left a bit of downtime before work, which I used to purge my room of High School Lu. I started with emptying racks of old clothes to make way for the boxed ones, but soon moved to upending drawers, clearing the surfaces of my nightstand and dresser, and emptying the bookshelves. I swept under the bed and found lonely socks, raffle tickets, hair ties, and an old magazine with Justin Timberlake on the cover. I took down posters and removed snapshots from my corkboard, starting with pictures of people I couldn't remember, but eventually nixing all of them because I didn't talk to anyone from high school anymore. In the end, I ditched the corkboard, too.

Gradually, my room began to look more Lu, circa now. I caulked all the pushpin holes and painted over the mauve walls with a light blue I found in the cellar. My bookshelf was bare of knick-knacks and memorabilia but for books. On my nightstand stood a picture of Gracie and her girls and a wedding photo of Mom and Dad. The room's only other ornament was the Crock-Pot on my dresser.

By the end of that next week, I'd settled on my next wedding story. I decided to journey to the opposite side of the wedding spectrum to Amanda and James, who'd dated for one year, been engaged for six months, and were waiting until their wedding day for their first kiss. I remembered youth group couples pledging this back in the day, but I was surprised anyone had followed through with it. Would their wedding feel different, given their choices? I was curious to see how it all went down, so it was unfortunate that I noticed their wedding invitation on my parents' fridge Saturday morning.

"What is this?" I held up the invite.

"Our invitation to the Bartlett wedding," Mom said. "We've known Amanda's family for years."

Grandma Pat squinted. "No, that's my invitation—see the tomato sauce smeared on the corner? I called in my RSVP while I was making stuffed cabbage."

"Wait, you're both going?"

"Of course we're going. The Bartletts go to our church, though Amanda is getting married in James' church because the Methodists have a larger fellowship hall for the reception, and frankly, their church is prettier ..."

As Mom droned on, I looked over at Nana, who kept silent.

"You didn't get an invitation?" I asked her.

"I did not," she affirmed.

Good.

"But, I am Patricia's plus one."

"This is unbelievable."

"Why?" Grandma Pat asked, missing the point entirely. "Bea is always my plus one to these things."

"It's unbelievable that I can't go anywhere without family trailing along." An unreasonable accusation, but I was starting to feel like my attic room and my metal desk at the bureau were the only places I could escape, which explained why I was spending so much time at both.

"We received our invitations before you returned home ..." Mom began.

"So, it's you who are following us," Grandma Pat finished.

"I'm uninterested in the timeline, ladies!" I shouted. "You keep to Amanda's side at the ceremony, avoid me at the reception, and we'll call it a truce."

I capped that little tantrum with a slam of the fridge door and sequestered myself in my room until noon when I donned a blue-and-white-polka-dot shirt, white linen shorts, patent yellow leather sandals, and twisted my crazy curls into a manageable chignon. The wedding didn't start until 2:00 p.m., but I wanted to stake the right vantage. My family walked in around 1:45 p.m. with Gracie, Ted, and the girls in tow. They ignored me (per my request) except Gracie, who slid in next to me.

"You're here, too?" I asked.

"Of course. The Bartletts go to our church."

"Everyone says that like it means something."

She shrugged. "Are we not allowed to talk to you?"

"You can," I conceded.

"You're such a teenager, Lu." She squeezed my hand before joining the family.

Fifteen minutes later, the piano crescendoed with Pachelbel's "Canon in D," the grandparents and parents walked down the aisle, the groomsmen entered, and the bridesmaids trickled in one-by-one in lavender chiffon. After a pause and music change to the "Wedding March," the back doors to the church opened and in walked Amanda and Mr. Bartlett, father of the bride and good friend to my dad, apparently. The preliminary wedding pleasantries ensued: a mini sermon and the exchanging of rings and vows before the awaited kiss—long, but not uncomfortably so, great posture, but not too stiff, and the right amount of lingering eye contact afterward. I wasn't sure whether the wait was worth it, but the kiss would look great in the photos.

I'd wrapped up my journalistic observations by the middle of the reception, and decided to conclude business with cake. Chocolate or vanilla? The decision kept me occupied, so I didn't see Jackson coming. I may have jumped at his approach. And reflexively put both hands behind my back.

He laughed. "Don't worry. Your hands are safe from me. By the way, have you figured out who I am yet?"

I nodded. "Did you know I didn't know?"

He smiled.

"Mean."

"I did exactly as you asked."

"Do we have to talk about it?" The awkwardness was killing my cake appetite.

"Yes, but only so we don't have to talk about it ever again."

"We could not talk at all."

"Well, we go to the same church," he pointed out.

"Not me, my family. And why does everyone say that like it means something?"

"Because it does to those people. How about we eat our cake together?"

I opened my mouth to object, but then he confessed, "It's my third piece."

"That seems a little rebellious for a preacher."

"Not rebellious. Fair. They have two flavors, and this is the deciding vote."

"Won't you have to taste both again?"

"Yes, and I need you as a decoy. Four pieces of wedding cake may look greedy." And with that, he cut in front of me, requested vanilla and chocolate, and held one out to me. I stared at it, unsure of what to do. Jackson smiled.

"It's only cake, Louisa."

"Okay, fine." I took the chocolate piece. "You may have one bite of this, but that's it."

"Yes, ma'am," he said, plucking two plastic forks and napkins the same pale purple as the bridesmaids' dresses as we exited the cake line. "Where should we sit?"

I scanned the room; my nine family members were strategically scattered around the fellowship hall.

"Outside."

It was humidity of the choking variety that August afternoon, but I welcomed the silence after the crowded buzz of the reception. We slowly moved past other reception exiles into the open field beyond. It had just been bush-hogged, which released a thick, sweet scent of cut grass, Queen's Anne's lace, and thistles, but offered no good place to sit. The Methodists hadn't thought to put a bench out here, but Jackson was prepared. After handing his cake to me, he unfolded a cocktail napkin and placed it on the ground—a gallant gesture that might protect half a butt cheek's worth of my white linen shorts. I decided to plop right down in the middle, figuring that if I couldn't avoid grass stains, I might as well aim for symmetrical green imprints on the outer rims.

I handed Jackson his cake after he sat down next to me, and held out my plate for him to claim his test piece before I dug in. He cut into about half of it with his fork and popped the wedge in his mouth.

"What the ...? You ... you ate half my cake!"

"I told you my plan upfront. You were merely a decoy."

"Well yes, but then you laid this napkin down all gentlemen-ish..."

"A decoy within a decoy," he explained before eating half of his vanilla in one bite.

"Can't you eat cake like a normal person?"

"Why do you think I brought you all the way out here?"

"To watch you eat cake like a shark, apparently. Where did you eat the other two pieces?"

"On the toilet."

I laughed—a real laugh that would have shot buttercream frosting out of my nose if I'd had any yet.

"Did you really eat cake on the toilet?" I managed to ask before I started laughing again.

"No, but I did make sure my mom wasn't looking before I wolfed it down. She hates how I eat."

"Your mom's here?"

"Your mom's here," he pointed out.

"That's not an explanation."

"We all go to the same church."

"That's barely an explanation."

"Says the girl who doesn't go to church. How come I don't see you there?"

I stalled with a bite of cake. I'm ever appreciative of what butter whipped with powdered sugar can do. The frosting was airy and sweet, and I carefully scraped all of it off the cake before digging into the cake itself, which tasted like chocolate cardboard. I should have stuck with the frosting.

"You want an honest answer?" I asked, setting my plate down.

"I do."

"I don't believe what my family believes."

"Do they mind that you don't go?"

"We've never talked about it. Though everything else seems up for discussion."

"Have you ever discussed what you do—or do not—believe with anyone else?"

This is the point at which I'd normally shut down the conversation. Usually, I'd never let a conversation get this far. I leaned back on my hands and looked at Jackson. I noticed his green eyes again, but it was the kindness behind them that struck me. And the openness. He was asking so many questions, personal questions, but I had the sense he was asking just to ask. It was nice to speak with someone who didn't have an obvious agenda, so I answered him.

"My ex-boyfriend, John, is Catholic, but in the Easter-Christmas tradition. He didn't care for it, and I was ready to break from the Sunday morning, Sunday evening, and Wednesday evening grind I'd been raised in. We never talked about faith other than to mutually agree not to go to church. After I left Dunlap's Creek, I was so happy not to be running into people I knew that I never got around to making friends—at least not good ones. John is like me. He's much more socially adept—quite charming when the situation calls for it—but also a loner by nature. And now that he's …"

I couldn't muster the word "gone." The thought of it instantly brought tears to my eyes, and I quickly wiped them away. I needed to end this line of conversation as quickly as possible.

"Now that he's there and I'm here, it's only me." It sounded lonely. It felt that way, too. I wrapped my arms around my knees.

"You always were in the thick of the crowds in high school," Jackson said.

"Yes, but that's because of Gracie, who's the most likeable person on the planet. Any friends I had were by association. It was never my preference. And we change, right? You used to fasten those buttons up to your Adam's apple," I said nodding toward the open collar of his blue shirt.

He laughed. "Back then I was under the impression that right choices—how I buttoned my shirts, for example—were important."

"Because of your church upbringing," I pointed out.

"Because of my misinterpretation of it," he corrected.

"And now?"

"Now I see grace—room to breathe, so to speak. And forgiveness. And my responsibility in it all. I'm guilty of more than inflating the importance of dress code, Louisa."

"Like what?" I asked. I couldn't help myself.

"Like dating a girl for years and insisting on seeing her as I wanted her to be instead of who she was. Kate left me, but I'm no less to blame."

He said it simply and without any of the excuses people usually offer to absolve themselves. And yet, the confession didn't seem to weigh him down.

"Is it hard for you to be back here?" I asked.

"Yes, but not in the way I think you mean," he said looking at me. "My family, my church—they've welcomed me back, or at least most of them. Divorce is complicated."

"So what are your thoughts on weddings like this where people wait to kiss until it's too late to turn back?"

"It's hopeful. You?"

"Odd, and maybe naïve? But I can't write that for the paper. I'm not even sure it's okay to say. Maybe I feel comfortable confessing it to you because of how you eat cake." And then came the vision of him eating cake on the toilet, and I started laughing all over again.

"You eat your cake weird, too," he said, standing and holding out his hand to help me up. I took it and brushed the field clippings from my shorts and legs. We headed back toward the church.

"What about how I eat my cake?" I asked.

"You mean your frosting."

"I should have stopped there. The cake was tasteless."

"I didn't notice."

"Because you didn't chew."

"If I eat cake at the pulpit tomorrow, will you come?"

"You're preaching?" I asked, as we stepped on the sidewalk. "This is all very tricky. A decoy within a decoy within a decoy."

"To get you to come to church," he affirmed.

"And save my sorry soul."

"Truth?" He leaned down, looking his green eyes straight into mine.

I didn't move.

"I don't even like cake." And with that, he walked away, leaving me to my laughter for the third time that day and the third time in a long, long time.

CHAPTER 6

Coming alone to church seemed like the right move, which meant getting up early. It was impossible to out-wake my family, but I'd set my alarm for seven, showered and dressed. A cool evening had followed yesterday's heat, leaving a fog that hovered above the cornstalks. I wanted to walk through it, so I nixed my plan for a skirt and sandals and went with shorts and sneakers instead. I took my breakfast of a coffee and two biscuits to go.

Two miles on foot, and I still arrived at church over an hour early. I nodded at the people readying the welcome foyer, but the sanctuary was quiet and cool. I ran my fingers along the tops of the pews as I made my way to a seat in the back right, far away from where I remember my family sitting. They were always front-and-center people. I hoped they still were.

I sat and checked my watch. Fifty-eight minutes to go and nothing to pass the time. I always keep an extra book in my purse for emergency downtimes, but I'd left that behind when I chose to walk. I scavenged the pew pockets, but found only Bibles, hymnals, and visitor cards. I wasn't interested in the first two and considered doodling away on the latter until I remembered—I can't draw.

Thankfully, Jackson entered from stage left to take his place at the podium. He cleared his throat and launched right in, treating me to a little sermon rehearsal. After ten minutes, I was wondering whether I'd even need to stay for the show when he squinted in my direction and cut short.

"Are you spying on me, Louisa?" he asked, right into the

microphone.

"I was here first," I noted.

"What's that?" he asked into the microphone.

"I was here first," I said a little louder, my voice echoing off the stone pillars and wooden pews.

"Sorry, can't catch it," he said again into the microphone. "Why don't you come forward?"

I sighed and walked to the stage. "I said I was here first."

He smiled. "I know; I heard you the first time."

"You remind me of my older brother."

"Ted? I like him."

"I don't."

"So, what do you think?" he asked, coming down from the stage and standing next to me.

"About your sermon? Mostly I was wondering whether listening to your rehearsal exempted me from the service."

"Sure … if you were listening."

Jackson had me there.

"You're consigned for the next round, then" he said.

"You can't blame it all on me. Beginning a sermon with, 'Please open to the book of Ecclesiastes,' is hardly compelling. If I started a news story like that, no one would read it."

"That's the normal start, and I guarantee you eighty percent of the crowd will follow suit."

"But shouldn't you be speaking to the twenty percent who aren't inclined to open their Bibles?"

"What would compel them?"

Nothing, I almost rejoined, but it was a thoughtful question that deserved more than reflexive snark. I took a moment to think it through.

"Something to answer the why," I offered. "Why should I open my Bible? What can it possibly say to me? How can it help me?"

"And if I do that, would you open it?" he asked.

"Why not?"

"You sound like you've got nothing to lose."

"There's nothing in there I haven't read before. 'The five poetic books of the Bible are Job, Psalms, Proverbs, Ecclesiastes, and the Song of Solomon,'" I recited in my best Sunday school sing-song.

"Careful, I might ask you to come forward with that one-woman show."

That threat, plus the approaching buzz of early birds, reminded me it was time to scuttle back to my section.

"Remember your promise," Jackson called out. I waved a yeah-yeah hand before returning to my seat and sitting still as a statue in the back of the church, which, as it turns out, is where families with small children sit. It was a gross place, what with the boy next to me foraging in his nose for a booger breakfast, but entertaining enough to carry me through the initial church festivities of singing, announcements, and prayer until Jackson resumed the podium.

"If you'd please, open your Bibles to the book of Ecclesiastes. While you're getting there, I've got something for you to look at." And then, the Welcome screen switched to a snapshot of a chubby little boy with his arms V'd in victory, his pants around his ankles, and his bottom front and center. I laughed, and then coughed, unsure as to whether my lowbrow humor was kosher, but then started laughing again when I heard other people do the same.

"It's okay. You can laugh," Jackson said, turning to the screen and laughing, too. "This is three-year-old me after the first time I used the outhouse at my grandparents' camp. I was terrified of it and stuck to the trees until number 2 came calling. I thought, 'If only I can use the outhouse, I'll be a brave boy.' But it turns out that where I was brave enough to go, I wasn't brave enough to stay—at least not long enough to pull up my pants."

He paused before turning to us.

"It's one thing to be caught with your pants down as a kid. Childhood is at least seventy-five percent embarrassment. Adulthood is different. Not in perspective—we're only slightly less naïve, unfortunately—but in the consequences of our naivety. The stakes are higher, and they usually don't end with a funny picture and a laugh.

"Tell me: How many of you have had 'If only …' thoughts recently?

"'If only I could move here, then …'

"'If only I had this job making this much money, I could …'

"'If only I'd been in this place at this time, then …'

'We've all thought this way, especially when our life hasn't turned out like we hoped. It's a natural response to disappointment. And it's logical to think we can solve our problems by swapping a few of the factors. This person for that one. An hourly paycheck for a salary. One less meal to lose a few

46

more pounds. And sometimes, it happens—our 'If only ...' comes true, and we get the job. Yes! And the rightness of our world lasts for ... what? A day? A week? A year?

"The demanding boss, bickering coworkers, long hours—they all factor into our growing dissatisfaction—but the real problem is that the job doesn't deliver what we were really looking for in the first place. Identity. Satisfaction. A sense of worth. A place to stand still. No job, no person, no place can deliver these things, but we can't stop seeking them. It's not long before we're back at it, seeking the next 'If only ...' as the antidote for our disappointment.

"Solomon, king of Israel and the writer of Ecclesiastes, calls out this naïve life pattern from the start of the book: 'Meaningless! Meaningless ... Utterly meaningless! Everything is meaningless.' He calls it as warning: If you limit your search for meaning to the horizontal plane of this world, you will not find it. And he calls it as a promise because everything that is here is not everything there is.

"If you haven't already, please open your Bibles to Ecclesiastes, chapter one, so that we can see what this king of ancient Israel has to say to us in Dunlap's Creek today."

Jackson had kept his end of the bargain, and I reached into the pew pocket to keep mine, looking like any other church girl with her Bible in her lap. But I felt conspicuous. In five minutes, Jackson pegged my state better than I had in all of my rehashing since I'd returned. How had John and I gone from that first morning six years ago to his cheating and my leaving? I'm not sure when John and I stopped playing our parts of the loving boyfriend and girlfriend, but it'd been a long time—long enough for me to feel like a stranger when I replayed our first kiss in my mind. And when I compounded that with my failed career and the city that didn't deliver ... well, then.

There was too much to feel—so much that I feared the emotions would drown me. I couldn't even begin to parse it all. I'd tried my best to tamp it down in the last couple weeks, but under it all, as Jackson had said, was disappointment. He didn't need to convince me of this. I could taste it.

I sat there, with my hand on the open Bible and not listening to another word until the people around me began to shift. I guessed Jackson's sermon was wrapping up.

"I always carry this photo in my pocket because even though

I'm a few decades beyond my three-year-old self, I'm not that much better at self-perception. I still think 'If only ...' thoughts. But now when I'm in the middle of that road, I stop. I pull out this photo to remind myself of where all these meaningless chases end—me with my pants down, figuratively speaking.

"The Bible gives us the same wake-up call—but some of you might not be ready for it. Maybe you don't believe the Bible has anything to say to you. Maybe you don't believe there's a God, or maybe you believe in a distant God who doesn't speak to us or who doesn't speak like this.

"Then don't open your Bible yet. Instead, find one of these pictures—of you at a particular time, in a particular moment and bring it with you next week."

And that was the reason my family retired to the family room instead of to Sunday naps after our meatloaf supper. By the time I'd put away the dishes and wiped off the counters, they were elbow deep in photo albums and boxes, and though I'd fully intended to tiptoe past and retreat to my room with my coffee, I noticed that even Nana Bea was picking her way through a small box perched daintily on her knees.

"What about this one?" she asked, brandishing a black-and-white photo of her in a floor-length gown with her arm around my mom as they both smiled angelically at the camera. My mother rolled her eyes. I'm guessing this wasn't the first beautiful photo of herself that my Nana had suggested.

"You're missing the point, Mom," she told Nana.

"We're supposed to find a photo from our past. Jackson showed a photo from his past," she defended.

"Yes, of his pants down," Grandma Pat cackled, still tickled by nude photos + church. "You're not looking for a picture where you're looking good."

"Why ever would I bring a photo where I am not looking good?"

"Because he's looking for irony," I interjected, inadvertently stepping into the fray as I stepped into the room. No one had mentioned my church attendance at supper, and I wasn't certain they'd noticed. I guess the jig was up now. "A picture where you think you're doing one thing but the opposite is true. More along the lines of the emperor has no clothes."

"Well, I don't have any nude pictures," she sniffed.

"Naked is not the only form of irony," I said.

"But it's the funniest!" Grandma Pat exclaimed, laughing all over again. She was sitting cross-legged on the floor with a swarm of snapshots surrounding her, all in which she was making a silly face, wearing something ridiculous, or striking a pose.

"You're more of a three-year-old in these pictures than Jackson," I said.

"What do you mean?"

"Have you ever made a straight face at the camera?"

"The goal is to find a funny photo," she pointed out.

"The goal is to find a photo that's funny now but probably not at the time it was taken, especially if you were aware of the greater context," I countered.

"The what? Stop speaking college, Lu, and help me out. But first go make me some of that tasty coffee."

I had nothing better to do, so I did as requested and spent the rest of the afternoon looking through old family photos. In the end, I persuaded each to take a photo she'd rather leave behind. For Grandma, it was a photo of her proudly smiling at her pierogie stand at the famer's market while some old dude dumped a plate of half-eaten pierogies in the trashcan behind her. It was 1972, and the man is most likely dead, but she vowed to refuse him pierogies if he ever stopped by again.

Nana's was of her in heels at the starting line of a walk-a-thon.

"How was I to know there would be an actual walk?" she argued, clearly still miffed.

And Mom's was a snapshot of bad 1980s judgment—one of her teacher school pictures complete with eyeglasses as big as her head, a perm, and a dye job gone orange. None of us could understand why she'd left the house, let alone smiled for a picture looking like that. Lack of vanity, she virtuously proclaimed. We voted her down.

I was still looking through pictures long after they'd left, having moved to the meticulous photo journaling of my own childhood. It was like turning the pages of a storybook, and at the next page of the photo album, I gasped. How could I have forgotten the tire swing suspended from the old oak tree in the backyard? I gently removed the photo from the plastic insert, thinking about the hours I twirled away, daydreaming I was in the stories I'd read when I wasn't twirling. Read, twirl. Read, twirl. That was the pattern of my girlhood days. I turned the photo over—*Lu, age 7.*

I heard the floorboards creak and looked up to see Dad walking into the room. He'd shown a group around the new church building after services and missed our afternoon's festivities.

"We should put the tire swing back up," I said. "I'll donate my spare."

"It's not good to be without a spare. Especially in your car."

"Not having a spare is the least of my worries with that heap. I should scrap it." I stood up and surveyed our afternoon's preoccupation.

"Why did you bring the photos out today?" he asked as he sifted through a stack on an end table.

"Jackson asked us to find a photo at the end of the sermon, remember? Mom, Nana, and Grandma got right to it after supper, and you should have seen what they came up with before I intervened. What would you choose for yourself?"

He crossed to where Grandma had been sitting and sorted through some piles. When he found the photo he was looking for, he tossed it Frisbee-style in my general direction. I caught it and looked.

"I don't get it. It's a young you in a suit smiling at the camera."

"Look at the back."

I turned it over and saw Grandma's slanted scrawl: *Mark— August 24, 1966.*

"That's the night of your mother's and my first date. Haven't you heard the story? Her family summered at the lake, where I commuted on bike to work at the old summer resort. Her family had the biggest place on the lake, but I hadn't met your mom until that year when she took a job—against Nana Bea's wishes—to teach kids swimming at the resort pool. The summer cottages around the pool were in constant need of repair, so our paths crossed a lot. It still took me all summer to work up the courage to ask your mom out—and save up the money. I wanted to pick her up in something other than my bike and take her somewhere nice.

"So you can imagine the surprise the boy in this picture felt when he finally did show up to her house in his secondhand suit in a car he'd worked on for two weeks to get it to start, and the girl of his dreams met him at the door in a ponytail and white T-shirt and suggested they hike to the lake for a picnic dinner."

"What did you do?" I asked.

"I put my coat in the car and walked with her down to the lake. I was grateful to keep the fifty bucks in my back pocket, I can tell you that. My car needed rear brakes."

He laughed and pointed to the picture in my hand. "Grandma Pat took that picture because I told her I was about to take the girl I was going to marry on our first date. I'd planned that first date all summer, but I couldn't have married anyone other than the girl who met me at the door and threw all my plans away with her picnic basket and bare feet. If I'd known, I'd have asked your mom out right after Memorial Day."

"What if it had gone the other way? If she'd met you in a dress and heels?" I asked.

He thought about that for a moment. "That's what makes this the right picture: a boy dressed up for a role he couldn't afford to play. Literally. Your mom and I grew up in very different worlds. She was the only daughter of the wealthiest family in town. I'm the only son of a single mother who worked days tailoring other people's clothes and nights catering for other people's parties. It took me all summer to earn enough money to have one dinner in your mother's world. That would have resulted in a pretty long courtship, don't you think? You might still not be born at that rate."

I looked down at the picture again. He was ten years younger than me, and he looked like a kid, a really excited kid. "It's the right picture," I agreed, handing it back to him.

"What picture did you choose?"

"I'm not past the single digits of childhood. No irony yet, just a lot of smiles," I said, choosing not to tell him about the photo of John and me in the Crock-Pot upstairs. I started to put the pictures back, but Dad interrupted.

"Let those pictures take care of themselves and get me your car keys."

"For what?"

"Your spare for your swing."

CHAPTER 7

It's an idyllic picture. I'm seven and wearing the perfect white, smocked dress for swinging on a summer evening. And I'm standing in the swing instead of sitting, leveraging my bare feet back and forth against the firm rim of the tire. Eventually, the swinging takes care of itself, and this picture captures me in a free-flying upswing with my head thrown back, my dress flowing behind, and a large smile on my face.

I smile and set it aside. It's the only personal item I'd brought with me to the office, but I didn't bring it for nostalgia. Digging through pictures yesterday got me thinking about how they tell stories differently than words. RJ wanted social media with the wedding beat, and I thought that if I gave up an afternoon to look through family photos, maybe people would do the same with other people's wedding photos.

I'm not the social media type, but it didn't take me long to figure out how to create the Instagram account, @creekweddings. I uploaded a pic of Saturday's wedding kiss, threw out some hashtags, and posted: "First kiss for @amandabartlett and @jamespshore52. Yours?" For followers, I invited the people who'd emailed me about the last two features.

Was there anything else to it? I wasn't quite sure, but Grandma Pat said dough never rises when you watch it, so I moved onto wedding and engagement announcements for the rest of morning. At lunchtime, I had ten followers, three of whom linked to their own smooch shots. By Tuesday morning, seventeen, and by the time I left work on Wednesday, I had twenty-five followers and ten pics. How come articles didn't leaven like this?

I couldn't help but tell Grandma Pat about it that night as I set the table for dinner.

"There's this thing called Instagram …"

"I know all about it," Grandma said, interrupting my Instagram 101 lecture. "Make sure you put spoons out for the applesauce."

"And I created the @creekweddings account …"

"Yes, I'm following it."

That messed up my spoon count. "You have an Instagram account?"

"@pierogiepat."

"You have an Instagram account?" I repeated.

"Two," she corrected. "One for the pierogies and one for the store—@pennythriftpat. You need to keep with the times if you're going to stay in business."

"I didn't know you knew how to use a computer."

"I don't like to brag."

"How did you find out about @creekweddings?"

"I'm keeping tabs on you, honey."

"Are you following me, too?" I asked Nana Bea, who'd been listening to our interchange from her place at the table.

"I am not."

So my world wasn't totally upended.

"Okay spoons," I stated, trying to reestablish normalcy. "Anything else different than the usual for dinner? You want me to get the iPad from under your pillow so you can update your status before we eat?"

"Go ahead and set an extra place," Grandma Pat said. A little too casually.

"Who's coming to dinner?" I demanded right before the doorbell rang. I didn't need to ask the question. I didn't even need to answer the door to explain tonight's midweek feast of pork roast, twice-baked potatoes, a roasted cauliflower crown, and homemade applesauce.

"I'd answer the door, but I'm carrying the roast to the table, and remember when you dropped the roast on the floor?"

"One time and I was six!" I shouted as I flung the front door open. Jackson.

"Hello, Louisa," he said, holding a bouquet of yellow

53

carnations.

"I can't believe this," I said, glaring at him and then toward Grandma in the dining room and then back to him.

"I know," he said gravely, stepping inside without an invitation—from me anyway. "I came up with the picture idea, and you stole it."

"You have an Instagram account, too?"

"@prodigalpreacher."

"Really?"

"No. @jacksonclearyABC."

"That sounds like a board book."

"Jacksoncleary was taken so I started adding letters until Instagram cleared me for access."

He smiled at me, and I smiled back without thinking. I had been wanting to see him again, but I didn't want him to misinterpret the dinner invitation.

"Jackson, I didn't invite you to dinner," I clarified gesturing to the flowers and closing the front door behind him.

"These are for @pierogiepat," he said before he brushed past me toward the dining room to hug Grandma and hand her the flowers. Nana didn't budge an inch and only nodded her head when he greeted her, which I took as a sign that she was on my side. Dad played no part in setups, and Mom seemed a bit surprised at his presence when she came downstairs, so I fully blamed Grandma Pat for our surprise guest.

I checked my reflection in the vestibule mirror and grimaced: typical six o'clock frizz-bombed hair that I'd run my hands through too many times today, makeup long gone, jewelry off, and me wearing cut-offs again. There was no sneaking away to freshen up, so I headed to the dining room where everyone was taking their seats around the table—with Jackson flanked by my grandmas and across from me, Mom to my right and Dad to hers at the head of the table.

I presumed dinner would play out uncomfortably. I was right.

"How long have you been divorced?" Nana asked Jackson immediately after grace, an irony totally lost on her.

"One year," he said not missing a beat, unfolding his napkin and putting it on his lap. I wondered how often he'd had to answer this question.

"But you only came back this summer," she noted after taking a small dollop of applesauce and passing him the bowl.

"Yes, ma'am."

"Well, we're glad you're here," Grandma Pat cut in, glaring at Nana and suddenly all concerned about what constitutes as rude. She carved a slice of pork and placed it on his plate with a side of advice. "You could wear jeans when you preach on Sunday, you know."

"I might get there, but I've only just started unbuttoning the top button of my shirts," he pointed out, winking at me. I ignored him and took a bite of pork drenched in applesauce. Amazing. Grandma was pesky, but she could cook.

She continued, "It's good you've loosened up; you always did seem like a stuffy little boy. And a bit pudgy. But, you've lengthened out now, so the girls will be trampling over themselves to get at you."

I wasn't sure whether Grandma was talking to him or me, so I ignored her and took another bite. Jackson also opted for the nonresponse and passed the cauliflower instead. Thankfully, Mom intervened to ask Jackson about his family, and since Nana had sniffed her disapproval and Grandma advertised her intentions, they let dinner proceed in a more polite direction. Jackson seemed unfazed by the introductory lightening round, and he chatted amiably with the family for the rest of dinner. His presence took the heat of questions and opinions off of me, but I was still rattled by his unexpected presence. I knew he wasn't here for @pierogiepat, but I didn't think he was here for me either, at least not in the way Grandma was scheming.

Regardless, by the time we finished dessert I realized I liked having him here. So, I brought him a cup of coffee after he helped clear the table.

"I don't drink coffee."

"If you're going to be my friend you do."

He took a sip. "This tastes horrible. Do you have any cream or sugar?"

I shook my head and nudged him out the back door before Grandma Pat could enact the next step in her matchmaker plan.

The hot day had given way to one of those summer evenings where the humidity starts working in your favor. The moist air felt cool enough on my arms to raise goose bumps, and I gently rubbed them as we crossed the deck to the backyard.

"I'm sorry about my grandmas."

"I like them."

"That's impossible."

"They say what they think. Now it's out there and done with."

"Out there but not done with," I clarified. "Nana will always disapprove of your divorce, and Grandma won't stop trying to set us up until you remarry."

"What can I say? I'm a catch."

I laughed and shook my head. "You're a pastor, not a rock star."

"Ahh, but in the church world, a single pastor is like a rock star," he countered.

"Then it's a strange little world. Is Dunlap Creek's Most Eligible Bachelor eligible for a game of cornhole?"

"Cornhole? I haven't played in years," he said, putting down his coffee to help me lug the boards from under the deck and pace them apart like a true gentlemen.

He slayed me in the first game, twenty-one to seventeen. I called him out on his crap. He laughed and suggested another game. It was on, but first I required he drink the rest of his coffee like a shot for hustling me.

"I thought it was only losers who had to pay penance," he said after he tossed back his coffee and coughed, pounding his chest.

"Did someone say Lu-ser?" Ted shouted, coming from next door with Gracie behind him.

"I did," Jackson said. "Do you want to join us for another game? Your sister could use some help."

"Was that a cup of Lu's coffee in your hand?" Ted asked him.

"Yes," Jackson responded.

"That's nasty stuff. Take this to wash it down." Ted handed him a beer, and the two immediately launched into baseball chatter while Gracie and I dug the corn bags from under the boards and took our position on the opposing side.

"Sorry," Gracie whispered. "Ted insisted on butting in when he saw Jackson out here. I thought tagging along might dilute him a bit."

"It's Grandma Pat who needs to apologize."

"Do you mind?"

"To the scheming, yes."

"And to him?" Gracie inclined her head toward Jackson and

smiled at me.

I looked across the yard at Jackson talking with Ted. His left hand was in his pocket, his right held a beer. He seemed at ease, and fit in well here, or at least much better than John ever had. John had always been meticulously polite—not in a false way, but as a means to an end, always looking for the nearest exit. Jackson looked like he could stay all night. From my vantage of twenty-seven paces, I could see Grandma was right; Jackson had lengthened out. Pastor or no, he looked good.

"He's fine." I shrugged. Gracie laughed.

"Let us know when you girls are done with your chatting so we can start playing," I shouted to the boys.

"She's mad because I beat her," Jackson informed Ted.

"I'll team up with cornhole shark there; Gracie, you're with Ted."

Of course, Jackson and I beat them, twenty-one to fifteen. Gracie was a hopeless yard gamer, and Ted, who dominated in every other sport, never could get the finesse that this arena requires. We played for the next hour, switching up the teams every game, with Jackson and I winning whenever we were together and competing head-to-head whenever we were against each other. We were dead even when Gracie called it quits on the fun.

"The girls will wake up at six o'clock tomorrow, regardless of what time I go to bed tonight," she said.

Ted shook Jackson's hand, which I thought was nice. But then he concluded with, "Great seeing you, Jackson. You're a much better cornhole player than the last guy Lu brought around."

Which was not nice at all. I didn't smack him, but that's because Gracie got to him first.

"One more game. The deciding one," I informed Jackson after they headed inside.

"Whatever you want; I can go all night with that cup of coffee you made me drink."

"Was it that horrible? I was a professional New York barista, you know."

"It might be time for option B."

I threw a bag straight into the hole. "That *was* option B."

"What was A?"

"Why doing fabulous writing for a fabulous paper where I would earn a fabulous Pulitzer, of course." The admission, surprisingly, rolled easily off my tongue. Jackson met my three-pointer with one of his own, which I followed with a toss onto the board. This was going to be another good game.

"But it didn't work out?"

"No. Nothing in New York worked out."

"Well, what can you expect when you move to New York with a guy who can't play cornhole?"

"Where were you when I could have used that advice?"

"With Kate."

"Was she a yard-game girl?"

"No. Not an outdoors girl, including backyards."

"I can see why!" I exploded as we crossed to the other board to collect our bags. None of his had landed on the grass. "You're merciless. Are your bags weighted differently?"

"Hey," he countered, holding up his hands in innocence. "Your bags, your boards."

I sighed and threw another—in the hole. But, so did he. "That's five in a row!"

"And you're playing like your brother," he said, laughing. "That was nice of him to come over."

"Oh, what—coming all this way to bug me?" I asked.

"He didn't come to bug you. He came to look out for you."

That revelation landed my next bag way left of the board.

"You're saying that because you're a pastor. It's your job to think the best of people."

"More like to see people as they are."

"And what do you see in me?"

"I'm not touching that landmine. Plus, am I a pastor of a girl who 'barely' comes to church?"

"I came this Sunday, I helped you with your sermon, and I did the homework."

"Which part: opening the Bible or finding the picture?"

"Come on, now," I said, rolling my eyes at him. "Do you carry that picture around with you all the time?"

He reached for his back pocket. "Want to see it again?"

I laughed. "No thank you. I have two pictures—one of me in a mid-cornhole victory dance with John looking baffled in the background. That picture is in the Crock-Pot upstairs in my bedroom."

"Do a lot of slow cooking up there?" Jackson asked as we

crossed back to the other side. He was beating me, but I blamed it on all the questions.

"It's sentimental, ex-girlfriend stuff. The Crock-Pot is the only thing I took from our apartment after John told me he cheated on me."

"He cheated on you?"

I nodded, because it was easier than admitting it out loud.

"And you responded by taking the Crock-Pot?" He laughed. "Sorry. I shouldn't laugh, but that's hilarious."

It was funny now, but at the time it seemed like my only option. John was confident and direct—he looked people straight in the eyes when he talked to them. But the night he told me he cheated on me, he looked at his hands. On and on his narrative went, and he never once looked up. I knew this because I stared at him the whole time, the sight of him anchoring me while his words undid me. Only after he shut up did he meet my stare. There were tears in his eyes.

So he was the one crying. I refused to join him, but swallowing against the boulder in my throat was like putting tape on faucet. I needed to get out of there before the whole thing blew open. I stood and surveyed our studio apartment. I'd never loved it, but I hated it now. All the "finds" I'd collected from thrift stores and flea markets—tarnished silver candlesticks, vintage posters, threadbare rugs—looked like the junk they were. John could take care of it. He'd probably already called the moving truck. He'd wanted to move for years, but I'd insisted on paying half of our living expenses, and the rent for this place was the best I could do on my barista income. It was one of our many fights.

As was the Crock-Pot on the drying rack. I knew how to make one thing: pork and sauerkraut, courtesy of my polish grandma. John had liked it when we were both broke, but then he became rich and eating leftovers day-in and day-out no longer appealed. That didn't change that it was the end of the month for me, and I was broke. He hadn't said much about Avery in his cheating confession, but I bet she didn't come to the relationship with a pea-green Crock-Pot.

I seized mine.

"I guess your new girl won't be needing this!" I declared, waving the ratty cord in front of his face before heading to the front door. I intended to leave without another word, but John followed me.

59

"Lu," he said as I stepped into the hallway. *"Is that all you're going to say?"*

I couldn't keep the tears from my eyes as I turned back to look at him. His confession was out of the way, and he looked more like himself as he leaned against the doorframe. My boyfriend, except that he wasn't anymore. He was with someone else.

We'd been together for six years. It was okay if it took me a little while to catch up to the new reality that John was no longer mine. But I did have something to say first.

"I hate that you did this, and I wish that hate was strong enough to drive out how I feel about you, but it doesn't. I love you, John. And if you have any feelings left for me at all, you will leave me alone."

It turns out I hadn't meant that last part. That's the problem with little speeches—they have a way of taking over. But it was done, and I wasn't about to piece together my smashed phone to call John and tell him I'd changed my mind.

I looked at Jackson before I switched my focus to the next shot. In the hole. "Leaving with the Crock-Pot was the best I could do at the time."

We were quiet for the rest of the game, which Jackson won twenty-one to nineteen.

"Seriously, is your life preaching and corn holing?" I asked as I collected the bags and Jackson carried the boards back to the deck.

"You've figured me out," he said. "You said you had two pictures. What's the other one?"

I stowed the bag bin next the boards, wiped my hands on my legs, and pulled out the tire swing photo.

"I know it flunks the assignment," I explained, "but I'm carrying enough other baggage. That disappointment you mentioned in your sermon? That's where I am. Maybe it'd be better for me to carry a picture of what I'd like to get back to."

"And what's that?" Jackson asked looking at me.

I looked at the picture.

"Happy. And free. New York wasn't great, but without John, there wasn't anything to keep me there—no real friends, no real job. And I'm tired. I know this seems like a ridiculous thing to say at the age of twenty-nine, but I couldn't come up with another plan right now if I tried. Coming back gives me time ... even if that time means Grandma Pat invites pastors over for dinner behind my back."

"That didn't turn out so bad, right?" Jackson looked at me.

I smiled in return. "Aside from Gracie, you're the first person I've talked to. Wanted to talk to. I laugh a lot more when you're around—probably because you call me out on my crap."

"The underbelly of pastoral work."

"So you're here as my pastor."

"No, as your friend and for similar reasons. I have a history with most of the people in this town, and being a divorced pastor stands in the way of making easy conversation. But you don't seem to have a problem telling me exactly what you think."

"Now you make me sound like my grandmas," I said, stepping off the deck to walk Jackson back to his car. "Thanks for coming over tonight."

"Maybe next time you could invite me instead of @pierogiepat?" he asked, opening his front door.

"You actually follow her on Instagram?"

"Heck, yeah. I've been a regular at her stand long before you came back."

"Didn't you come back when I did?"

"A month before. That's four Saturdays of pierogies."

"I'll be at the stand this Saturday."

"You make pierogies?"

"No. Grandma won't even let me pinch them, but she has a trunk show at her shop, so I'm on farmer's market duty."

"That's nice of you."

"I'm only doing it because she's paying me. My rent check is due in a couple weeks."

"You have to pay your parents rent?"

"Don't get me started."

"You want some company at the stand?"

"Yes," I said before I could second-guess myself.

Jackson got in the car and backed out of the drive, the gravel popping under his tires. I waved goodbye and turned toward the house. I was surprised all the lights were off, save the front porch light. Gracie's house was still, too. I checked my watch—11:47 p.m. I closed my eyes, enjoying the quiet of the night but for the cricket chatter. I should go to bed, but I headed toward the backyard for a midnight swing instead.

CHAPTER 8

"Pierogies," Jackson shouted, in the most drawn out way possible to the Farmer's Market crowd that Saturday morning. "Get your pierogies, one for one dollar or two for one-fifty."

I shushed him. "It's already a three-syllable word; you don't need to make it five. And can't you quiet down a bit? Not everyone woke up ready to hear your shouting."

He laughed at that, totally unfazed by my seven o'clock, one-sip, Saturday morning self. "You keep to the back of the stand cranky pants and let me handle things up front until you're caffeinated," he said.

I clutched my coffee mug like a life preserver and set up a folding chair by the coolers holding potato pierogies and potato and cheese pierogies and cottage cheese pierogies and sauerkraut pierogies.

It'd been awhile since I'd worked this scene, but Jackson operated it like a pro. He knew most people's names, and if he didn't, he asked. "What's your name? Where are you from? Where are you headed on this fine Saturday?" Ladies old and young ate it up, and I'm convinced Grandma's sales to the thirty-and-under female crowd spiked with Jackson at the helm. Him and his unshaved Saturday morning self.

Coffee finished, I set my cup aside to help. "What can I do?"

"Why don't you sauté while I take orders?"

He handed me his spatula and white apron. I tied it around my waist as I moved toward the griddle. The smell of pierogies frying in butter and sweet onions made my mouth water, and I popped a potato and cheese in my mouth without even thinking.

"Hey, those aren't for you. They're to entice the customers."

I hid my smile with my hand, but I couldn't stop myself from turning to look at him.

"What?" he asked.

I took his measure with my eyes. The poor man didn't realize what was attracting our newfound customer base, and to point it out would probably embarrass him, so I kept quiet and ate another pierogie.

"I can't help it, Jackson. The smell makes me feel like I've been on a hunger strike."

"You want something to wash that down?" he asked, handing me the cup of coffee I'd brought him, but he hadn't touched. His loss.

I sipped, sautéed, and scoped the crowd. I think we were on our fifteenth day of ninety-plus heat, but the market was hopping with consumers wearing straw hats and toting reusable produce bags. They seemed in no rush, perfectly happy to talk heirloom tomato varieties and hormone-free sausage links. Sally, the gluten-free, dairy-free cupcake lady across the way, was doing as brisk a business as us. The idea of Grandma Pat's stand across from such dietary restrictions made me chuckle.

"What's so funny?" Jackson asked after he'd sold a baker's dozen of kraut pierogies.

I nodded toward Sally's stall. "Grandma Pat's million and one opinions about that."

"Should we buy a sample?"

"So you can swallow them whole and leave me with the crumbs? No thanks. The fact that her cupcakes sell for three times as much as Grandma's pierogies is funny, though."

Business swelled, and I was grateful for the extra layer of deodorant I'd swiped, given the combined heat of the morning and the griddle. I didn't have to do much—all of Jackson's smiles and chatty left me to simply direct customers to the pierogie varieties so they could try and buy. Most did, and our coolers were empty by market close at noon.

"Do you think @pierogiepat will be happy?" Jackson asked, beaming over his salesman success.

"At selling out, yes," I said carefully choosing my words.

"What aren't you telling me?"

"That she normally sells them for one dollar each."

"But I set one for one dollar and two for one-fifty," he pointed out.

"And how many people bought just one?"

He had to think about that, though I suppose it was hard for him to crunch the numbers with me laughing so loudly.

"She'll probably take it out of my pay," I said, unable to stop myself from needling him further.

"Will you make rent?" he asked.

"Don't you worry about me, Pastor Jackson. I'm headed to a wedding later today, and hopeful something there will spark another brilliant @creekweddings post or inspire me to create a blog or Facebook account or … something like that," I petered off.

"You don't know what you're talking about do you?" he asked, stowing the coolers this and that way so they'd all fit in my '85 Cutlass. Every time I took it out, it felt like a risky maneuver, but it had survived today's mile into town square without something falling off.

"I don't know what I'm talking about," I admitted.

"How are you the only person in our generation not on social media?"

"Maybe you haven't noticed, but I'm not much for people. I set up a couple accounts in college, but I barely used them. And right now, there's not much to post: 'Sold pierogies today. Stop. Went to another person's wedding today. Stop. Went back home. Stop. To hang out in my room by myself. Stop.' I don't even have a phone."

"Where's your phone?"

"I smashed it with a hammer."

He shut the car door (not as gently as I would have liked) and laughed his head off. "More ex-girlfriend stuff?"

"Boys don't do this?"

"No."

"No?"

"No. But my grandparents' camp with the outhouse? I lived there for six months after Kate left and wore a flannel shirt every day, grew a beard, and chopped a lot of wood."

"Did you hunt and gather all of your own food, too?"

"More like reheated frozen burritos and pizza rolls and packed on a gut," he said, patting his stomach. I kept my eyes on his face, already aware that whatever gut Jackson had developed was long gone.

"So whose wedding are you crashing today?" he asked, putting the last cooler in the front passenger seat.

"Eric Carson and Ashley Tipton. It's a second marriage for both. Do you know them?"

"Nope."

"Amazing."

"They don't go to our church."

"This morning proved that you know way beyond that radius," I said pointing back toward the thinning crowd.

"What do you mean?"

"You knew almost everybody's names right off and asked the rest theirs."

"A radical idea, I know. But you should try it."

"Try what?"

"Asking people their names. It's not exactly a rude question."

I stopped by Grandma's shop to drop off her pierogie profits, and as soon as I stepped through the spring green door, time stood still. I stood still. Out of all the memories I'd reluctantly encountered, I'm surprised I hadn't sought this one out. Penny Thrift was my latchkey growing up; when Mom had to stay after school, Ted and I would walk the half mile here. Ted always breezed through the store, stopping to hug Grandma and grab some fresh-baked-something-or-other before heading out the backdoor to throw baseballs at targets Dad set up for him in the lot behind the store. I happily remained inside, helping Grandma ready fabric for sale or dreamily wandering the shelves of the ever-changing inventory.

Penny Thrift was Grandma's second child ... or maybe her second spouse. She'd married young to her first husband, Bill Tate. Six months after the wedding, Dad was born, and eight months after that, Bill was gone. Grandma Pat was an open book about everything, except for him, so of course I was always dying to know more.

"Do you wish your husband had stayed?" I asked once.

She'd snorted at that and said nothing. I'd persisted.

"Wouldn't it have made things easier? Two incomes? Two

parents to raise Dad?"

"I'm sure that man would have continued to drink away our money, and he couldn't keep himself to the line, let alone raise a kid to walk it. Leaving was the kindest thing he ever did for me."

"So why were you with him in the first place?"

"Because he was good at making babies," she'd said, effectively cutting my line of questioning.

After Bill left, Grandma went on her own downward spiral, but around Dad's third birthday, she found Jesus in a ditch and hedged all her bets in that corner. She swore off men, swore off drink, and moved out of her parents' home. She didn't even have a high school diploma, but Great Grandma Sokolowski had taught her how to cook and how to sew—so that's what Grandma did.

For years, she worked days as a seamstress for Laundromats and then tucked Dad in at her parents' house to waitress nights. Her reputation with a needle and thread grew, and she eventually cut out the middle man to take in sewing directly, boosting her income enough to quit waitressing and try her hand at catering pierogies and other Polish fare. She made enough to pay her bills and save two dollars each week.

After Ted was born, she moved in with my parents and turned her old home into Penny Thrift. The shelves were stacked with fabric that Grandma had re-purposed from vintage tablecloths and curtains and anything else that caught her eye. It was cloth most people wouldn't look at twice in their original form—allowing Grandma to thrift it for pennies—but once she'd ripped the seams, washed it, pressed it, folded it, and placed it in the right section of the shop, or combined it with the right fabrics in a quilt, women suddenly had to have it. And were willing to pay for it.

"How long are you planning on standing there, Lu?" Grandma asked, bringing me back to the present.

"Just remembering," I said, turning my eyes from the shelves and handing her the money bag.

"Come on down to the cellar; I want to show you something." We crossed the shop—which did look more shop than house, thanks to Dad's renovation skills in opening spaces and replacing walls with display shelves. She opened the cellar door, and the cool humidity and comforting hum of the dryer greeted me as I carefully navigated the steep wooden steps. The left half was as I remembered—washer, dryer, ironing board and mounds of fabric in various stages of prep—but the right half now hosted a computer and stacks of cardboard boxes. And, there was a large rectangular table with address labels, packing tape and a large, sleek monitor in the middle of it all.

"You ship?" I asked in disbelief. "And is that a Mac?"

"It's refurbed."

Not even "refurbished" but "refurbed."

"I have a shop on Etsy. Want to see?"

I did, and she proudly took me to her online storefront advertising quilts, pillows, table runners, café curtains, and stuff I didn't even know existed.

"What's a tea cozy?" I asked.

"Like a cap for your teapot. It keeps it cute and sort of warm."

"Will you get thirty-five dollars for it?"

"Oh, those sell like hotcakes."

Grandma eventually got antsy with all the sitting and bustled to her ironing table, so I took over navigation, clicking on every picture. I'd always loved what she made, but now I marveled at her business sense.

"How do you have time for all of this?" I asked. I'd kept my visits to home sparse and short while I lived in New York, and my phone calls the same, excepting Gracie. When Grandma did corner me on the phone, it was to pepper me with questions. She wasn't one to talk about herself or her work, and I'd never thought to ask.

"Other ladies work the shop and do most of the sewing, so I only come in a couple of days a week to fuss around with fabric. I have a lot of free time to try this Internet stuff."

"What was your trunk show for today?" I asked.

"There's a girl in town who cuts up old cotton T-shirts and sews them into something special—look at this," she said, tossing me a package made from a brown grocery bag and decorated in a graffiti of spray paint. I opened it, and inside was a skirt, broadly formed from five vertical panels that I assumed were cut from different indigo cotton T-shirts given their slightly different hues. The sewer had expertly stitched circles of various sizes around the skirt and cut out a reverse applique to reveal the white cotton lining underneath. I'd witnessed enough of Grandma's creative process to know that hand stitching like this takes time. The skirt could have easily veered into a hot mess, but it was beautiful. I'd never seen anything like it.

"I want this," I breathed, running my fingers over the soft, worn cotton and chunky embroidered seams stitched with thick cotton thread. She hadn't even hidden all her ties, leaving tails of cotton thread exposed here and there to add another dimension to the exquisite garment. I couldn't decide which I liked better—looking at the skirt or touching it.

"Good, I got that for you."

"I can't imagine how much time this took; it must have cost you a fortune."

"Well, I'm pretty sure she'll be able to make rent, thanks to this morning's show. She has a little baby at home, and lots of time and talent, but is short on cash. The baby's dad isn't in the picture."

I looked up at her, wondering how I'd missed this about Grandma—how she was always helping women in tough situations to get back on their feet. Some of the women had thrived, many had walked away, but Grandma never stopped.

"You're a good woman, Grandma Pat," I said.

"Blessed to be a blessing," she automatically replied.

"Well, thank you. It's beautiful." I carefully refolded the skirt and put it back in its spray-painted packaging, keeping it on my lap.

"So, how'd my other business do today?" she asked.

"You sold out."

She hollered. "It's been awhile since that happened. People don't appreciate pierogies like they used to."

"Well, it may have been partly to do with an accidental sale. Jackson set them at two for one fifty."

"And the other part?"

I hesitated, mentally slapping myself for even starting this line of questioning with my wording. "Also Jackson."

She hollered at that. "I told you the ladies would trample over one another to get at him."

"Yes, but while he and I were sitting across from each other at a blind date you never informed me about. That was not okay."

"Something else that's not okay is what you're wearing," she said, gesturing at the loose tank top and khaki shorts I'd chosen for this morning's pierogie duty. "You're not even putting up a fight against those other girls."

"Would you stop and listen to yourself?" I nearly yelled at her. "If there's a fight, I'm not in it because I'm not on the market. Please stop trying to set me up, and let me be his friend. Honestly, that's what I could use right now."

"I don't want you to wind up like me, honey," she said, which diffused my anger a bit. She released her iron in a cloud of steam, carefully folding the pressed fabric into a neat square before grabbing the next scrap from the pile.

"You always said Jesus was your husband," I reminded her.

"He is," she acknowledged. "Still, if I'd met a man like Jackson, I might have tried to make room for both."

"Well, why don't you scratch that matchmaking itch of yours and set up an eHarmony profile," I said, standing and holding my present. "Thank you again for the skirt. I think I'll wear it to the wedding I'm covering tonight."

"Maybe you'll meet someone there," she said.

"That would be rude to my date."

She put down the iron. "Who?" she asked hopefully.

"Gracie."

She rolled her eyes. I headed up the stairs.

"Jackson's not going to be on the market forever," she shouted.

"EHarmony!" I shouted back.

Gracie might not have been Grandma's first choice for my wedding date, but the little time we'd had since I'd returned had been spent on my parents' deck, so it was nice to take our friendship out on the town, even if it turned out to be on another person's deck. Instead of spending money on a big wedding, Eric and Ashley had invested in a deck and limestone patio as the backdrop for their ceremony and reception. It was a small gathering of thirty friends and family and very casual. There was no big bridal reveal, just Eric and Ashley walking hand-in-hand from inside the house at the appointed hour—her in a simple ivory sheath and him in an ivory shirt and navy blue pants. They welcomed us and then turned things over to the officiate, who guided them through the vows, ring exchange, and kiss. Start to finish, the ceremony lasted ten minutes, and then it proceeded like any other party.

They'd set up a random assortment of tables with no assigned seating, so Gracie and I quickly claimed a table for two at the back of the patio. Wedding dinners for a crowd of thirty is way tastier and timelier than a reception for three hundred, so we were happily feasting on Chilean sea bass within moments of the ceremony ending. I was still enjoying how the first tender bite mingled with the tangy mango salsa when I realized Gracie had already shoveled half of hers in her mouth.

"Slow it down, girl," I said. "I think the reception will last long enough for you to finish at an adult pace."

"Sorry. I'm used to eating with little kids. I swear, every time my butt touches the seat, they spill their milk and ask for more. I'm up and down, up and down, throwing food in my mouth whenever I get a chance. Half the time, I don't even finish."

"I promise not to ask you for more milk, scout's honor." And I made the requisite symbol with my fingers.

"Were we scouts?"

"Brownies in Kindergarten, I think. But to prove my point, I'll go and fetch you something from the bar. What do you want?" I asked, placing my napkin on the table.

"A Shirley Temple?"

"Isn't that what we ordered when our parents took us to that fancy restaurant for our sweet sixteen?"

"I'd forgotten all about that!" Gracie exclaimed. "I think I ordered a Caesar salad, and not even topped with grilled chicken or shrimp. Salad only. Now that was lame."

"And my allergies were so horrible that day that I kept blowing my nose on the cloth napkins." I stood up to get our drinks. "It's still okay to get the umbrellas in it, right?"

"And don't forget the cherry and plastic sword," she said before shoveling another forkful of fish.

I crisscrossed my way up the deck stairs and through the maze of tables and soft clinks of people eating and drinking to the bar set up beside the French doors leading into the house. I smiled at the other people in line but turned to look at the party instead of attempting small talk. The white tablecloths with white rose centerpieces and white candles and twinkle lights all around made for such a pretty scene that it felt more like a bridal magazine shoot than a wedding. And then I laughed, because of course it was both, and I was the journalist covering it. The summer evening carried a light breeze, and I closed my eyes to tune into the stringed music playing softly through speakers camouflaged in the landscaping. I had no idea what Ashley's first wedding had been like, but her second was lovely.

I opened my eyes again, and there was Ashley, the bride herself. I stepped aside.

"Hello, Lu!" she exclaimed, giving me a quick hug before accepting my place in line. "Is everyone giving you all you need for the story?"

"Yes, though I do most of the interviews before the wedding so that people can enjoy themselves without my bugging them. But how can you be standing all by yourself only minutes after saying your vows?" I asked looking around.

"Because I only invited people who know I like space even when I'm supposed to be the center of attention," she said before thanking the bartender for her champagne and then stepping aside for me to order two Shirley Temples.

"Those were great vows, by the way," I said. "I haven't been reporting weddings for very long, but yours felt honest. More like a love letter and less like a recitation."

"The first time I got married, I recited the standard vows without giving much thought to what I was saying. It wasn't that long into my first marriage that I realized neither my first husband nor I were committed to keeping them. This time around, I wanted to give more thought to what I was promising."

At that, another wedding guest approached, leaving me to return to Gracie.

"Chatting it up with the bride?" she asked, leaning back against her black rattan chair and taking a sip of her cherry red drink. She'd cleaned her plate while I was gone. "Do you choose which weddings you go to based on the caterer? Because this was so good."

"Nope. Remember last Saturday's wedding cake?"

"Cardboard."

"Exactly. Whichever wedding pitch makes me roll my eyes the least wins. Ashley put some serious thought into the, 'Why should *The Daily* cover your wedding?' question on our form. Her hope in the second time around even tugged at my cynical heartstrings."

"Are you cynical, Lu?"

I took a sip of my drink, wishing I'd order something with less syrup and more strength. "No."

"Talk to me."

"It's hard for me to do that."

"Why?"

71

"Because for all of you, it's over and done. John wasn't right for me, and you didn't like him in the first place, right? But it's not like that for me. I loved John, and he cheated on me. I'd welcome cynicism—anger, even—if it helped me move on. But hurt is all I've got. If John came back for me, I'd go with him."

I wiped the tears from my eyes. "I miss him. And because I didn't take anything from our apartment, all I have is this one picture of us, which I don't even like, in my Crock-Pot upstairs, and I was going to use it for the sermon homework, but then I decided otherwise."

Gracie shook her head. "What are you talking about? What picture? What Crock-Pot? What sermon homework?"

"Remember? He asked us to bring our version of the pants-down picture to church this Sunday. Don't you pay attention in church anymore?" I asked.

"I wasn't aware that you did. That's the real news here. And, I didn't even know you went to church last Sunday."

"I went early and sat in the back. And, I wasn't paying attention in church; I was paying attention to Jackson."

She smiled.

"Not like that," I defended. I should have shut up, but felt compelled to continue. "He gave us two options: open your Bible or find a picture. The latter seemed like the lesser of two evils."

She leaned in and looked at me, still smiling. "If you ever opened your Bible, you'd realize that what you said makes no sense. So what picture do you have in your Crock-Pot? And why do you have a Crock-Pot in your bedroom?"

I explained those backstories. We didn't say anything for a while, but I could tell she was processing as she pleated her cloth napkin back into its original fan shape.

"Lu, you could always pick up the phone and call the man. Girls do that, you know."

"Not when the man has cheated on them."

"You said you'd go with him if he came for you. Don't wait for that. Call John and tell him how you feel."

"So that he can tell me he doesn't feel the same way about me anymore? I don't think I could handle that, Gracie."

"Then at least get rid of the stupid Crock-Pot."

"I know it's ridiculous, but ..."

"No," she interrupted, reaching across the table for my hand.

"You're hurting, and it's a piece of the man you miss, the life you miss. If you're not going to run after it, then let it go. Let him go. And get rid of that Crock-Pot."

I would have started crying again, but thankfully, another wedding guest bumped into our table with his hip, sloshing our Shirley Temples about. The ensuing apologies and cleanup snapped me out of my sadness, for which I was so grateful I could have kissed him.

Gracie and I resumed our seats, and I resolutely dug into my half-eaten bass that was no longer warm, but still tasty. "Are you going to find a picture?" I asked, deflecting the conversation back to her. She paused, probably weighing whether she should press the issue of John, but she let me have my way.

"I don't need to. Walk into my house at any moment, and you'll find someone running around without pants. That's my life."

"Well by that reasoning, my picture can remain in the Crock-Pot, too. I chose another one—of little girl me on the tire swing. I thought it'd be better for me to have a vision of what I'd like to get back to."

"I can't believe the swing's back up! I took a few turns on it the other day when the girls were napping, but I had to get off because I started feeling nauseous."

"Yeah, I can't stay on it too long before my butt goes numb. What a couple of old girls we are. How long have you been married now?" I asked.

"Eight years this December."

"Do you think you'd do it differently if you did it now?"

"No church basement reception the second time around," Gracie said without hesitation.

"What about your vows? Would you change those?"

She thought. "No, those I'd keep. It'd be nice to say them again, now that I have a better idea of what they mean."

Gracie somehow finagled another sea bass from the waiter, and we ordered a second round of Shirley Temples before leaving the party. I had her home by ten, and then trudged up the three flights to my room, exhausted from the day. Lights from the street filtered through the two dormer windows at the front, and I leaned against the doorway, staring at the shadowy outline of the Crock-Pot.

It was one thing to laugh it off as stupid ex-girlfriend stuff and another to look at it as ballast. My exodus with the Crock-Pot had been a ridiculous but bold gesture—the most decisive thing I'd done in years—but since then, what? I'd fled my life in New York with John, and now I was home, but for what? I missed John, but I also missed the girl I'd been when I met him.

He'd told me he never met anyone like me. John was raised to go to the best schools and work for the best people. The man knew how to sail and pick wine with a knowledge that went beyond choosing the flashiest label. We came from different worlds, though I'd gone to enough country club parties with Nana Bea to know that, yes, I wasn't anything like girls he would have met in those circles. I'm much more of a scrapper, and when I met him, I was in my element—determined to make a life away from Dunlap's Creek and my family. My ambitions were self-formed. I'd worked hard to land my first job after college, and I was working hard for the next one at a bigger paper in a bigger city.

John and I were kindred spirits in our determination. We went after what we wanted. We moved to New York for his job and assumed mine would follow. I took the job at Starbucks to bide my time until I found something better. Nothing better had come along. That's what I'd thought, what I'd said—but the more honest answer was I'd stopped looking. Instead, I channeled that determination into digging in my heels, wearing my menial work and minimum wage as a badge of pride to protect me from my failure.

I never realized that girl I'd wanted to become, but in this showdown with the Crock-Pot, I saw that I was also far from being the girl John had fallen in love with. I didn't deserve what he'd done, but the time for do-overs with him was also done. I wasn't going to call him. So I followed Gracie's advice and yanked the Crock-Pot off its perch, carried it downstairs and tossed it in the trash by the garage. It landed with a resounding thud that lent a nice, dramatic touch to the whole thing.

I went back inside and dusted off the top of my dresser to remove the evidence of its existence. Of course, I could still see the Crock-Pot in my mind. I even traced the outline of it with my finger, but I assumed that memory would fade. The picture of John and me I slid in my top dresser drawer. Maybe I should throw it away, too, but I wasn't ready for that yet.

I opened my laptop. The wedding story wasn't due for another week, but today had me thinking about do-overs. Did a second chance ever come from a place we would have willingly put ourselves in if we'd had the choice? I hadn't wanted John to cheat on me, and I didn't want to be living with my parents. Grandma hadn't asked to be a single mom or to scrape by on her sewing skills, and Ashley hadn't entered her first marriage thinking it would end. Yet now, Grandma was in a place to help other women with their second chances, and the white lights of Ashley's second wedding still twinkled in the back of my mind. My second chance didn't go much past clearing John artifacts from my dresser, but it needed to be done before I could take the next step, whatever that may be.

I closed down the day by posting the first tweet for @creekweddings on Twitter: "Wedding vows the second time 'round—change or repeat?"

CHAPTER 9

If Saturday night ended on the high note of second chances, then Sunday's sermon landed like a bucket of cold water to the face.

"There are no second chances, not really. But we think there are. We think, 'This time ... this is the time I will ...' We create this weary cycle of relying on ourselves to change or relying on our circumstances or the people in our lives to change or to change us. It's August. How many of you are still keeping your New Year's resolutions? How many of you even remember them?"

He got a laugh at that, but not from me. Maybe it was because my resolution of less than twelve hours was still fresh, though long enough to warrant my disagreement with Jackson's conclusions.

My Twitter followers also disagreed. They were more than happy to share their vow do overs, an eagerness not lost on RJ.

"I need you to do more," he announced when I jingled into work.

"Good morning to you, too," I muttered, suddenly and urgently requiring another cup of coffee, though there was not enough caffeine in the world to deal with this man. I glanced at the glop put out by the Mr. Coffee and opted for a cup of water instead. I booted my laptop before answering RJ. "Okay, so what do you want?"

"More," he repeated.

"More what? I've done everything you asked: two weddings a month plus social media. What kind of 'more' do you want?"

"You decide. Everywhere else on this paper, I'm cutting

content to make room for advertisers, which still doesn't make up for the lost circulation revenue. But people are responding to you. I don't know if this will translate into dollars, but I'm willing to risk it. I don't care what you write. Keep it coming and do more of it."

This was ego-boosting in a certain light, but tempered by the suspicion that covering weddings every Saturday would render me the twentysomething equivalent of the cat lady. I shoved this thought and RJ's directive aside to draft the story of Saturday's wedding. Given the Twitter response, and my newfound hopefulness, it seemed that second chances was the angle to take. Problem was, Pastor Jackson's downer of a sermon on Ecclesiastes 1 kept getting in the way.

"You believe in second chances, don't you?" I blurted to my dad while we cleaned the dinner dishes.

"Sure."

"So you disagree with Jackson's sermon?"

"No."

"Then you disagree with yourself?"

He smiled. "No."

"Explain yourself, please," I said, taking my frustration out on a spot of grease on the glass casserole dish.

"What did I used to say when you'd mess up?"

I hadn't thought about that in years, but I parroted the verse straight from memory. "1 John 1:9—'If we confess our sins, he is faithful and just to forgive us our sins and cleanse us from all unrighteousness.'"

"And how many times could you do that?"

"As many as I needed."

"Why?"

"Because God never gives up on me."

"There's your second chances."

"So you're saying without God, there's no second chances?"

"Shades of them, but nothing like the second chances that come from God because only God can really change a person or a situation."

"Some people would say that your chances are what you make of them," I pointed out.

"Some would say that, but Solomon would say that's like chasing the wind."

"How would you say it?"

Grandma Pat came in carrying a load of table linens. "Well, I know what my mom would say," he said, smiling.

"About what?" she asked, opening the door to the laundry closet.

"About people trying to change themselves," Dad said.

"That's hogwash. Haven't I told you about the time Jesus found me in a ditch?"

She'd told everybody. Multiple times. And the conclusion was always the same.

"No one else could have rescued me."

"You could have crawled out of that ditch," I argued.

She slammed the washing machine door and turned around to point her finger at me. "Now you see here, Lu. Sure, I could have crawled out of that ditch, eventually— once I could tell my head from my behind. But it would only have been a matter of time until I fell into another."

I crossed my arms. "Literally or metaphorically?"

She crossed her arms back at me. "A ditch is a ditch."

I conceded. "So, how do you know it was Jesus who saved you?"

"Because I saw him, plain as day. And, I never again felt the need to do any of those things that had sent me into that ditch in the first place. That's the kind of rescuing Jesus does. It's complete and final. Anything else is hogwash."

By Tuesday, my Twitter followers were well into the double digits, and they had so many interesting responses that I'd decided to include a sidebar on second vows next to the main story in Sunday's paper. By the end of the day, the feature was ready, but I was still frustrated.

I decided to take it to the source himself, thought it felt weird to walk into church on a Wednesday. I'd done it every Wednesday night as a child, but to do it as an adult and by choice? Strange. I held my breath as I walked around, worried that any oxygen intake would signal the Four Horsemen of the Apocalypse, or worse, one of my old Sunday school teachers. I was certain everyone knew I was in the building, but Jackson didn't even look up when I came to his door. I knocked, and he looked at me.

"Hey, Louisa," he said, not seeming as surprised by my presence in church as I was.

It was a teeny office, made smaller by bookshelves lining three of the walls. The remaining space barely fit the desk and two chairs in front of it. Entering felt like an invasion of his personal space— it was certainly a violation of mine—but he gestured to one of the chairs in front of his desk anyway.

"It's good to see you," he said.

"Great, because I came here to pick a fight about Sunday's sermon."

"Let's have at it," he said, settling back into his chair while I launched into my problem.

"I disagree with you that there are no second chances without God and that a life without God is without meaning. You can't prove that."

He folded his arms on his desk and leaned into them. "Prove what you said."

I sat back. "What do you mean?"

"This goes both ways. How can you demand proof for my conclusions without offering up yours? Plus, I already presented my proof on Sunday."

"Which was?"

"Ecclesiastes 1:3-11."

"Your proof seems unnecessarily pessimistic; life isn't a cycle of toil and no gain followed by death. That's leaving some things out."

"Of course it is, but to get people to acknowledge what really drives us—the work behind the work, so to speak. Think back to when you left New York. You were probably asking yourself, 'Now what was the point of all that?' You moved for a boyfriend, a job, and a place and they all fell short. Now you're back out there, questioning more than your circumstances.

"We don't search for the next opportunity so much as we search for what that opportunity says about us. We want to know we matter, but we look in all the wrong places for the proof. Doing this again and again isn't a second chance. It's more like *Groundhog Day* with us making the same mistake every morning."

"So, same crap, new day?" I summed up.

"Something like that. But I'm not saying that's all there is. There's joy, too. I love my job, God loves that I love my job, but my job doesn't validate my existence. And if I was looking for it to do that, it would only be a matter of time before the job disappointed me and I was looking for another. We can only find our worth in God."

"Our one chance …" I murmured, without really thinking.

"What's that?"

"Something my dad said the other night—that God's our one chance out of the cycle you described." I sat back, rubbing my hand across my forehead as I thought about what was really bothering me. I sat back up and looked at Jackson. "Your conclusion seems limiting."

"It seems freeing to me," he countered.

"And not very fair."

"What's not fair about a way out?"

I had to laugh. "Because I don't like *that* way out. And I'm not sure I agree with it."

"Well at least you admit it. This Sunday, I'm talking about some of the other escape routes we try." He reached behind him for a Bible and tossed it to me. "Why don't you read up on it beforehand?"

I tossed it back to him like a hot potato. "I have my own Bible."

"Then read the rest of Ecclesiastes one and two, and let me know what you think."

"I don't need to open it to tell you I don't like what it says."

"But you're smarter than to counter with 'I don't like it.' Read up. I'd hate for you to lose this like you lost at cornhole."

"I demand a rematch. How would you like to come over for dinner tonight?"

"You cooking?"

"Never. But Grandma Pat is reheating leftovers, and I can't think of a better way to get back at her for last time. That, plus beating you in cornhole would kill two birds with one stone."

It was hard to tell who was most surprised by Jackson's presence at dinner that night. When he rang the doorbell, even I was still mildly surprised at having invited him. His hands were empty this time.

"No flowers?" I asked.

He grinned. "You probably should have bought some to make peace with @pierogiepat for this."

"I'm more interested in getting even right now. Thanks for being a pawn in our game."

"More of a starving bachelor than a pawn," Jackson said before leading the way into the dining room. Grandma looked up, startled at his presence, but he went straight to her and gave her a bear hug, almost lifting her off her feet.

"Louisa was really anxious to have me over for dinner tonight but felt badly about asking you to make something special," he said. "But then I told her that your leftovers are better than most people's cooking the first time around."

She beamed, while I looked around for something to throw at him. Too bad Grandma Pat wasn't years younger. Those two deserved each other.

But, I did bean him with a cornhole bag as soon as we set up the boards after doing dishes. He tossed it right back—in the hole of course—before leaning down to straighten his own board.

"You deserved that," he said. "My family raised me to respect my elders."

"Yeah, but did you have to throw in the 'Louisa was anxious to have me over for dinner tonight' bit? She's been trying to set me up with you since the morning I came back."

He shrugged. "People tend to think that moving on from a past relationship means moving on with someone else."

"But your sermon on Sunday is going to be all about how that doesn't work?" I asked, rehashing the same question I'd been asking all week.

"I'm not going to call out blind dates specifically, but you could lump them in."

"Because the only true move forward is with God, right?" I rolled my eyes and sighed in frustration. Time for a topic change. "Have people tried to set you up?"

Jackson laughed and nodded. "Almost immediately after they stopped telling me divorce wasn't an option."

"And what do you think about that?" I asked, stepping away from my board and toward him.

"I think anything is an option if someone wants it to be." He looked at me. "Kate wanted out; I couldn't force her to stay. She agreed to a couple of marriage counseling sessions, but she basically had both feet out the door by that point."

"What happened?" I tossed the corn bag back and forth between my hands, uncertain about this venture into new territory.

"Honestly, I still don't know. I don't know if she knows. We were both raised in this church and town—a totally sheltered environment. We were together from before I could even remember, and it seemed we always should be. We got married and then moved away for seminary and my first job—and all the new and different was like a shock to the system. She fell apart, questioning everything, and I was too busy with the church to notice her or what she was going through. By the time I got around to caring, it was too late. I was not a good husband."

"Did you ever question what you believe about God in all of this?"

"It's more like the divorce brought what I believe into sharp relief. I could be bogged down by my failure and retreat," he paused, leaning against the side of the deck, "or I could move forward in faith that God could work through it—work through me in it. So that's what I did."

"After you cut wood for a little while?"

"Exactly."

"Do you ever think you'll remarry?"

"I don't know." He shook his head and shifted his weight. "Certainly not by my own courage. I was thinking about what you said earlier today in my office—about how one way out seems limiting. And I can see your point, especially since that one way out is by accepting God's work on our behalf instead of us having to do anything. We like to know we won the fight, right? But only God has the power to create new outcomes, and because I believe in him, I also believe that a second marriage wouldn't have to go the way of my first."

"People can believe that without believing in God."

"And what do you believe, Lu?"

"I'm about as convinced that the Bible solves my problems as another man would at this point."

"Have you cracked open your Bible lately?" he asked, staking his position at the opposing board.

"Why do you ask?" I staked mine.

"You seem to think that because you read it as a child, it's childish. Try reading it as an adult. You might be surprised at what you find."

We finally settled into our game—best out of three, and I won. But after he left, I took stock of the Bibles on my bookshelf. It was quite the library, starting with the Precious Moments King James Version given to me as a little girl and up to the teen adventure

Bible I'd received at a high school youth retreat. I think we were supposed to leave confirmed in the faith in which we'd been raised, but it had only confirmed my distaste for cabins, bunk beds with inch-thick mattresses, singing around campfires, and trust exercises where you fall backward into the arms of strangers. Who does that? Not me, and I never went to another one.

The paperback NIV seemed the most all-purpose of my assortment. I plucked it from the shelf and sat cross-legged on my bed, pausing to get my bearings. I opened to the first third of the Bible, landing in Psalms. I shuffled a little farther until I found the blaring "Meaningless! Meaningless!" of Ecclesiastes 1:2. I started reading, which quickly turned to skimming. I started over, this time using my pointer finger to train my focus, but I still found myself skimming.

"At least my little girl self could read this stuff," I muttered, folding the upper left corner of the page and putting the Bible on my nightstand. I chalked my scope creep to the late hour and went to bed, determined to give it another go in the morning. I needed some ammo in my next conversation with Jackson, but I also wanted my questions answered. Surely I could read two chapters in the four days before the next sermon.

CHAPTER 10

Solomon sought meaning in pleasure, wisdom, and work, but found them meaningless.

This was the subject sentence I pulled out of my back pocket when I took my seat in the back right of the church. Every day, I'd read my Ecclesiastes assignment, but this was all I could glean. I wondered how Jackson was going to squeeze sermon out of this one. The book had already begun with Solomon's big reveal that life was meaningless, so the fact that he now pinpointed specific things in life as meaningless was hardly a shocker. And somewhat redundant. Sloughing through it had been a chore, so I appreciated that Jackson opened his sermon with the question I'd been asking myself all week.

"Why are we reading this?" he asked the congregation. "Does Solomon need to say specific things are meaningless when he's called everything meaningless?"

Nope.

"Yes. Yes he does because we easily forget. Solomon began Ecclesiastes with a proclamation that life is meaningless and in today's passage from chapters one and two, he also finds pleasure and wisdom and knowledge meaningless. No surprise there, right—since pleasure, wisdom, and knowledge fall under the umbrella of "everything"? But he's not beating a dead horse, and he's not repeating himself. He's blocking off the escape routes we try to make meaning in a world that—separate from God—has none. Solomon is a wise man, remember? So, he knows we're going to counter. 'What about this?' 'Have you thought about this?' 'Have you ever tried this?'

"We are always looking for the exception to the rule. Please open your Bibles to Ecclesiastes to see how Solomon responds."

Jackson spent the rest of his sermon taking each escape route in turn. I filled up the rest of my cheat sheet with notes. Jackson, no surprise, came to the same conclusion as Solomon: Any pursuit outside of God was meaningless. We can't enjoy our way out of death, we can't think our way out, and we can't work our way out. A dreary assessment, but it agreed with my subject sentence, so I gave myself an A. Literally. I put a big A at the top of the paper and circled it before folding the sheet and putting it in my pocket as I stood to leave. I had other work to do.

This past week, I'd taken stock of my lemons and what I could squeeze out of them. There wasn't anything more to do about John, now that I'd thrown out the Crock-Pot. I assumed as time went on, I might even stop opening the top drawer of my dresser to look at the picture of us. But right now, there wasn't enough sugar in the world to sweeten my breakup lemon, so I set it aside.

Next was my housing lemon. Living at my parents wasn't ideal. There were plenty of opinions about how I should live my life—more than I could live out in several lifetimes—but no real micromanaging beyond that. I could come and go as I pleased. And I don't think I would have liked living by myself. It was nice coming home to people, even if I sought the empty spaces. But those times were lessening; I'd started coming down a bit earlier in the mornings to talk with my parents before leaving for work and helping Grandma Pat prep more dinners, to which she always readily agreed and then quickly rescinded when it became evident I couldn't chop or stir for anything. And the other day, I even offered to continue helping Nana Bea with cleaning out closets at the manse.

"Whatever for?" she asked, looking at me like I'd proposed we drive her Caddy to the moon.

"Because you're thinking about moving ..." I reminded her.

"Why ever would I do that?" she asked innocently. "It's such a lovely place, and I wouldn't want to live anywhere else."

"Then why do you live here?" I wanted to shout. But I let that one go, as well as the idea that I could bond with each of my housemates.

The last lemon was the job. I had one—a plus—but it came with crappy pay, a crappy boss, and a crappy beat. Once I set those three factors aside, I saw three more. One, I was writing. This was all I've ever wanted to do, and the only thing I ever could do. I'm a uni-talented individual, excluding cornhole, but that offered even fewer job opportunities than journalism. Second, the job was going well. Thanks to social media, but mostly to Grandma Pat, who was shamelessly offering a ten percent discount if people chose to follow me when they checked out on her iPad at Penny Thrift. Lastly, RJ had given me a blank check to do "more." I wasn't sure if this came with more pay, but I took it as creative license to try something new.

So, I decided to exploit myself on a blog. I'm an erratic journaler at best, and the few journals I'd filled, I'd eventually thrown away after re-reading a few pages—appalled at what I'd written and even more appalled that someone else might stumble upon it. Why anyone would blog their personal life to the world was beyond me, but there was something inherently funny in my lemons—the jilted, twentysomething girl living at her parents and consigned to writing about weddings for the local paper. RJ wanted more, but I wasn't looking to cover more weddings. Maybe the more could be my perspective in all of this.

I walked home after church, grabbed an odd assortment of leftovers from the fridge for lunch, left a note on the counter about my whereabouts, and then walked to work. The paper came out today, and since today was also a Sunday, it was a whole new level of quiet: no ringing phones, or burbling Mr. Coffee, or whirring fans. No overhead fluorescent lights. I presumed I'd be the one and only in the office today, and I welcomed the solitude of this space to hash out my plan.

By five o'clock I was no further along. I hadn't even created an account because I couldn't think of a name, and looking at all the other wedding blogs out there hadn't helped because I was no longer convinced I had anything to add to the conversation. I wasn't funny like some or particularly witty or thoughtful. I buried my face in my hands in frustration, remembering why I'd made the choice to work at Starbucks all those years ago. The work was less frustrating, and it paid better.

When I looked back up, the sight of Jackson's face smushed against the front window made the decision for me. I laughed, closed my computer, and left the office.

It was a beautiful summer evening with a light blue sky not yet touched by the colors of sunset. I could feel the promise of fall, and one deep inhale of the cool air cleared my senses and dissipated the frustration of my afternoon. I looked up at Jackson. His face was smeared with dirt.

"I'm pretty sure RJ has never had that glass washed," I observed, rubbing a smudge off his nose. I dropped my hand once I realized what I was doing. "How did you know I was here?"

"I called your house, and decided to return the work visit."

"Did you come to pick a fight, too? Oh, and that reminds me." I flourished my cheat sheet and notes of this morning's sermon from my back pocket.

"Well, will you look at that," he said, scanning it. And then he laughed. "Is that a grade you gave yourself at the top of the paper?"

"Yes, an 'A' since my subject sentence aligned with your conclusion." I reclaimed my paper and put it in my back pocket. "Where are you off to?"

"Your house, and I'm in charge of dinner," he said, steering me toward his car. "Your family has fed me twice; it's time to return the favor."

I raised my eyebrows. "You ran this by Grandma Pat?"

"Of course."

"She doesn't like people in her kitchen other than to clean it," I warned him, but of course she was a doll with Jackson.

I never pictured Grandma playing the role of sous-chef, and yet here I was sitting on a kitchen stool and munching on a carrot stick while she happily diced veggies for his pork lo mein. I looked over to Nana Bea, who was sipping a before-dinner martini at the kitchen table, and she raised her right eyebrow. I took that as a sign of solidarity and raised my eyebrow right back at her like it was our secret handshake.

"So, how long do you sauté these vegetables?" Grandma cooed, her cooking experience of the last hundred years suddenly escaping her.

I almost rolled my eyes and said something snarky, but I decided to make myself helpful instead and set the table without someone having to ask me first. Mom beat me to it and was filling the water glasses when I came in with the superfluous place settings.

"That's nice that Jackson cooked us dinner."

"Yup," I said, about to offer to finish filling the glasses for her.

"You think you two …"

"Nope," I said, then escaped the room in emergency mode, only to bump into Gracie's family coming through the back door.

"Hey, Lu-ser. I hear a boy called the house today," Ted shouted.

Caroline's seven-year-old eyes popped out of her sockets, and she gave a little jump and clap. "Oh! Does Aunt Lu have a boyfriend? Where is he?" she asked, scanning the kitchen until she landed on the one man who wasn't her dad or grandpa. "Wait, aren't you the pastor?" she asked Jackson, wrinkling her nose. Which is exactly how I felt about it, too.

I leaned down and put my arm around Caroline. "We have to forgive him for that, honey," I said. "Aunt Lu is holding out for a fireman."

She nodded because that explanation made perfect sense. And then we all piled into the dining room as Jackson and Grandma Pat served steaming plates of lo mein and pot stickers and sticky rice. My cold lunch of cheese cubes, a hard-boiled egg, and apple slices was long gone, and my stomach growled while Dad said grace.

Dinner finished almost as soon as it began. We gobbled our Asian feast quickly, and quietly, thank goodness. In between bites, the men discussed new church building stuff while us womenfolk took turns answering the girls' random questions. And then Gracie's family left since it was the first school night of a new year. The girls' reluctance to conform to an earlier curfew required both parents' full attention in shuttling them out the door, and Ted somehow left without flinging any more potshots in my general direction. I had to remember to buy my nieces a pony the next time I saw them.

The older folk retired to the family room, leaving Jackson and I to clean up. Jackson offered to do dishes, but I insisted he chill at the bar instead while I did dishes. We didn't talk as I loaded the dishwasher, but I caught him in midyawn as I filled the sink with warm water and soap for hand washing.

"You look bushed, J," I observed.

"J?" he asked.

"Well, you insist on calling me by a nickname."

"Louisa is your full name."

88

"And the only time Mom trotted it out was when I'd done something naughty. Everyone calls me Lu."

"Would you rather I call you Lu?"

I thought about that as I scrubbed and rinsed the rice cooker. "No. Would you rather I call you Jackson?"

"Yes."

"J it is then! Can I force a cup of coffee on you?"

"No, but if you want to make some for yourself, I'm happy to sit with you while you drink it."

"I'm afraid you'd fall asleep and teeter off that barstool. It takes work to pull off what you did this morning and then cook a whole dinner for my family. I'm impressed."

"Let me see that cheat sheet again," he said, holding out his hand.

I gave it to him, and he read it while I scrubbed and rinsed.

"It's interesting to see the sermon through your notes. You work on something for so long and start to wonder whether it makes any sense," he said after a few minutes.

"It did to me. I don't agree with your conclusions, but your sermon had logic and depth. I mean, look at my sentence. I took those verses a bit at a time each day and that is all I could come up with. I wondered at how you were going to fill thirty minutes, and you did."

"You do something similar—somehow tying peoples interviews and your observations into a cohesive story. What are you working on now?"

It's not easy to talk about my writing, especially if I'm about to start something important, which for some reason this blog seemed to be. But Jackson was a safe space. He looked at me while I talked and listened without interrupting, which gave me freedom to process all that had been clanging around my head this afternoon. He must have been exhausted, but he was listening to me like he had all night.

"Do you normally second-guess yourself when you start a story?" he asked after I'd finished.

I shook my head.

"So why with this?"

I let the next pan soak in the soapy water for a minute while I thought about that. "I think because it's me on the line—a shift from objective observations to writing from a personal angle. I can see the irony of my situation—cuckolded single girl consigned to the wedding beat—and I can see how it would work for editorial, but I'm not sure I'm ready to be the subject."

"I don't think you've described the real you."

That snapped my gaze to him. "What do you mean?"

He leaned onto his arms and looked at me. "What you described is a pitch, to borrow from your lingo. Maybe it's something that sells a story, but that's not the full story. I don't see just irony in you. I also see a humor that comes from the humility of being able to laugh at yourself, which is more gentle than sharp. You're willing to grow and change. Look at the notes you took today from a sermon you're not even buying. And you're not so hard as you make yourself out to be ... except when you're forcing coffee on people," he said, smiling.

"So what would you suggest?" I looked back down. His kind assessment had turned my cheeks red.

"If you're going to write about you, then write about you. Not what you think will sell and not from behind a persona. One of the most special things about you is that you're very real. What you see is what you get; you just don't let a lot of people see it." I peeked up at him, and he laughed. "But these are only suggestions, Louisa. I'm not a writer; I certainly can't write like you can."

"No one can write like our Lu can," announced Grandma Pat, swinging back into the kitchen. "You look awful tired, honey," she said crossing the room to put her arm around Jackson and give him a squeeze. "Before you go, I want to show you something. It won't take but a minute."

Jackson looked at me, and I shrugged. She rummaged in her rooms off the kitchen and emerged a short time later holding a thick white binder. I had no clue what was inside until she opened the thick plastic cover to reveal the first story I'd written—"Tails of Red & Blue"—about Nana Bea's pugs, whose real names were Eliza and Theodore, but I'd insisted on calling Red and Blue because of the color of their collars. And probably because I knew even at that young age how horrible it was to name your dogs Eliza and Theodore.

Grandma gently removed the book from its plastic insert like it was an archival document.

"Have you washed your hands?" she asked Jackson sharply.

"Yes, ma'am."

She reluctantly handed the book over, keeping a hawk eye on him as he turned the first page. "Now you take care—this is the only copy I've got."

Jackson looked at me. I could tell he wanted to laugh.

"A limited edition," I said gravely.

He did laugh at that but then tucked in for what I remember as quite the riveting read.

"Now what do you think?" Grandma asked, reclaiming the book and returning it to the insert before he could properly close it.

"I think it's good I stopped illustrating," I said.

"No one asked you," she snapped. "Keep quiet and let Jackson speak."

"I'm going to need to see some more of Louisa's work before I form an opinion."

What a punk.

Grandma happily settled on the barstool next to him, eagerly relaying the backstory to every piece of writing she'd squirreled away since my writing career began at the age of six. This included the legit stories, a la "Red & Blue," but also programs I'd written to accompany Gracie's many in-house musicals and some writing assignments for school. I had no idea she'd been doing this, and it was sweet, but I was also glad I'd tossed my hidden journals before she could somehow acquire them.

I finished cleaning while they walked down my literary lane. The early years' stuff was cute, but the high school section of the portfolio was so awful, I needed to vacate the premises. Nine o'clock in the evening was as good a time as any to drink coffee, and I gestured to the French press in between stories to see if the peanut gallery wanted any. Grandma nodded enthusiastically, Jackson shook his head. I placed a cup of water in front of him instead. A few minutes of boiling and brewing later, I gave Grandma her coffee and pleaded one more time on Jackson's behalf.

"Let the man go, Grandma. He's exhausted."

She shooed me away like a pesky fly. "Off with you."

"Yes, off with you," Jackson echoed. I guess he'd found his second wind.

I thought about retreating to the deck with my coffee, but headed to the family room instead to see what the rest of my family was up to. They were all immersed in reading, and only Dad broke to give me a brief smile when I entered. I sank into a chair by the front window and removed my cheat sheet from my back pocket. I hadn't given it much thought since this morning, but reading Jackson's thoughts seemed like a decent return on his favor of reading mine—at least the thoughts of my six- to eighteen-year-old self.

At first, the notes all blurred together—like how my Bible reading had gone this week but after half a cup of coffee, I noticed something. Solomon wasn't talking about pleasure, wisdom, and work from a philosophical viewpoint. And, he wasn't talking about it with a moralistic finger wag. He was speaking with the "I" of first-person experience.

As a little girl, I'd turned up my nose at Grandma Pat's Polish food. No other girls I knew had to eat sauerkraut. But she'd always respond: "Try it. If you don't like it, fine. But if you don't try it, you've got nothing." Solomon had tried it, which lent a certain validity to the whole argument.

"You want a Bible to go with that?" Jackson asked quietly as he sat in the chair next to me. I hadn't heard him come in, and I glanced at my watch. Thirty minutes had passed.

I did want a Bible—I wanted to check out some of Solomon's verbs—but I shook my head. "All done?"

"Through the high school years anyway. The funny thing is, I remember reading some of that back then."

"You read my stuff in high school?"

"I read the school newspaper in high school," he clarified. "Especially in math class."

I laughed, which jolted my family from their reading. Jackson stood. Dad, Mom, and Nana paused long enough to thank Jackson for the meal and say goodnight before lowering their heads again. I walked Jackson to the front door.

"Sorry Grandma Pat kept you out so late," I said, opening the door.

"Tomorrow's my Sunday; I can sleep as long as I want. What about you?" he asked, nodding toward my coffee mug before he stepped onto the front porch.

"I'm immune—five minutes and I'll be sleeping like a baby."

"That's good because it's a big day for you, right? You should check out your grandma's binder; she has a few ideas that might help you …" Jackson started to say, but then he stopped and stood there, smiling at me.

"What are you talking about?" I asked, leaning into the doorway.

He put his hands up. "I'm the messenger."

"A messenger who isn't saying anything."

"The signaler, then."

"To what?"

He crooked his finger at me to lean in closer. I did, and he whispered, "To tell you to check out your grandma's binder before she hides it."

We said goodnight, and I closed the front door as quietly as possible and tiptoed back to the kitchen so as not to alert Grandma, who'd joined my family in the front room. The kitchen lights were off, except the one above the stove, but I could see the outline of the binder on the bar. I grabbed it, furtively looked around for booby traps I might trigger by moving it, and then carried it to the stove so I could see what Jackson was hinting about.

I noticed this time that the cover had a title—"Lu #1"— scrawled in Grandma's slant with almost faded pencil. So there were more—a scary enough thought that almost sidetracked me on another mission to ferret them from her room. I opened the binder instead and quickly flipped through the plastic inserts. Nothing out of the way. And then I took one story out—a two-page assignment I'd written in ninth grade about my most prized possession. I flipped the cover, and there they were—a colorful assortment of Post-its containing Grandma's suggestions of different wording and angles I should have taken. I put the story back and took out another. Same. And then another. Same. This binder was as much Lu's Literary Museum as it was Pat's Editing Hall of Fame. Definitely salty and sweet, that Pierogie Pat.

I returned the binder to where she'd left it, but glanced back before I left the kitchen. Lu #1. I had no idea how many other binders were out there—probably several given my prolific output in college and postgrad—but this one reminded me of all the writing I'd done as a little girl without giving much thought to what I was doing. I hadn't done it to make my mark or to set myself apart; I'd done it because it's what I did. Writing was my contribution: a program for Gracie's song and dance routines.

Writing was how I spent my Saturday afternoons while Ted played baseball outside.

But at some point, writing had become my ambition and my failure. Grandma's other binders would track that rise and fall. But this white binder, with its faded title and eclectic content and colorful Post-its … this binder was like a talisman. I picked it up.

"I'm taking this," I announced to Grandma Pat as I walked by the family room and marched up the stairs to my bedroom, hugging the binder to my chest.

"But it's mine," she protested, getting up from her chair.

"My name is on the cover."

And so it was.

CHAPTER 11

My blog, *Creeking*, debuted that Monday to little fanfare, notwithstanding the silent drumroll of my heart.

I'd thought about calling it LuUpTheCreek as a nod to one of Grandma Pat's favorite hillbilly expressions, but after my conversation with Jackson, I knew being up the creek without a paddle wasn't the whole story. My lemons were details, certainly funny details that uniquely underscored my life and work, but in the broad strokes I wasn't much different than other girls—wading into each new day to walk the familiar streams of who we think we are, what we think we're doing, where we think we're going. But sometimes the light breaks on the surface in a new way, our toes feel a difference underfoot, and we spy a shadow of something yet unseen that causes a break from walking along our patterns and perceptions so that we can kneel and discover what's under the surface.

Which is what had happened to me. I'd relied on muscle memory in my current iteration in Dunlap's Creek. Ask how it's going, and I'd respond, "typical" to every experience and person I'd encountered. But, I was wrong—,as wrong as when I'd hunt for mudbugs with my dad and give up after a half second of searching the creek bed with my little girl fingers.

"There aren't any," I'd shout in frustration.

"Try again," he'd patiently urge.

And we'd repeat this exchange as many times as it took until I found my first one, which was all I needed to sustain an afternoon's worth of exploration.

I'd followed last night's binder march with a couple of hours of looking through it. And thanks to the content therein, as well as the grandma who'd hoarded it, I opened my laptop on Monday morning resolved to two things: 1) To write what was of interest to me, and 2) To write in a way that was true to myself. Follow these guidelines and I figured I'd at least please an audience of one—which was good, since the second person to peruse Creeking was not impressed.

"Isn't creeking some extreme form of whitewater rafting?" RJ shouted from across the office about five minutes after I clicked "publish."

"It's also this."

"It sounds like a science class field trip," he persisted.

"The pictures of wedding cake and people kissing will clear that one up," I hollered back, effectively ending the volley, but not before he muttered something about one blog in a sea of millions.

In my inaugural blog week, I decided to shadow Anne Jameson, a middle school science teacher getting married this Saturday. Maybe pictures of fireflies lighting up the night sky as the scientist bride and farmer groom said their vows in an open field would appease the naturalists who inadvertently surfed to this space expecting a treatise on backyard biology.

Anne agreed to pose in the actual Dunlap's Creek for the blog's first post: "T-Minus Six Days with the Bride up the Creek." With *The Daily* not publishing daily, I could never have done something like this for the paper, but publishing in the blog world didn't cost anything, and blog readers seemed to expect the inane and quirky insights about everyday people that traditional journalism doesn't deem newsworthy. The Monday lunch hour I spent creeking with Anne was the most fun I'd had on the job, and the mix of beautiful pictures punctuated with excerpts of our dialogue was my favorite feature. Tuesday's post, "On the Farm," introduced Rob, the groom, and offered a sneak peek of the wedding's location on his farm, and for Wednesday's post, "In It for the Free Cake," I accompanied them both to the cake tasting in full hopes that some of that cake love would come my way. It did, and in two flavors: dark chocolate raspberry and lemon white chocolate. The baker sent me home with a box of each, and I took them straight to church.

Jackson wasn't in his office when I arrived, but his mess was— open books all over the desk, and some loose sheets of paper that had trickled to the floor. I stepped forward to pick those up and shamelessly peek at their contents.

"Spying?" Jackson asked from the doorway.

"Trying to, but I can't seem to make sense of any of it," I said, bending down to pick up the last few papers and put them on his desk.

"The Greek or the Hebrew?"

"Your handwriting," I said, holding up a sheet and rotating it. "I honestly don't know which way is up." I put the paper on the desk and turned a few pages of the various books in their strange languages. The paper was thick, yellowed, and musty. I wrinkled my nose at the smell. "Who knew you were such a nerd, J."

"And here I'd always thought women loved men who know different languages."

"More in the whispering to us in Spanish context. Speaking English with an accent also works. This though … you'd better stick to cooking meals like you did on Sunday if you want to nab a girl."

And then I shut my mouth, one sentence too late. I looked at him, and neither of us spoke or moved for a brief eternity.

Eventually, he cleared his throat. "I've been meaning to ask you something."

He took a step forward, and I took a step back.

"Has Grandma Pat said anything about me?" he asked in a breathless rush.

That question cut the tension, and I laughed. "She passed me a note asking me to invite you for stuffed cabbage tonight. I brought you some cake to tide you over until then."

"What's the occasion?" he asked as I opened the two cake boxes.

I smiled. "My thank-you for encouraging me."

He smiled back. "Anytime—and I mean that," he said as he reached for the chocolate like a flash. But I was ready for him and smacked his hand away.

"Hold it cake shark. We are splitting these. And do you even like cake?" I asked as I cut each in two, shuffled the halves accordingly and handed him his carton.

"I guess we'll never know," he said.

We sat on either side of the desk, eating our first bites in perfect silence.

"Sermon stuff?" I asked, nodding toward the books.

"Research."

"On Ecclesiastes again?"

"Until the bitter end," he said. My thoughts exactly.

"So riddle me this. You are one of the friendliest people I know. Why are you preaching from such a cranky book that throws around 'meaningless' like it's the word of the day?"

"Other translations use vanity. Would you prefer that?"

"Like in the 'Mirror, mirror on the wall' sense?"

"More like in the futile sense. It's probably the better translation, but since we keep NIV Bibles in the sanctuary, I'm using that for the sermon."

"And why this book?" I asked again.

"It's the book I read right after my divorce."

"To self-flagellate?"

Jackson gave a shout of laughter. "No, not to … Man, you don't hold back, do you?" He picked up his cake, but then put it back down to laugh again. After another minute and a bite of cake, he answered.

"God led me to it," he said simply, like that wasn't a strange thing to say. The look on my face said otherwise, and he backpedaled. "I'll put it another way. For you, the Bible is another book—maybe a stranger book than most."

I nodded.

"But to me, the Bible is God's words. I read it, but it's also accurate to say that I open it to hear what God has to say to me. Right after Kate left, I could barely tell my right from my left. I knew the Bible would have words to help me with my grief, generally speaking, but I also knew God had something specific to say to me. I prayed for direction, and he led me to Ecclesiastes. It's similar to how you might go to a friend and ask, 'Remember that one thing you said that one time that helped me …?' That's how I was asking God about what to read."

That made some sense, and I nodded. "Why do you think he led you to Ecclesiastes?"

"I needed tough love. I'd misappropriated and made much out of my work and my position instead of making much of God. And a lot of the repair work I'd been doing in the fallout of my marriage was still to salvage those things instead of come back to him. What I'm covering this Sunday was a real turning point for me—chapter three."

"Why?" I asked, feeling like a nagging toddler.

"Because I needed to stop patching and fail and let God pick me back up."

"So it'll be another doozy." I sighed. Jackson laughed.

"Have you given anymore thought to last week's sermon?" he asked, leaning back into his chair.

"Yup, and you'll be happy to know I'm busy making like Solomon."

"How so?"

"I'm exploring all the nooks and crannies of my current lot to see whether I can sniff out any meaning. I hope to have a harem by week's end," I said, alluding to one of Solomon's exploits. I settled back into my chair, put my feet on Jackson's desk, and gave my full attention to eating cake. I couldn't tell whether I liked the tangy raspberry or tart lemon best.

"You let me know how that goes," he said. And then a beat later he nodded toward the doorway. "Hey, Dad."

Not mine.

His.

I'd always been scared by Pastor Cleary when I was a child, and a quick check of my vitals showed I hadn't grown out of it. Of course, he'd caught me with my feet on his son's desk, talking about harems and eating cake. I lowered my feet, one at a time— suddenly and supremely thankful I only had two—and swallowed the cake that now felt like a lump of wool in my esophagus.

I looked at Jackson. He smiled, knowing exactly how freaked out I was and reveling in every second it took me to stand, turn around, and face his dad. Pastor Cleary was very tall, very thin, and wearing small wire glasses that did little to camouflage eyes that pierced my soul. I wanted to tell him I was joking about the whole harem thing. I meant to say something, anything, but I couldn't seem to form words. So I stood there.

After awhile, he cleared his throat and handed Jackson a book.

"I think this is what you were looking for, son. Nice to see you again, Louisa. Say hello to your family for me."

He left, while I continued to stand, staring at the space he'd vacated.

"Hey," Jackson said, very softly, very kindly.

"What?" I asked, following the thread of his voice to escape the twilight zone.

"I want you to try something."

I turned to him. "Okay."

"Take a deep breath and say, 'Hello, Pastor Cleary.' Or, 'Hey, Paul.'"

"Who's Paul?"

"My dad."

"Yeah, I'm not calling him Paul."

"You haven't called him anything, yet."

"Because he's scary."

"No, your family is scary. Mine is quiet."

"He's a pastor!" I accused in a sharp whisper.

"So am I."

I groaned, sitting back in my chair and burying my face in my hands. "Stop reminding me."

"Are you going to eat your cake?" he asked.

"Have at it, Pastor," I muttered, pushing the box across the desk. I wasn't hungry anymore, but Jackson was, and he happily chowed it down while I took deep breaths.

"I'd suggest you put your head between your legs, but your tail is in the way," he said.

I glared at him to show I did not appreciate that comment.

"And may I remind you that your nana asked me point-blank about my divorce the minute I sat down to dinner at your house? I can still talk to her."

Wondering what his parents might know made me dizzy. "What does your dad know about me?"

"I don't know."

"Well, what has he said?"

"Nothing."

"What have you told him?"

"Nothing."

"Nothing?"

"Nothing. We don't sit around and talk about you."

"I guess your family is different than mine. If I so much as think about you, they're ...

"You think about me?" he interrupted, somehow fitting a piece of cake as big as his head in his mouth.

"Oh yeah. Like right now, I'm thinking a lot of things about how you're eating that cake."

"You're the one who brought it … and to church might I add. You were bound to bump into my dad at some point," he reasoned, scraping the last of the frosting from his container.

True. This was not a safe space. I stood to leave but then hesitated. "Is anyone else milling about that I should be aware of?" I asked under my breath.

"The elder board."

That didn't sound good.

"Am I still invited to dinner tonight?" he shouted to me as I left.

I shook my head no.

"Great, I'll see you at six."

CHAPTER 12

There is a time for everything, and a season for every activity under heaven...

Jackson brought me a piece of chocolate cake and this verse, along with the rest of Ecclesiastes 3, written on a sheet of notebook paper when he came to dinner on Wednesday night.

"For Sunday's test," he'd explained.

Of course, I'd had to decipher his scribble against the print of my NIV, but what I found didn't require me to train my finger to the text:

A time to be born and a time to die;
A time to plant and a time to uproot,
A time to kill and a time to heal,
A time to weep and a time to laugh ...

I read it again and again, and not because the words blurred. I now understood why Ecclesiastes was considered poetry:

A time to mourn and a time to dance,
A time to scatter stones and a time to gather them,
A time to embrace and a time to refrain,
A time to search and a time to give up ...

On it went. I wasn't in a rush to make sense of it, and I didn't want to uncover something that would make the verses play less beautifully in my mind. So play they did as I wrapped up the workweek and dressed for Saturday's wedding in my new favorite skirt from Grandma Pat. Was there a time to repeat your wedding outfit? I guessed yes, and as I found myself once again marveling over the design, I decided it was also time to publish. I leaned on Dad to take some pics, posted on Instagram under "My Wedding

Skirt," and happily paired it with the same off-shoulder, white shirt and jute wedges I'd worn to the last wedding with Gracie, then left to fly solo at this one.

I caught the breeze of fiddles the moment I stepped out of my car and followed their harmonies from the fallow-field parking to the old red barn that would serve as the backdrop for the ceremony. The bride and groom had opted for hay bales over chairs, and after a brief inspection, I chose an innocuous looking one in the back. I didn't want any wayward hay strands poking my skirt.

Ten minutes into the festivities, I realized hay bales were more cute than comfortable, but I kept to mine after the wedding finished to brainstorm the feature. Beautiful details surrounded— from bluegrass strings to the bride's brown and turquoise cowboy boots peeking out from under her cream wedding dress to the bonfire smell of fall in the air. A clear start to the story eluded me, however, and the goosebumps on my arms reminded me to start bringing cardigans to outdoor weddings. The lantern lights strung along the barn rafters beckoned against the fading twilight, and I tucked my notes in my purse before heading to the reception.

A friendly hum and touch of warmth welcomed me as I stepped into the barn doorway, realizing too late that it was open seating— a fact, that if I'd remembered, would have made me the first to bolt from the ceremony to sit at a table in the back. As it was, I attempted an unassuming pose in the yawning barn doors as I searched for a lone seat amid tables already crowded with friends and family—but none familiar to me. It felt very "high school lunch room," an awkward situation I'd always buffered by shadowing Gracie, and I kicked myself for thinking I could leave her at home tonight. I instinctually stepped toward a free chair not yet claimed by a purse or jacket at a table of polite looking baby boomers, but the laughter from a table of people my age turned my wedge sandals left before I could consult with my brain as to whether this was a good idea.

I autopiloted toward the empty chair, and the group of seven fell silent when I gestured to it. A couple seconds passed with no one saying anything, and I thought that if I could melt away at the rate that the sweat was now melting off my pits that would be a good way to go.

"Can I sit here?"

"Sure, but let me get a look at that skirt first," the woman across from me said. I complied, and the two other women at the table joined inspection. One of the men correctly interpreted the embarrassing red of my cheeks and encouraged the women to sit it back on down.

"I'm Tom," he said as he stood and reached across the table to shake my hand. He round-robined with everyone else's names. They were all friends of the groom— township folk who shared my class year, but not my school. We filled the minutes before dinner with polite back and forth, but once we tucked into the prime rib, stories of their yesteryears came forth. By the end of dinner, I concluded that country folk are crazy. It was amazing any of the people at this table were still alive, given their high school driving escapades. Bill, sitting three to my left, claimed he took Dead Man's Curve on 732 going fifty in his dad's Ford pickup, but I wasn't buying it.

I felt a slight letdown when the unassuming background dinner music turned to dancing volume, and my tablemates paired off to the paneled floor in the middle of the barn. The fun was done. I was about to push my chair back to stand and leave when I felt someone else do it for me.

"Want to dance?" Tom asked.

I smiled up at him, and surprised myself again by realizing I did, and I took his hand. Of course, I blamed this sudden desire on Solomon, for putting a time to dance in my head in the first place, and then on my skirt, which demanded a twirl.

I cannot dance. I have no natural rhythm, or coordination, or bravado, or any of the other things required to move one's body in a fluid motion, but the song was slow enough to get away with a basic step-touch. Tom seemed much surer of himself, with his right hand planted firmly on my lower back and his left gripping my right.

"When will I get to take a closer look at your skirt?" he asked, smiling. So, it was a time to flirt—his, at any rate.

Not mine. I shook my head, but smiled back to the cut edge of my denial.

"You can't blame a man for trying."

This was starting to remind me of my first interchange with John, but I blocked that memory to stay in the moment. "I'll forgive you, given your dinnertime rescue," I responded, and we bantered like this for the rest of the song. It made for a light three minutes, but I wasn't sorry when the song ended.

"Can I take you home?" Tom asked as we headed back to the table.

Right. Home to my parents and grandmas. I laughed at that sexy proposition, but said, "After those fast and furious stories from dinner? No thank you."

"Can I have your number then?" he persisted

I picked up my purse and looked at him. He was handsome, objectively so—dimple on the right cheek, blond hair, blue eyes. And by how he smiled at me, I think he knew it, too. He probably wasn't used to being turned down, but what could I say? I didn't have a phone.

"Thanks for the dance," I said by way of rejection, and turned to leave the barn which suddenly felt a little too warm, a little too light, and a little too loud. I happily left my foray into friendliness for the cool quiet of the evening as I walked alone to my car. I'd had fun.

And, I had my story.

Saturday's wedding proved that the right barn with the right fiddle playing the right song on the right night might just move anyone to believe it's their time to dance, their time to romance. But this night belonged to Anne and Rob, no matter how their wedding may have persuaded the rest of us to think it was ours . . .

CHAPTER 13

I slipped early into my seat at church that next morning and played tic-tac-toe with a little boy, probably about seven-years-old, sitting next to me—after a quick eyebrow check with his mom, of course. She seemed relieved for someone else to step in as cruise director, and the little man and I fit in five games during the church preliminaries. He started drawing a hangman's noose after the last song, but I pulled my ear and nodded toward the front of the church. It was time to listen. He put down the game. His mom smiled. What can I say? I had the touch.

Jackson took the stage, and I took Ecclesiastes 3 from my back pocket.

"Would you please open your Bibles to Ecclesiastes 3 ... and would you please do this without sighing?"

The congregation and I laughed. On this, at least, we were at least in agreement.

"I know it's been a tough road these last few weeks—not much to write home about, unless of course you wanted to make your family cry. Someone asked me why I'm preaching from this book, and I said, 'Because it's the book I read after my divorce.' She then accused me of self-flagellation."

Another laugh. I hoped the red on my cheeks didn't give away my anonymity.

"Maybe so. At that time in my life, I was asking what my life was for, and reading this book was like pushing a bruise, which when you're in pain, is somehow what feels best. My years of dating and engagement and marriage seemed like a total waste, and Ecclesiastes responded to me like an empathetic friend, nodding with me at every turn: 'Yup. You're right about that. Life is the worst. Totally and utterly meaningless.'

"I thought we were in complete agreement, Solomon and I. Then I came to Chapter 3 and realized that what I'd read as empathy, he'd intended as an argument to lead me to a point of decision. He was effectively saying: Take God out of the equation, and there is no meaning to what had happened with you. Or, to anyone.

"That's how pain stands without God. That's how life stands without God. That's the point of Ecclesiastes 1 and 2.

"But, what if God is in the equation? This is what Solomon poses to us today in Ecclesiastes 3. What if God was there when I was dating a girl I wanted to marry? What if he was there when I asked her to marry me? If God was there on the day we were married than he was also there when the fighting started, and I turned away from my wife, and she walked out. If he was there on the day I signed the divorce papers and lost my job, then ... what? What did this mean for me? What does it mean for you?

"The existence of God changes the equation completely because it means that the world Solomon describes in bleak black and white in Ecclesiastes 1 and 2 is not all there is. There is more. And God is lord over it all.

"Ecclesiastes 3:11 says: *He has made everything beautiful in its time . . . .* Because of God, not some things, but *everything* is beautiful in its time—not just the laughing, and dancing, and mending, but also the weeping, and mourning, and tearing. Each bookend from verses two through eight has its purpose, its time, and because of that, we don't need to avoid it. We don't need to pretend it doesn't exist. We can lean into it . . . ."

I released my grip on my paper, sat back in the pew, closing my eyes. These words had pierced me and spread like a balm, though I hadn't known why. I understood now. My family had said much in the aftermath of New York, mostly in their negative opinions about John or how I should move on from him. I'd heard it and even understood it. Wouldn't it be great if I could be that girl who moves on without looking back? But just because I'd smashed my phone didn't mean I didn't wonder whether he'd called.

My family's intentions were good, but they didn't meet me

where I was. Ecclesiastes 3 read like an invitation to reality—not to what had happened or what should happen next, but to what was happening, right now. My grief.

I stood and left, not caring how it looked to leave church midsermon. It was my time to cry. Finally.

CHAPTER 14

I was waiting for Jackson on my front stoop that night, though I didn't realize that's what I was doing until his car turned into the drive. We hadn't made any plans, but I'd been hoping. I walked toward him as he exited the car, and we turned together to walk down my street instead of back to the house.

"You okay?" he asked after a few footsteps of silence.

"Are you referring to my bloodshot eyes, red nose, and puffy cheeks?" I reached into my back pocket for a tissue to blow my nose. Crying all day had released a well of snot that I couldn't seem to fully expel.

"A gentlemen does not mention such things."

"And a lady doesn't blow her nose like this," I said before foghorning into the tissue. "Does Ecclesiastes 3 allot a time to make noises like that?"

"The footnotes mention it." He put his hand gently on my back—a gesture that surprised me almost as much as my reaction to it. I wanted him to keep it there.

"Are you okay?" he asked again before taking his hand away.

"Tomorrow I will be, but today's sermon seems to have unleashed a crying dam. I was afraid it would overtake me at some point this afternoon, but despite evidence to the contrary," I said, gesturing to my face, "I think it's dissipating."

"It's good to know your grief hasn't affected your vocabulary," he said, laughing.

"What are you talking about?"

"I'm talking about you throwing around words like 'dissipate' when you're a mess."

"Shut it, Jackson."

"That's better. That I understand." He stopped walking and turned to look at me for a long time. It should have felt uncomfortable. No one wants to be inspected at close range, especially when her face is a blubbering train wreck, but the kindness in his eyes felt like a hug. I started crying all over again.

He rubbed a tear from my cheek with his thumb. "You're going to have stop."

"Solomon didn't put a timetable to the time for weeping."

"I meant that I didn't bring any Kleenex."

"That's two strikes against you, then!" I said, blowing my nose into my used tissue, not caring that it could fall apart at any blow and explode snot all over me.

"What's the first?"

"Causing all of this with your little Ecclesiastes 3. I feel like everyone else has been trying to push me forward, but this ... This is telling me to stand still and live what's going on inside of me instead of shutting it out. Other than the day I found out, I haven't really cried since John told me he cheated on me. To grieve for grief's sake felt weak. But something about these verses and what you said today are telling me different. There's a time for what I'm feeling right now, and I need to get this out."

He smiled.

"Not that I think you have to believe in God to believe this," I clarified.

He kept smiling. "Use that big vocabulary of yours and describe me."

I chose my words carefully. "You are friendly, fun, laid-back, honest, and humble, even though you seem to have an answer for everything."

"Does any of that remind you of me from high school?"

"Not at all."

"Describe that boy."

"Quiet. Maybe stuffy? You always seemed ill at ease, and I don't think I ever saw you smile."

"And that's exactly how I was until my divorce. As a preacher's kid, I grew up with a healthy fear of sin. I tried to do everything 'right.' My relationship with Kate is a perfect example of this. Give me a checklist of what makes two people compatible, and we fit it. Tell me everything a couple should do before deciding to marry, and I can prove I checked every box.

"But it wasn't enough—despite my best efforts. And this is what kept running through my head as I split log after log, month after month. I was not enough. And then it hit me—God already knew I was a loser! And, he loved me anyway. Nothing in what happened with Kate took him by surprise, but it needed to take me by surprise so I could finally admit it, apologize for it, and move forward, trusting in him to make me right instead of trying to do it myself."

"So that's the gospel? We are losers?"

"Every one of us, but none of us have to be because of what Jesus did for us. That last part is very important."

"And without the gospel this idea of everything being perfect in its time doesn't apply?"

He spread his hands. "Why would it? Under what authority? You tell me what in this world says failing is okay? This world says failing is okay only if you make something of it later. But in the Gospel, failing is a prerequisite."

"Why?"

"So that you can be rescued."

We didn't say anything on our walk back to the house. I wasn't sure whether I should invite him to stay, but Jackson made the decision by opening his car door. He paused before getting in. "You look tired," he said.

I blamed that on him with my eyes, but he shook his head. "I am not taking the fall for this one. Didn't I read something about 'A time to romance' in this morning's paper?'"

I groaned and put my hands to my face, having forgotten about last night's hay bales and fiddles and boy. "Did I write that?" I asked, too embarrassed to look at Jackson, but I peeked at him through my fingers anyway as he got in his car and drove off.

Boys. Boys and phones. I'd smashed one phone to prevent John from calling me, and I wouldn't have given my number to Tom if I had one. But Jackson? My eyes followed his car until it turned out of sight.

CHAPTER 15

"Have you noticed your Instagram post on the skirt is going gangbusters?" Grandma Pat asked me over coffee and chocolate-chip banana bread the next morning.

Her lingo shouldn't have surprised me, or the iPhone she wielded from her back pocket. It was a new day, but Grandma was still hipper than me. She handed me the phone, and I saw my Instagram account on the screen, but the stats were too small to read. I casually V'd my thumb and pointer finger like I'd seen everyone do everywhere over the last decade. A page for weight-loss secrets popped up.

"Give me that," Grandma said, swatting my hand and reclaiming the phone. I was no better at navigating smart phones than pinching pierogies. I peeked over her shoulder as she navigated back to the account and zoomed in.

"Is that double digits I spy?"

She nodded.

"Cool." And I turned my full attention to enjoy my coffee and bread. I'd take a banana over plain banana bread any day, but banana bread with chocolate chips is an evolved creature. I'd cut myself two thick slices and slathered them with butter and was now alternating bites of gooey, chocolate deliciousness with sips of bitter coffee. Heaven.

"That's all?" Grandma demanded.

"What, you want some?"

"Not that, this!" she said, thrusting the phone back in my face.

She wasn't talking about banana bread. I sat back in my chair, taking my coffee with me. I was going to need everything it had to offer on this Monday morning. I took a sip, looking at her over the rim of my mug.

"You want me to do something about so many people liking the skirt picture."

She nodded.

"Then why don't you set up an interview with the skirt lady?"

"Her name is Virginia Stanley, and she'll be at my shop today at ten o'clock."

I smiled and put my cup down, shaking my head back and forth. "You've been busy, Grandma."

"I was trying to help you out, honey. Now how about you go and make me a cup of coffee."

I obliged, but her small hand grasped my wrist before I could rise from my seat. I sat back down and looked at her. She was small all over, but small in the stick of dynamite sense.

"You okay?" she asked.

I wasn't surprised she'd noticed yesterday's cry fest, but that she asked without offering up any opinions was new ground.

"I'm okay. Better than okay." I squeezed her hand and stood to make coffee.

"Good. John was no good for you. Jackson is what you need."

And just like that, we were back on familiar ground.

Since I was all big time, I nixed going into the office in favor of lingering over a third slice of banana bread and a second cup of coffee before heading to Penny Thrift to meet with Virginia, a diminutive woman my age, but with a baby and a fashion collection.

Virginia was one of those introverts who made me look like an extrovert, which is to say I liked her, despite her kindred spirit stonewalling all my questions with a shrug of the shoulders or a soft, "I'll have to think about it." At least now I had the answer to how she found the time to hand-stitch all this stuff; the girl didn't talk to anyone.

I'd done enough journalism to expect the initial interview awkwardness. The early questions are for working out the conversational kinks. But thirty minutes into my interview with

113

Virginia, I was no farther along, which was doubly frustrating given the story's potential was strewn about me in her jackets and skirts and shirts. Pictures wouldn't cut it. I needed her to say something. Anything.

Grandma must have caught the scent of my despair because as I was about to bail, she breezed back into the room with one of Virginia's garments in tow.

"Virginia, honey. Can you show me how you tie off this knot for your applique stitches?" she asked.

I didn't know a stitch about sewing, but I did know there wasn't a technique a twentysomething girl could reveal to someone who'd been sewing for one hundred and fifty years like Grandma Pat. Virginia probably knew this, too, but she jumped on Grandma's question like it was a lifeline. I tuned it out, but after several minutes, I tuned back in because she was still talking. Talking about sewing technique was Virginia's familiar ground, and my broader questions about how she'd started her business and how she intended to grow it were too much.

I rerouted my approach.

"Where do you thrift these T-shirts you use for your fabric?" I asked, touching a corseted top formed by ten hourglass panels of soft, faded black cotton and appliqued with ivy shapes of dark gray.

"Oh, I have three favorite stores. I go to each of them on three different days."

"Because of their sales ..." I finished for her. I bet she frequented the same stores where I'd scavenged my high school wardrobe.

"Do you know about the new one on Dunlap-Farmland Pike? Twenty-five percent off every Monday," Virginia said, offering her first tidbit of unsolicited information.

"Let's go then!"

"Okay!" she exclaimed. But then, "Wait, what?"

"Let me shadow you. You won't have to do anything other than what you usually do. You won't know I'm there."

"I'll watch little Danny," Grandma chirped.

Virginia looked at her six-month-old son sleeping in a Pack 'n Play and looked back to us, her face uncertain over this spontaneous field trip. I didn't want to strong arm the poor thing, but I needed to get her to her mother ship if I was going to redeem the morning's efforts. She nodded, and within five minutes,

Grandma Pat and I had her loaded in my car.

It'd been years since I'd entered a thrift store, but the familiar smell hit my nostrils like a forgotten perfume. Valley Thrift was way bigger than the stores of my youth, and so well organized by style, color, and size that shopping here almost felt like cheating. You could be in and out with cool stuff in a half hour easy.

I glanced at Virginia. She hadn't said a word during the ten-minute drive, and she stood paralyzed now.

"Do you always look like a deer in headlights when you come here?" I asked her.

"No, but ..."

"But, what?"

"I normally come in here to find stuff to sew, not so someone can write a story about me for the paper."

"Forget about the paper, forget about me. Do what you do, and if I have any questions, I'll ask. But I'm going to try to keep quiet, okay?"

Virginia nodded, and halfway through the rack of short-sleeved T-shirts, she started humming to the songs on the store radio and forgot about me. She plucked shirts in a range of color from the rack, and just as I thought her thin arms might break from the weight, she carried the bundle back to the furniture section and laid out the shirts according to color along the back of a faded brown corduroy couch.

She moved from humming to singing as she revisited each color pile, beginning with the yellow, to weed out the shades that didn't jive. I assumed what remained would form the main panels of each garment, but I didn't ask because she was scooting a kitchen table into her workspace. She spread out her reject shirts, and brought over her color piles to pair complementary applique colors with the base colors: mustard and azure with black, taupe with light cream, white with navy blue. Here, the low tones of her alto voice stopped, and a one-way conversation began as she mused and questioned each piece.

"You could go with ... no, not this, but maybe that? Yes, that works. Get away from there; go here instead. I'm not sure why I ever took you off the rack. Sorry. You're beautiful by yourself; no other color needed."

Virginia repeated these conversations until she'd worked through every pile. The humming resumed as she put her hands in her pockets and took a final survey of her choices. She made some minor changes before giving a satisfied nod. She pushed the table back to its place, returned the rejects to their racks, and headed to the cashier with her finds.

"$11.50," said the cashier after a loud pop of her gum and squeeze of her unnaturally red ponytail.

"Did you take the twenty-five percent off?" Virginia asked.

"Sure did." Another gum pop.

"Would you consider taking off more? They're just old T-shirts," she said, flipping through the pile with a poker face that belied the forty-five minutes she'd invested.

The cashier looked at her, silent but for the chewing of her gum, Virginia stared back, and I felt like the journalist covering the showdown at the O.K. Corral. This was a nail biter.

It was the cashier who broke. "Make it $10.50."

Virginia waived a ten dollar bill in response.

The cashier rolled her eyes. "Fine. $10.00."

"I sure do appreciate it, ma'am. Thank you." And she handed over her money, but with enough reluctance I wasn't sure whether she was done negotiating. She released the bill in exchange for a plastic bag stuffed full of T-shirts and stapled at the top with a receipt.

The sliding glass doors closed behind us, and my laughter ricocheted across the cement parking lot.

"Wow," I said, my voice full of admiration. I needed to bring her home to talk down my rent.

She smiled, but then she stopped walking and looked at me. "You're not going to put that in the paper are you?"

"And ruin your game? No way."

Our excursion thawed Virginia, and she filled our ride back with conversation about her plans for morphing thrifted cotton T-shirts into designer garments. Grandma had lunch waiting when we arrived, and Danny was back down for his afternoon nap, so Virginia spent the next couple of hours showing me her process, from the initial cut of the T-shirt to the knotting of the final applique. Any uncertainty from the morning had faded; the Virginia of the afternoon was confident, decisive, and enthusiastic. And unbelievably talented. She saw these T-shirts for what she could make of them, and then moved faster than a sewing machine to get it done.

Seeing Virginia in her element made me excited to get back to mine, and I narrated my five-minute drive to the newspaper with different pitches to persuade RJ to let me write this story. He'd made it clear he wanted me to cover weddings, but if I pitched this from the angle of wedding wear, he might clear it.

I was excited to invest the rest of my afternoon with drafting the story, and since it was late in the day on a Monday, I didn't expect anyone in the office. But there was RJ with a demand.

"You need to do something about that skirt post. There's over one hundred likes now," he said instead of hello.

I couldn't have set that up better if I'd planned it. I pitched my idea for the feature.

"Fine," he answered. "I have another idea."

Nothing good could come of that.

"Your second highest post after the skirt is the cake pic you posted this past Wednesday. Do you know what this means?"

"People like clothing and cake."

He rolled his eyes.

"More advertisers?" I suggested, though I didn't think he was going to squeeze much out of Virginia. He'd probably end up paying her somehow. I laughed at the thought.

RJ wasn't amused. I coughed.

"I'm thinking of something bigger," he continued. "The paper is struggling, and anything we can do to increase our exposure will help. I think a wedding expo to bring vendors together could work. The paper can sponsor it, but I need someone to pull it off," he said.

I looked around the room. RJ looked at me.

"Not me," I said, stepping back.

"Yes, you."

"Even if I could do this, I'm not sure I want to."

"You didn't want to do the wedding beat," he pointed out.

"Yes, but at least it's in my wheelhouse. It involves writing. What you're describing is a big thing better suited to ... anyone but me. I'm not a girl who does big things like that ....." I trailed off. The excuse sounded lame. But it was earnest.

He didn't say anything.

"Can't you find someone else?"

He gestured to the empty office in response. "And if I could, I would still want you to do it."

"Why?"

"Look at what you've done."

I thought he was going to follow up the compliment—or was it an observation?—with something more, but then he turned back to his computer like we weren't midconversation. I took out my notes and computer, and we worked in silence for the next hour.

By five o'clock, I wasn't sure where we'd left the expo offer, but as RJ left the office, he said. "You don't have to do this, Lu. I have my own reservations about whether it will work, but I can see where we're headed. At worst, the expo will get us there sooner. But at best, who knows? It's a risk I'm willing to take. Think about it."

He hadn't given me a timeframe, but knowing him, he'd want my decision soon. I locked up the doors and decided to leave my car behind and walk home. It was the end of August, but the top leaves on the largest trees were already starting to change. I took the long way home along the quiet side streets to muse over their colors instead of thinking about what RJ wanted me to think about.

I didn't get home until after six o'clock, which put me late for dinner. Still, I didn't expect my dad to be cleaning the last of the dinner dishes.

"There's a plate in the fridge for you, kiddo. We ate early tonight because I'm off to a walk-through of the new church."

I nodded and sat at the bar, resting my chin on my hand.

He came around and put his arm around me. "You okay?"

I leaned my head against his shoulder. "Are you asking because of all my crying yesterday?"

"And you seem distracted now."

I told Dad about the day, beginning with the thrifting and ending with RJ's proposition.

"It sounds like a good day," Dad summarized.

"It was. It's just ..." I paused, searching for the right words to describe my feelings. "It feels like every time I get comfortable, something comes along to shake it up, and I'm unsure of myself all over again."

He nodded but kept quiet—this one family member of mine who was more content to listen than to offer advice. A long while passed without either of us saying anything. My mind was too full to articulate any of it. Dad squeezed my shoulders.

"How about you come with me? You haven't been to the new church, and there's something I'd like to show you."

CHAPTER 16

Five minutes into our drive in Dad's old pickup, I realized I had no idea where we were going—that's how little I knew about what he and my brother had been doing while I'd been so immersed in my own world since I'd been back.

Fifteen more minutes, and we arrived at the site. Had I given any thought to the new church, I wouldn't have conjured the chapel before me. It was narrow and tall, with large windows that reflected the grove of the trees around it and wooden supports that suggested maybe the building had also sprouted organically from the ground.

But, no. It was my father's and brother's handiwork, and the inside continued the illusion I was in a forest, though walls of wood and glass surrounded me. The outside door opened straight into a large sanctuary, and I walked to the middle and circled to take in the panorama. Move-in date must still be a while away: loose wires marked the spot for future lighting and shavings covered the floor, filling the air with the sweet smell of freshly sawed wood. Plastic tarps, spot lighting, and power tools aside, I could see how it would be—the unassuming beauty of this space.

Square wooden columns rose along the height of windows before beaming to meet their sister columns on the opposing side in reversed concentric V's to support the cathedral ceiling along the length of the sanctuary. I spied a shadow of detail and walked closer to inspect the left column closest to the front door. It was the geographic etch more common to stained glass windows.

Carved into the wood, it took on a new feel. I had enough Christmases to recognize the scene of Jesus and the manger. I moved along the left wall toward the altar, pillar by pillar and scene by scene—Jesus and Mary, Jesus and twelve men, Jesus and a boat. The last was Jesus and the cross, and I ran my finger along the groove of the etchings.

"You did this?" I asked my dad, who'd followed me on my survey.

Dad shook his head. "Ted. And, I don't think it was easy."

And then walked in the devil himself—my brother, the master carver. Behind him trailed Jackson, his scary dad, and a handful of other older men.

"You want to join us?" Dad asked. I shook my head and Dad left to greet them. As they headed outside, I crossed toward the right wall to inspect those scenes—Jesus and the tomb, Jesus and the Resurrection, and so on. I finished my pillar walk and repeated it, finishing for the second time as the men came back inside to inspect the sanctuary.

I slipped out the front door and took a seat on the limestone steps, musing over what Ted had accomplished. I vaguely remembered him taking art classes as his high school electives and sketches taped to his bedroom walls, but I had no idea of what he was capable of. I'd lumped him in my lot—another returner to home when his plan A as professional baseball player hadn't worked out. But the pillars proved he hadn't been languishing at all. He'd been busy. He'd done well.

The front door opened, and I looked behind me. Jackson. I exhaled his name in my mind, and smiled as he sat next to me on the steps.

"You're looking better than yesterday," he said, smiling back at me.

"It's amazing what not crying all day will do for a girl."

"So you've had a good day?"

I told him about it.

"Have you decided what you're going to do?"

I shook my head. "I don't want to fail again, Jackson. Especially over something I'm not sure I want to do."

He nodded, and was about to say something when Ted joined us. "Did you come here to check out my handiwork or to check out Jackson?"

121

I swallowed my retort and stood to hug him. "I had no idea you were so gifted, Ted. Your carving was a bit of an inspiring kick in the butt. Thanks."

Even Ted couldn't be mean after my little speech. He cleared his throat. "Have you guys had dinner yet? I guess it's been a long day at home. Gracie got Mom to watch the girls, and she's demanding a meal she doesn't have to cook or clean up. Want to join us for dinner at Creek's?"

I hadn't ventured out to eat since I'd returned, and the mention of Creek's set my mouth watering. I had to have a slice of their double pepperoni pizza that dripped grease down my chin.

The place itself was a pizzeria relic, complete with Tiffany-esque lights that emitted no light whatsoever, private wooden booths with high backs, and a phone at each table to call in the order. Ted and I raced to it, but of course he got there first and placed the order for two extra large double pepperoni pizzas while I chucked a stale crouton at his face. He caught it and popped it in his mouth, not minding I'd found it on the table.

"Should we order four pizzas?" he asked Gracie. "I'm so hungry, I could eat an extra large all by myself."

She rolled her eyes, and he kept it to two. "Ted still thinks he can eat like a high school boy," she informed Jackson and me.

"There's all sorts of things I can do if you'd let me show you, Grace," Ted said, pulling her close and planting a firm kiss on her lips. "I'm sorry you had a rough day with the girls."

Her eyes filled with tears and their conversation assumed low tones. Jackson and I —gave them some space and headed to the salad bar in the middle of the restaurant. This was health as defined in 1985, but to Creek's credit, they'd added some better options. There was now a spinach bin next to the iceberg lettuce, but I built my salad according to my preferences from yesteryear—light on the lettuce and heavy on the hardboiled egg, mini corncobs, cheese, ham cubes, and water chestnuts. I finished with some token broccoli florets, a generous helping of blue cheese dressing, and a prayer that none of this had been sitting out so long to cause food poisoning. I also made Gracie a salad according to her healthier adult leanings and brought back both to the table. Ted's arm was around her shoulders, and her eyes were red, but she'd stopped crying. I slid into the booth across from them and Jackson sat next to me.

Turns out, Gracie and Ted had reached a parenting decision while we were gone. "We've decided one of our girls has to go. Who would you like to take, Lu?" Ted offered.

"Remind me of their names again?" I asked. Gracie laughed, and I smiled, glad to have provided her with some comic relief. "Do you want to talk about your day?"

She shook her head and took a bite of her salad. "Let's hear about your day."

"My day feels like small potatoes compared to what I uncovered about Ted's artistic abilities," I volleyed. "Should we talk about that?"

"Lu, listening to him talk about engraving is about as interesting as baseball statistics," Gracie said. "Believe me, it's better to look at it. Now spill it."

I rehashed my day for the third time, ending with my indecision over RJ's offer. "It's not like it's going to be crazy. Dunlap's Creek is the biggest of the small towns around, and yes, a lot of people come here to get married because of all the pretty churches in the town square, but it's still a small town and ..."

"Lu, this is a big deal," Gracie said. "Of course you can do it, but you should think about whether you want to do it."

"What do you think?" I asked, turning toward Jackson. He started to answer, but an older woman I didn't recognize came to our table.

"If it isn't Pastor Jackson!" she exclaimed. My heart skipped at the volume, but Jackson handled it calmly enough and stood to shake her hand.

"It's nice to see you, too, Mrs. Johnson."

"Oh, call me Judy, please. Your family must be so glad you're back and so proud! I can't wait to hear what you're going to say this Sunday. Aren't his sermons so uplifting?" she asked us. The looks on Ted's and Gracie's faces told me they felt as put on the spot as I did. Gracie recovered first and started nodding her head.

"Absolutely," Ted affirmed.

"Love them," I said.

That set Jackson to coughing, which is when he realized Judy Johnson hadn't released his hand. He tugged it away from hers and put both in his pockets. I'd yet to see him off-kilter, and he was embarrassed now. I angled my body to watch the show.

"My husband and I were saying how we'd love to have you over to dinner."

"That's kind, thank you."

"And it just so happens my Mary—you remember my daughter, right? She was a few years behind you in school? She's home from college this weekend."

"From college?"

"That's right."

"How great to have the family all together," he said in a tone meant to conclude this conversation. Judy didn't take the hint. I took a bite of salad and chomped away.

"How about you come over to dinner this Sunday so the two of you can catch up?"

"Well, Mrs. Johnson ..." he started.

"Do you have something going on?"

"I ..." He ducked his head, and a small measure of compassion set in over his predicament. I suppose it's hard to come up with an excuse when the bachelor pastor won't lie.

"He's having dinner with me," I interjected. I'd felt brave in saying it, but the look Judy shot me turned me small. Thankfully, my brother rescued me.

"What my sister meant to say was Jackson is having dinner with our family this coming Sunday."

"Your family?" she repeated dumbly.

"They're babysitting our girls while Ted and I go out to dinner," Gracie finished.

"Another time, then," Judy said to Jackson. He sat back down, and the four of us looked at each other, dying to laugh, but not at the expense of the woman who was sitting two tables away. Instead, we asked the waiter to box up the pizzas. Heckling Jackson was better suited to my parents' deck.

By the time we licked the last of the pepperoni grease from our fingers and set up cornhole, Ted and I were prepared to reenact the roles of Jackson and Mrs. Johnson, respectively.

"Why hello there, you fine young pastor, you!" I shrieked in the same octave as my muse.

"I am fine," Ted said with mock seriousness.

"And may I tell you how awesome you are in general?"

"You may," Ted deadpanned.

"How would you feel about marrying my daughter this Sunday?" I proposed, and Ted looked toward the heavens while weighing the decision with a balance of his hands.

"No! He's mine!" Gracie tantrumed in the role of me before tossing a cornhole bag straight to my kisser. I fell down and thought I might puke from laughing so hard. Jackson was a nonparticipant in our theatrics but a game audience. He called for an encore of me getting beamed with a corn bag.

Needless to say, no serious game of cornhole ensued, and Jackson and I abandoned the notion once Gracie and Ted called it a night.

"So, you want to grab some pizza with me tomorrow?" he asked, leaning back on his elbows and stretching out his legs as he settled next to me on the steps.

"I don't know if I'd have the courage to rescue you again, J. Judy Johnson has a price on my head." I laughed. "I'll admit; it was fun to see you squirm. You win the most awkward conversation award. And you proved your argument."

"What argument?"

"A single pastor is like a rock star."

"There is a time to be a rock star," Jackson said with sham gravity. "Apparently, this also applies for a single journalist."

"I blame that one on the skirt," I muttered, picking invisible nothings off my jeans so I wouldn't have to look at him. I'd been heckling Jackson all night, but it took one comment from him to embarrass me. "But my short dance at the wedding reminded me too much of the first time I met John, so that wasn't going to work. How did you meet Kate?"

"You want to know?" he asked. A pause followed the question, and I lifted my eyes to look straight at him. I nodded.

"Sunday school. Second grade."

I laughed, which at this point was cashing a check my stomach muscles could not afford.

"She was wearing a pink dress and pigtails, and I was smitten," he continued in a wistful tone.

"Leave it to you to put that cute little word to your G-rated romance," I said, turning toward him.

"At least in the early years."

"Do you ever wonder what it would be like to speak to Kate again?"

"I don't have to wonder."

He responded casually, but it was quite the reveal to me.

125

"You … you don't?" I asked.

"She comes with her parents to church whenever she's in town. So, I've seen her about …" he shifted his weight to his left elbow to do a quick finger count with his right hand, "five or six times since our divorce."

"And?"

"And what?"

"There has to be more."

"No there doesn't. Why? What would happen if John came back?"

"I'd die," I said instinctively.

He laughed. "I hope not."

"Or melt."

"Isn't that another sort of death?" he asked.

I ignored his comment to get back to the matter at hand. "So you're telling me when you see Kate, you don't suffer from clammy palms, a pounding heart, faintness of breath, a quick outfit check, or anything like that?"

"No, but it sounds like her coming back might freak you out."

I raised my eyebrows.

"Well, let's hope she and John don't come back on the same day, then," he said.

"Oh, John's not coming back."

Jackson looked at me and opened his mouth to say something, but closed it again. After awhile, he said, "I wouldn't be so sure about that, Louisa. But if he does, Gracie and I will be ready to star in the re-enactment."

"You're a good sport, J."

"Have you decided what you're going to do about the expo?"

I shook my head and leaned my elbows on my knees, looking at my hands. "No, but I'd like to know what you think."

"Do it."

I waited for an explanation or a justification. "That's it?"

"Sure."

"What about the part about me never having done this before?"

"I don't think it's so out of your realm as you think. Writers articulate an idea. Here you're articulating a concept—an event instead of a story."

"And the part about me failing?"

He smiled, and I pushed back from elbows and stood with my

hands on my hips. "You want me to fail!"

"Nope."

"You want me to succeed?"

"Nope."

"Then what are you telling me?"

"Everything I said yesterday."

"Oh, what? Doing this event is going to lead me to Jesus? Be gone." I shooed him from his sitting position and off the deck. "Or I will call Judy Johnson and sign you up for a date with her daughter this Sunday."

He turned toward me, taking a couple of steps until he was right in front of me.

"You don't want me to go on a date this Sunday," he said.

"No, I don't," I said.

Jackson smiled and turned to leave.

"Who else would help me babysit three girls?"

He laughed and left.

CHAPTER 17

I woke up Tuesday morning knowing I'd say yes to the expo, and knowing I would need help.

I started by crossing the backyard with my French press in hand.

Ted was in the kitchen putting away dishes, their clatter muffled somewhat by the stampede of little girls upstairs.

"Here I thought you were being a good guy," I said, nodding toward his chore before inclining my head toward the ceiling. I'd choose morning dish duty over wrangling those little girls into their school clothes any day.

"Don't tell Grace," he said before handing me the utensil caddy. "Make yourself useful."

"Sure, if you do something for me." I grabbed a mug from the cabinet above the sink, filled it with my black gold, and handed it to him before attending to the silverware. "Drink this."

He obeyed, and let out a small grimace at the bitter beans hitting his taste buds. But then he took a smaller second sip. As he lifted his mug for a third go, I thought my coffee love was taking effect, but then he lowered it and looked at me suspiciously.

"What's this about?" he asked, swirling his mug.

"Oh not much, but I'm going to need you to drink coffee if we're going to work together," I said casually, like I was discussing a prior agreement.

He took his third sip. "Go on."

"What are your thoughts on designing the logo for the wedding expo?"

"You've decided to do it?"

"Yes, but I need help. I have an idea of the feel and tone I want for the event, but my artistic abilities never graduated past the stick figure stage."

"Doesn't the paper have someone who can do it? And isn't it a little too early to be worrying about this part?"

"For peace of mind, I want to know the marketing is in process. The paper has a graphic designer who can morph what you design into various multimedia, but not an artist."

"An artist ..." he probed.

"An artist like you," I rushed in.

He smiled. "See, that wasn't so hard, Lu-ser."

"Can you please stop calling me that?"

"It's a term of affection."

I shook my head and handed him the caddy. He put it in the dishwasher and closed it, and we assumed our standoff with both our arms crossed over chests. If he didn't agree to help, I was totally taking my coffee back.

"Fine. I will call you Lu, or should I call you Louisa?" he asked with a wiggle of his eyebrows.

"And you have to stop teasing me about Jackson," I quickly added.

"Not happening. But I will agree to your condition, *Lu*, as long as you do something for me, too. I'd like for you to watch the girls for the rest of my baseball games this season. I'll send you the schedule, but we're talking one evening a week and one weekend afternoon."

I nodded, not for Ted's sake but for the snapshot of Gracie with red-rimmed, tired eyes that replayed in my mind from last night. I wished I'd thought of the idea first. "You know you're getting an unskilled laborer, right? I'll feed them all the wrong things and let them play with all the wrong things—except for when I'm letting them watch too much TV."

He shrugged. "As long as Grace gets a break, I don't care."

"Deal."

"My first game is Thursday night."

"I want a mock-up by the end of the month."

We shook on it. Ted got to keep his coffee, and I headed back to my house with what remained in my French press to draft the rest of my team.

"Well, hello ladies!" I said maybe a bit too brightly, as attested by the startled look Grandma Pat and Nana Bea gave me after I swung through the screen door. Either I'd tipped my hand, or they weren't used to seeing me up so early and initiating conversation.

I surged ahead, and poured them the remaining coffee. Grandma Pat drank hers black, and she looked at me suspiciously as I eagerly fetched cream and sugar for Nana Bea's coffee. I started to dole it out myself, but Nana covered her cup protectively, which left me to recap RJ's proposal without further schmoozing.

I assumed Grandma would be the easier sell, and I turned to her after I summarized the project.

"We'll post ads in *The Daily* for vendors, but I'm not sure that's enough to convince the locals to purchase booth space for an event in its first year, especially if they pinch pennies like Virginia. Can you call in favors from your farmer's market and Penny Thrift connections?" I asked.

Grandma responded by pulling her iPhone from her apron and scurrying to her room to get to work.

Nana Bea was predictably less enthusiastic. She hadn't said a word or moved her hand from the top of her coffee cup.

I forged ahead.

"You've thrown so many gatherings, amazing parties ..." I began, remembering the spread of black-and-white photos of luncheons and bridge parties and charity benefits we'd unearthed when searching for Jackson's sermon homework picture.

Nana Bea nodded.

"And I've thrown ... well ... none. The detail is beyond me. I'm not asking you to do it, but if you could give me a checklist of things I need to take care of, I'd appreciate that." I poised a pen above my yellow legal pad and adopted a position I hoped brokered no refusal.

And yet, the woman remained silent and took another sip of her coffee. After another minute and another sip, she gestured toward the notepad with her perfectly manicured and bejeweled hand.

"Give me that," she commanded.

I obliged, and she tossed it on the chair next to her. It was a definitive gesture; I just wasn't sure what it meant. Several seconds passed, and she remained close-lipped, like there was nothing more to say.

I gestured toward the legal pad. "Is that a 'yes' or a 'no' or a 'maybe' or a ..."

"It's an 'I'll take care of it.'"

"You'll take care of it?"

"You figure out the date, the time, the estimated vendors and crowd, and I'll take care of making sure everything goes smoothly."

I was grateful. I was also flabbergasted.

"Why would you do that?" I asked.

"Because you're in over your head ... and because you're my granddaughter."

She'd never called me her granddaughter before, or ever said anything remotely affectionate, come to think of it. Using it now felt a bit like a hug. I sensed tears pricking the back of my eyes, but suspected they might repel her generous offer, so I sucked them back and left the room.

I reclaimed the legal pad on my way out and spent the next couple of hours cross-legged on my bed, organizing my thoughts. The key to my wedding beat success seemed to lie in its underwhelmed stance toward weddings. It was important the event continue in this understated vein. Ted's art would help, especially if he opted for the geometric etching he'd used in his pillars. Regardless, the man wasn't going to go all wedding crazy on me, and neither was I. I wasn't sure I wanted the word "wedding" in the expo title.

By the time I arrived at the office, I had a clear idea of what I was willing to sign up for, which was good since RJ's ideas were more stereotypical than mine—think tulle as the main fabric on every vendor table. He also wanted to attract the big, out-of-town vendors because they'd pay a premium, but I firmly believed it was the local artisans who would make our expo ring different, so we needed pricing to accommodate them, too. In the end, we compromised on most points and conceded on some.

"We need to build on the success of your beat and social media. Get over your issues, call it Creek Wedding Fest, and be done with it," RJ said.

We settled on the Saturday after Thanksgiving—Shop Local Saturday—as the date, and made it an afternoon affair. We set the publishing and advertising timelines, but ended the meeting with a lot of TBD—that is, to be determined by me. RJ waived me away from our two-hour planning meeting with a *carte blanche* to "do whatever I saw fit so long as I didn't screw up." It wasn't the vote of confidence I'd like from my boss before embarking on a new venture, but it wasn't a surprise, either. And not having to brainstorm with him anymore made my new role of Lu, The Wedding Expo Planner, almost palatable.

"One more thing," I said before returning to my desk. "Virginia Stanley gets a free booth."

"Why?"

Because I want her to. Because she's a single mom struggling by on her sewing skills. Because she won't come otherwise. Because ... I had many good reasons, but none would resonate with him. So I threatened him instead.

"Because her work inspired me to take this on. And without me, you've got nothing."

He consented, and a season began like I'd never experienced. September and October flashed by in a whir of all the normal journalism plus event planning logistics that required an extra cup of coffee to see me through working 11-hour days. I don't know if the busyness moved me on from New York and John or didn't allow for me to dwell on it. I was aware of the picture of us in my top dresser drawer, but when I walked the two flights of stairs to my room after a full day, I was too tired to pull it out.

I couldn't so easily defend against all the memories, though— the unexpected song on the radio or one night at dinner when Ted had sat back in his chair and draped his arm around Gracie's shoulders. He always does this, but I went to bed that night missing John with an intensity I hadn't felt since I first came back. I saw him when I closed my eyes, and I could feel his pull when I reached out my hand. I wanted to heal, I willed myself to heal, but moments like these told me I still wanted John. His conjured presence haunted me, and I don't think I've ever been so grateful for a sunrise. I unfolded in its beam, releasing the grip on my knees and stretching out my legs before I stood. The exhaustion from these moments ran deeper than lost sleep, but I couldn't afford to lose both a night and a morning. There was too much work to do.

But it wasn't all on me, thankfully. I'd suffered some doubts following the initial adrenaline in enlisting my family. The pressure of working together could snuff out my re-awakened affinity for them, but we were all too busy getting along with our jobs to get on one another's nerves. My trust was well-founded. Ted's linear silhouette of a bride perfectly captured the feel I wanted for the expo and morphed beautifully into the postcards, signs, banners, and every other promotional item we scattered around Dunlap's Creek in a twenty-mile radius.

We attracted enough vendors to warrant renting the largest venue in town, the municipal building: an eyesore of mustard brick, designed in the 1970s to prioritize energy efficiency over aesthetic. I wasn't thrilled at the choice, but Grandma Pat assuaged my concerns with plans for how we could make it look more welcoming.

Plus, she reminded me, it was the vendors who were the real stars, and working with them formed the core of my work. Grandma Pat solicited them, Nana Bea figured the logistical ratios of their booths to aisle space, and I worked with the vendors to brainstorm the booths according to my vision for the event. The more prominent vendors—the ones who ran their own shops and regularly rode the expo circuit—didn't need help, but the Virginia Stanleys did. Sometimes all it took was one pep talk, but others needed several phone calls and even house calls to bandy ideas for branding their wares or services. I usually took one or preferably, both, of my grandmas with me on these visits. Grandma Pat had a creative eye, Nana Bea a polished one, and we three made quite a team trolling around town in Nana's Caddy to convince the small-timers they could do what they'd signed up for.

RJ had agreed to a deeply reduced rate for booth space for the locals, and this "local artisan alley" of designers, jewelers, florists, caterers, and bakers accounted for about twenty percent of the expo, which exceeded my expectations, as did the advance ticket sales. Everyone was coming. I tried not to think about it.

Spearheading such a large event for such a small town put me out there in a way I'd never have wished upon myself. I even broke down and purchased a cell phone with a Dunlap's Creek area code, a maneuver I instantly regretted since people used it like a twenty-four-hour hotline. By early November, I couldn't go anywhere without being accosted in person or via text with questions, suggestions, well wishes and all manner of feedback from the peanut gallery, which in Dunlap's Creek, is everyone.

"I think more people know you than me," Jackson noted after our conversation was interrupted for the 267th time as we played tag with the girls on the sidelines at Ted's last baseball game, an exhibition game pulling out all the stops to entertain the crowd as a thank you for their support. Everyone was here.

"Check that," he corrected. "I think you know more people's names than me."

As I started to answer, one of the musicians who would be playing at Fest—Billy, the lead singer and banjo player of a bluegrass quartet—catcalled in front of us, "You gonna go for the cheek this time, Jackson?"

Jackson and I deflected his allusion to our Kiss Cam with matching smiles, which didn't help our platonic defense. But this remark had occurred at least once in every baseball game, and we were used to it.

"Nice to see you, Billy," Jackson responded, as he always did.

"We're friends, Billy," I said, as I always did.

And it was true. We were friends—friends who saw each other most days and wondered what the other was doing on the days we didn't, at least for my part. It was an unnatural inclination for an introvert like myself. I like quiet. Being alone has never felt lonely. So it surprised me that even in these people-infused times, my favorite way of capping a day was by being with Jackson. I'd even gotten used to him looking so good. Almost.

"Why did you kiss me in the first place, J? You could have prevented all of this by letting me keep my hands to myself."

"I believe you demanded it," he said turning toward me.

I scrunched my forehead while I rewound time. Surely he was wrong, but … no. I had done that.

"So what are you preaching on this Sunday?" I asked, to change the topic. Jackson clued me into the coming Sunday's passage midweek, but it was now Friday night, and he hadn't told me a thing.

In the last two months, he'd picked up the pace, and I assumed we were a few Sundays away from finishing. The remainder of Ecclesiastes had read a bit more innocuous than the first chapters—less talk of meaninglessness and more on Proverbs, like "the sleep of a laborer is sweet, whether he eats little or much, but the abundance of a rich man permits him no sleep." I wasn't as rattled, and I suppose I should be grateful. I couldn't have Ecclesiastes 3 moments every week and get anything done, but I wasn't sure I liked this ambivalence either. Going to church was starting to feel like going through the motions. Maybe this Sunday would fire me up.

"I'm not preaching this Sunday or next," Jackson said. "I'll be in Phoenix visiting my sister's family."

Well, that fired me up. Jackson wasn't allowed to leave without telling me. Or to leave at all. The thought had me opening and closing my mouth like a guppy.

"When are you leaving?"

"Tomorrow morning."

"What about church?" I asked with affected calmness, though my mind was asking a more honest question. *What about me?*

"It's going to close down for the next two Sundays."

"Really?" That thrilling prospect took the edge off his leaving.

"No." He laughed. "Dad's preaching. We're tag teaming. I'm gone the next two Sundays, and then I'll finish preaching Ecclesiastes the Sundays he and Mom are in Arizona for Thanksgiving."

"So you'll come to our place for Thanksgiving."

"Is that an invitation or a command?"

"It's a … a …" I looked at him with what I hoped weren't puppy dog eyes, but that's how they felt as I tilted my head back, noting the laugh lines along his mouth, the green of his eyes, the dark scruff on his chin. Was he growing a beard or had he taken a break today from shaving? I guess I'd know in two weeks.

"It's a 'Please spend Thanksgiving with us,'" I said.

"I'd love to spend Thanksgiving with you … and your family," he added a moment later.

Now, what did that mean? I didn't have much time to ponder because a man I hadn't met came up, presumably to talk to Jackson, but after an initial hello, he stood there looking at me instead. And that awkward situation of the two of us looking at each other would have continued for who knows how long without Jackson's help.

"Justin Thompson, this is Louisa Sokolowski. Louisa, Justin was in my graduating class at school, and now works as a math teacher at the junior high. Louisa returned to Dunlap's Creek this summer and works at the paper."

"Nice to meet you," I said, shaking Justin's hand.

"Have I read anything you've written?" he asked.

"I don't see why you would," I replied. "It's mostly wedding

135

stuff."

He cleared his throat. "So, umm, are you enjoying the game?"

"I don't like baseball."

We resumed our silence until Jackson intervened for the second time. "Louisa, you may not know this, but Justin goes to our church."

I smiled, and Justin gobbled up that information with some quick nods.

"How are you enjoying Jackson's sermons, Louisa?" he asked, attempting a new line of conversation.

"Enjoy isn't the word I would use," I responded.

"What word would you use?" he asked.

"You don't want to know. Trust me."

That startled him, and after some polite murmurings, he left.

Jackson started coughing, but from behind his hand, I could see he was smiling. "You could throw the man a bone, Louisa."

"What are you talking about?"

"Justin didn't come over here to talk to me."

"I've never seen him before."

"He's seen you. And those other guys who are sitting next to him," Jackson pointed to where Justin had resumed his seat. "They've seen you, too."

That gave me pause. I'd laughed when Jackson claimed his rock star, single pastor status, but the last couple months had proved him right. Girls didn't exactly hide how they looked at him, though why a girl wanted to chase after him because he was a pastor was beyond me. Yet until now, I hadn't given any thought to how men in this town might be seeing me.

"Justin did not want to hear my thoughts on your sermon. Or anything else, for that matter. I was being plain with him."

That set him laughing, and in a contagious way that left me laughing at myself, too. Why did he have to go away for two weeks?

"I am the way I am, J. Guys who can't handle that should stay away," I concluded.

"That's not going to happen. Look at you," he said, so simply and with certainty—like it was an objective fact. I opened my mouth to say something, but then shut it because I had nothing other than the flush creeping up my neck. I looked over at him.

"It doesn't seem to affect you much," I said after a bit.

He met my stare. "I wouldn't say that."

The last strike of the game was swung, which sent my nieces scurrying to me in their happy dance that Daddy's team had won. Jackson and I had driven separately, and it was time to call it quits for the night. And for the next two weeks.

"Well …." I said, at a total loss for words. "Have fun in the desert."

"Try not to break anymore hearts while I'm gone, Ms. Sokolowski."

CHAPTER 18

Breaking men's hearts was put on the back burner, but the sound of Nana Bea speaking in heightened tones on the phone that first Monday Jackson was away almost stopped mine.

I'd slept in that morning and the extra hour left me feeling groggy as I came down the stairs. But her sharp, "What do you mean?" set my feet moving to the kitchen. Nana looked up at me from the table, her right pointer finger tapping the wood as she listened to what seemed like bad news.

The tension was thick enough to keep me standing at my place in the doorway.

"Explain to me please this 'double-booking,'" she asked as if it was a brand-new term. When Nana started asking for definitions, it was about to rain down.

"I made this reservation for November 24 over two months ago. Who else would reserve this building?"

How that ugly place could be double-booked was beyond me. And Nana, too.

"What do you mean that's not my concern? And don't you bother apologizing to me, either. I will expect our deposit returned to me by the close of today with a handwritten apology, and I will never do business with you again, do you understand?"

She set down the receiver and smoothed an invisible wrinkle from her heavy tweed skirt, an odd outfit choice for a warm morning that promised a hot day. But Nana dressed for the season, not the temperature. Her skirt reminded me that it was fall ... and

Fest was three weeks away.

She looked at me. I still hadn't moved from the doorway because I didn't know where to go next, figuratively or literally.

"You heard?"

"I heard."

"We will fix this," she said.

"We will fix this," I parroted. "I shouldn't tell RJ, right?"

"Best not until after we come up with another solution."

Nana stood and smoothed her tweed again. "You go about your day, Lu. I will take care of this. I am sure you're busy tending to other tasks."

She was right. It was already a full week without this snafu. I was covering a wedding this Saturday, and the bride, a local florist, was doing her own flowers. I was meeting her each morning this week to cover her floral countdown for the blog, beginning today with the boutonnieres. When she would inevitably ask how Fest was humming along—everyone did—I'd have to respond with a smile and "Fine." "Fine" is not my strong suit; it's not in my lexicon.

I adopted a calm veneer all morning, returning calls for miscellaneous expo business, and wishing RJ a nice evening as he left the office for the day—all without belying that my innards were in a twist.

A terse shake of Nana's head when I returned home for dinner told me nothing had been resolved. I swirled chicken noodle soup around my bowl while she and Grandma Pat brainstormed a Plan B. Dad was working late, and Mom had school conferences, so they got to miss my reenactment of Lu, The Teenage Years.

"What about the Methodists?" Grandma mused. "They have the largest church in town."

"Booked for a wedding," Nana said.

"I hate weddings," I grumbled.

"The Shady Nook?" Grandma forged ahead, ignoring me. "A lot of people have large wedding receptions there."

"Not half big enough," Nana said.

"I hate wedding receptions," I said.

"Dunlap's Creek doesn't have many options. The largest spaces are the big churches, the municipal building, and courthouse. Maybe we'll have to go out of town and closer to the city," Grandma said.

Nana and I shook our heads at the same time.

"Why ever not?"

"Because it's 'Creek' Wedding Fest, and transplanting it would ruin the point," I said.

"But desperate times ..." Grandma began until Nana interrupted.

"Lu is right. It needs to stay in town."

None of us said anything for a minute. "This is a matter for prayer," Grandma Pat concluded.

I understood the sentiment, coming from her, but it didn't feel like the most useful course of action. Grandma bowed right then and there. "Lord, we need your help to find a place for Lu's expo. You know what we need; please show us how to get there. Amen!"

She waited, peeking out of one closed eye until we offered our "Amen" too.

The interlude hadn't helped my appetite, and I pushed my soup away. Nana Bea looked uncomfortable. I presume she preferred praying behind the privacy of a closed door, but the prayer seemed to revive Grandma Pat, and she dove into her soup.

"You two need to start thinking outside the box," she said between slurps. "You'll see. God will lead us to a place close enough, big enough, and free."

I groaned and put my head in my hands. What she'd described wasn't going to sprout out of the middle of nowhere, but ... wait.

"I've got it!" I shouted, smacking my hand on the table. "Get in the Caddy, ladies. We're going for a drive."

Fifteen minutes later I swerved Nana's car into the gravel drive of the new church.

"See?" I said. This was it; this was the spot. I knew it.

They did not. I ignored their underwhelmed reaction and headed inside. Dad and Ted were working away. Ted was pushing a long piece of baseboard through the table saw while Dad held the end piece. I waited until the shriek of metal against wood stopped, and they removed their safety glasses.

"How's it coming along?" I asked, like check in here was a regular thing. Ted raised an eyebrow and said nothing, but Dad obliged.

"Great, kiddo. I think we'll finish this job on time."

They carried the cut baseboard to the right exterior wall to check the measurement.

"Another centimeter," Dad said, marking the line with his pencil.

"And when is that date again?" I asked as they positioned the baseboard for another cut.

"Early December," Ted said before starting the saw. I waited while they made the cut.

"What are your thoughts on a soft opening on November 24?" I asked after Ted knelt over the piece to blow away wayward sawdust.

They looked at each other before looking at me.

"The date of Creek Wedding Fest?" Dad asked.

I was about to answer with the full re-tell when Nana Bea spoke from behind me. "The municipal building was double-booked."

He gave me a sympathetic look. "The pews won't be in yet…"

"Open floor space is better," Grandma Pat responded from my other flank.

"Yes, but there are a lot of other finishing details that might prevent us from getting this place up to code and cleared out before you could hold a public event."

"You let me handle the permit," Nana said like the government owed her a favor after the whole municipal building fiasco.

"And I'll do whatever I can to help you finish," I jumped in.

Dad pressed on. "Even if we can get the permit, the church will need to agree. There were plans to christen the building before we held this first service, and the expo could conflict with that. Plus, there's the potential damage a large crowd could do. Are you going to talk to Pastor Cleary? It would be a conflict of interest for me to do it."

I nodded, ignoring that I couldn't form one word in his presence during our last encounter in Jackson's office. I headed to church first thing the next morning before I could overthink it. He wasn't there when I arrived, and I took a seat outside his office and attempted to hone my foggy morning thoughts. It'd been a late night. The grandmas and I plotted the hypothetical layout of our hypothetical space after we returned from the church. We closed the party down with some reheated soup around eleven o'clock, which is why I found myself now dozing outside Pastor Cleary's office, though I didn't realize it until he spoke my name.

"How can I help you?" he asked, gesturing to a chair in his office and then taking a seat behind his desk.

"I don't have a harem," I blurted, alluding to my reckless talk from the last time I'd encountered him.

A promise of a smile pulled at the right corner of his lips, which reminded me of Jackson. "Is that what you came here to tell me?"

"No." I took a breath and launched into my request. He listened and leaned forward on his elbows when I finished.

"Is it a problem for you if the space isn't done?" he asked.

"Not for us. It might be with the government, but Nana Bea said she'd take care of that."

He laughed, again reminding me of how much I missed his son.

"Will holding the expo there be a problem for your father's deadlines?" he asked.

I shook my head.

"Then it's not a problem for me, either. The space is yours."

"Wait, what?"

"I said the space is yours."

"Just like that? I know what I'm asking can turn out to be a huge hassle for the church. You can tell me no ..."

He held up his hand and smiled. "Lu, I've known your family a long time, and our church is not a building, but the people who fill it. Churches close their doors every week, but we're in a blessed position to require more space on Sunday mornings. This expo isn't what I envisioned for 'breaking in' the new church, but I'm not going to say no to that many people coming through our doors. If you want it, you can have it."

"Thank you, sir."

"Paul," he clarified.

"Paul," I repeated. "How much would you like to charge for the space?" *The Daily*'s sponsorship wasn't generous, and I'd measured every expenditure against the tight budget over the past two months. I knew what we could afford to the penny.

"Nothing."

"Nothing?"

"That's right."

"But ..." I began. It's against my nature to get something for nothing, and I straightened my shoulders to argue, but Pastor Cleary's unexpected laugh dinked my swagger.

"Jackson said you were a fighter," he observed.

I sat back and smiled—at the mention of Jackson's name and that he had talked about me with his dad. Jackson was busted.

Still, I shook my head. I had the budget to pay at least a little something, and I wanted to pay it.

Pastor Cleary countermoved.

"The church is available and free," he said again, but this time in a tone that brooked no argument and synced more with my scary picture of him.

"Thank you, Pastor Cleary," I surrendered.

"Paul," he said again.

"Paul."

I rode on my adrenaline from using Pastor Cleary's first name twice in one conversation to take care of my last piece of finalizing Creek Wedding Fest, the Beta version—telling RJ, who growled like a bear at the double-booking and questioned my proposed solution.

"You are going to hold the expo in an unfinished church on the outskirts of town? What if it isn't done? What if you don't get the permit? What about the PR material advertising the municipal building? How do you plan to handle...?"

His voice escalated with each question, which paradoxically calmed me down. I'd asked all the same questions, and I didn't have any of the answers, I was 24 hours further ahead of him. I waited until he ran through the rant and smiled when he came up for air

"Well, do you have anything to say?" RJ demanded.

"I wanted to make sure you're finished before I answer."

"I'm finished." He took another breath.

"Creek Wedding Fest will be at the new church on Saturday, November 24," I said.

"You know this?"

I didn't. I figured the next three weeks would show me the extent of how much I didn't know. But I had a new understanding that all of this wasn't falling on me. I left the office to go and help my family get it done.

CHAPTER 19

The previous two months' workload was a mere warm-up to the next two weeks. I set my alarm earlier and earlier and my bedtime crept later and later each day until the time between these bookends was four hours.

The other twenty were spent resolving the promo advertising the old location, finalizing the event itself, and writing. I'd rerouted the direction of my blog to explore my new night gig as a construction worker. I titled the series, "Underbelly of Wedding Expo Planning." My grumbles (like why Dad and Ted used the metric system) and foibles (like how I messed up the metric system) kept the followers coming and helped me keep writing amidst all the other work.

Dad and Ted relegated me to mundane grunt work, but even my unskilled self could see our chances of reaching the November 24 finish line needed an extra set of hands. So, I recruited more worker bees from my family pool—Gracie to help me, and Mom to watch her kids.

Gracie was happy for any excuse to get out of the house without the girls, and working with my best friend made the late nights fun. She and Ted also pitched some classic fights, which provided comic relief, as well as more blog fodder, like the one I recorded under "Why Married People Shouldn't Plan Wedding Expos."

"Hand me the Phillips screwdriver, Grace!"

"Which one is that?"

"We've been married eight years, and you have no idea what a Phillips is?"

"I bet we'd have the same problem if I asked you to find something in the kitchen."

"If you'd ever clear out the cupboards, I could!"

Gracie holds up a dozen screwdrivers like a bouquet—evidence that someone else in the marriage is a pack rat.

"The Phillips is the one with the red handle," Ted says.

She tosses it. Ted catches it with his right hand, and winks at her.

"Love you, Grace."

I included a later picture of the two of them kissing to show that no marriages were harmed in the making of Creek Wedding Fest. The likes for this post topped the rest. Because my family was cool; I'd just been the last to realize it.

"Have you heard from Jackson?" Gracie asked me the Friday night before he was supposed to come back. We were crawling along the baseboards, spackling holes and talking about all manner of things.

She wasn't the first person to ask me this question. Jackson and I'd spent enough time out and about Dunlap's Creek this fall that people as much assumed the answer to this question as asked it.

I responded to Gracie as I did everyone else.

One, swallow. Two, answer as simply as possible. Three, change the topic.

I swallowed.

I spoke: "I haven't heard from him."

And deflected: "How are the girls doing in school?"

Gracie ignored me. "When does Jackson get back?"

"Tomorrow night," I responded. "Do you know what you're wearing to Fest?"

She ignored me again. "Have you been counting down since he left?"

I sighed. I gave up the ghost, as well as any pretense I was working, and sat crisscross applesauce in front her. She did the same, and our lightening round commenced.

"I've been counting down since he left."

"Have you decided what you'll wear when you first see him?"

"My cream wrap dress."

"So fancy?"

"Church clothes, since that's where I'll be when I see him."

"Have you decided what you'll say when you first see him?"

"I won't say anything."

"That's not very friendly."

"I don't talk to him at church."

She laughed. "You say that like it's a rule."

I shrugged. It was.

Then Gracie leaned in and whispered. "What will you say on the inside when you see him?"

A shout from Ted to get back to work stopped our powwow, and my answer to her question shifted in my mind over the next thirty-six hours: a blur of phone calls and writing and sawdust and total exhaustion. On Saturday night, we pushed to finish the last of the construction, which would give us a good week to clean the church before Fest.

I didn't get to bed until two o'clock, and I set my alarm for as late as possible while still allowing for a shower before church. But then I forgot and pressed snooze three times. Around eight-thirty, the memory of Jackson's reentry roused me from my slumber. The planned dress would have required makeup and a curling iron to pull off. And a shower. But jeans and a T-shirt don't require anything other than a ponytail, so I pulled on the ones with the least amount of sawdust and caught a ride to church with my parents.

I hadn't sat with my family at church since I returned, so my prechurch pleasantries with the regulars distracted my anticipation over seeing Jackson again and my attention away from an important fact: his ex-wife, Kate, was in the congregation.

I noticed her when everyone stood to sing. She was sitting with her parents to my front left; I presumed she was in town for Thanksgiving. Her presence hardened me like a statue, a not so-subtle shift in my demeanor that drew the rest of my family's attention to her like a magnet. Church started, and their attention turned to the service. Mine remained fixed on Kate.

She was pretty, and in that moment, I remembered she always had been—in a meticulous way. Not a hair out of place and makeup applied so subtly it appeared her cheekbones actually looked like that and that her lips were glossy pink. She looked attractive in the blue dress she was wearing, having the unfair advantage of looking good in blue as all blue-eyed people do.

For the first time since I'd come back, I paid no attention in church. Zero. I kept looking from her to Jackson and then back again, thinking what a good-looking couple they'd make. Surely she regretted leaving him. How could she not? Look at him. Surely he'd take her back if she asked. Look at her.

And who was I in all of this?

In what was both too long of a time for my comfort and too short of a time for my curiosity, church ended. Everyone around me broke after the final song to small talk, grab their stuff, and go. But I stood still, my eyes transfixed in the space between Jackson and his ex-wife, wondering when the gap would close and who would be the one to close it.

It was Jackson. Of course, it was Jackson. He went straight toward her with the openness and ease that's such a part of him, and though they didn't touch, they chatted a hair's breadth apart for a fifteen-second eternity.

I couldn't handle it; I couldn't handle the reason I couldn't handle it. As I started to turn away, I felt a hand on my arm.

"Now you listen here, my girl," Grandma Pat said. "Don't you turn away. Not yet. Look on back."

And there Jackson was—in the same place with the same girl— but looking at me. Grandma's grip steadied me there as I breathed in and out. In and out. Someone else claimed his attention, and he turned, but not before he smiled at me.

"Do you see?" Grandma asked me.

I saw.

"All right then. Now we can go."

The moment we got home, I collapsed on the couch. I should have gone to bed, but it was two whole flights away. I also thought sweat pants would accompany my nap better than jeans, but again, they were far, far away. My exhaustion overrode my preferences, and it turned out I didn't need a bed or sweats to sleep the day away.

A gentle shake lulled me out of my deep sleep. My throat was on fire, and my head pounded so badly I couldn't lift it off the pillow. I was also seeing double, which was okay, since it was

Jackson's face I opened my eyes to. I'd missed him so much, I would take two of him—though it was a little weird.

"Jackson," I whispered. "I missed you."

This was an unplanned admission I'm pretty sure I was supposed to have relegated to my inside conversation. I was too tired to care. And too nauseous. I closed my eyes to give them a break from focusing.

I felt him take my hand, but as soon he touched it, he shifted his hand to my forehead. "Louisa, you are burning up."

I nodded and puked all over him.

The next few days were a feverish, puking blur. Sleep was my constant companion. Once in awhile I emerged to ask about Fest, only to be shushed by whichever of my family had drawn the short straw to force pills and water down my throat. Basically, I wanted to die. I may have said a few dramatic prayers to that effect.

But one day I woke up. I wasn't sure what day it was, but the sun was shining through my western dormers, so I knew it was afternoon. I sat up, testing the depths of my equilibrium. When the movement didn't set my stomach to vomiting or my head to pounding, I exhaled. I was done being sick.

And I wanted out of this sickroom. I wasn't sure how to go about it since I felt weak as a kitten. I scooted down the stairs on my butt and stumbled to the living room to grab a blanket. Then I journeyed through the hallway, dining room, and kitchen to the deck—grasping furniture, and walls, and counters like a tow cable the whole way. I used the remaining shreds of my energy to wrap the blanket around me in a recliner and turn my face toward the afternoon sun. I was happy to know Indian summer had continued though my convalescence. The warm breeze on my face felt like a caress, and I fell back asleep.

I awoke before sunset to the clang of dinner preparations in the kitchen and the sight of Jackson again, this time sitting a bit farther from me than he had on Sunday. I smiled at him.

"Keeping a safe distance, J?" I asked in a low voice. My throat felt better, but it wasn't used to speaking.

He crossed the space between us, and leaned on his heels so his eyes were level with mine. "I'm a pastor, so I'm used to people puking on me, Louisa."

"I think you're confusing yourself with a doctor."

"I was referring to the rock star part of my job."

"That sounds plausible then," I murmured, closing my eyes. I kept them closed for the next question, which I wasn't sure I had a right to ask. "Have you seen Kate?"

He waited until I opened my eyes before answering.

"No." And then he stood up. "Want to go for a drive? I brought a barf bag."

"What day is it?"

"Wednesday."

"What did I come down with anyway?" I asked, as I unraveled from the recliner.

"The plague," he said in total seriousness.

"Is everyone else, okay?"

"Yes, despite your best attempts to infect one of us," he said, gesturing to his shirtfront. "I'd say I don't mind, but I do."

I wanted to laugh, but I wasn't sure my stomach could handle jostling of any sort. He offered his hand, and I wasn't in a position to argue since I wasn't sure I could exit the chair, let alone walk to his car, without it.

It was a beautiful night, and we put the windows down for the drive. The fresh air, plus the box of oyster crackers and can of ginger ale he gave me, revived me. Not to mention the sheer pleasure of his company. I could have listened to him talk about Arizona—or anything for that matter—all day long. By the time we arrived at the new church, I was sufficiently energized to get from the car to the church on my own.

"I want to see what's in here, right?" I asked, though I knew he wouldn't have brought me here if I didn't.

He opened the door in response, and I felt like a bride taking in her first sight of the church on her wedding day. I'd planned Fest to death, I'd worked myself sick over every nook and cranny of this space, but I caught my breath all the same. The construction equipment was gone, and in its place was a simple, clean, and beautiful space with rows of empty tables awaiting vendors and their wares. I could see how it would look this coming Saturday when all the vendors set up shop.

I jumped and clapped. I couldn't help myself. Then I hugged Jackson, trying not to think of how long it'd been since I showered and how sick I'd been in the interim. This was more a hug of sheer joy and gratitude than affection, and I gave a similar one to each of my family members when we returned home.

I thought the gesture was well received, but then Grandma Pat, who was last in line, wrinkled her nose. "Honey, I love you, and you need to fill that belly. But before you sit down at this table, I'm gonna need for you to shower."

I hugged her before complying, and when I returned, they were halfway through plates of beef and noodles, while my place setting held a lone cup of chicken and rice soup.

"If you can keep it down, then we'll talk about you having some Thanksgiving dinner tomorrow," Grandma Pat said, noting the forlorn look on my face.

I'd forgotten about the holiday. "I assumed it'd be a working Thanksgiving, but you guys took care of it."

"Your Nana hired industrial cleaners to take care of it," Dad clarified. Nana had lived with us for so long I forgot she had an empty mansion across town and plenty of money to throw at situations like this.

I ended up making it through about five spoonfuls of soup, partly because that's all my stomach could handle, but mostly because I was too excited to hear how they'd done what they'd done. All that was left to do was pull the thing off.

"Thank you," I said to Jackson as I walked him to his car after dinner. He'd kept quiet about his role in it all, but I had a feeling it was considerable. Though it was Wednesday, his sermon probably wasn't close to started. "Do you need me to help you with your last Ecclesiastes sermon for this Sunday?"

"You're saying that much too happily."

"Your dad preached on Jesus feeding the five thousand while you were away. It made for a great Thanksgiving story."

"Don't you mean 'Paul'?" he asked. My conversation with his dad seemed like on eon ago, but his allusion to it reminded me that this wasn't their first conversation about me.

"Keeping tabs on me while you were away?" I asked and smiled.

"Thinking of you in general," he said, producing a lone, miniature cactus in a small clay pot from his back seat and handing it to me.

CHAPTER 20

It was the sight of this cactus that made me smile the next morning when banjos and slide guitars blaring from the kitchen speakers woke me up. Grandma Pat was in an Appalachian mood this Thanksgiving.

I buried my face in my pillows, wondering why this holiday required a slow-cooking bird that needed to enter the oven at ... I paused to check the clock ... seven o'clock. I groaned, considering returning to sleep, but then I smiled, remembering what I had in store for this day.

So, I swung my legs out of bed, pulled my feet into my fleece slipper socks and my arms into my thick, gray jersey robe before grabbing my Bible to see what Solomon had to say today. An Ecclesiastes skim had become my unintentional morning habit since Jackson began clueing me into his sermon passage for the coming Sundays. I turned to Ecclesiastes 12:

Remember your Creator
In the days of your youth
Before the days of trouble come
And the years approach when you will say,
'I find no pleasure in them' —
before the sun and the light
and the moon and the stars grow dark,
and the clouds return after the rain ...

"Happy Thanksgiving to you, too," I muttered, stopping at verse two. Solomon wasn't pulling any punches. Today was not the day for his doom and gloom. On a whim, I flipped back several pages to the Psalms, many of which read beautifully. I landed on Psalm 107:

Give thanks to the Lord, for he is good;
His love endures forever …

I stopped there and laid my hand flat against the page. About giving thanks to God, I still wasn't sure, but I had a lot to give thanks for today. I swung my legs out of bed to get to it.

The morning was a flurry of the cleaning my mom insists on doing before every holiday dinner and the cooking my Grandma insists on doing for every holiday dinner. Of course, I wasn't allowed to help with anything involving food preparation, but multiple courses made for a lot of dishes to clean, as well as many forgotten ingredients to forage. Nana Bea and Dad somehow had flown under the fray, reading in the family room. I needed to tap their wisdom before the Christmas draft.

At noon I called it quits, leaving me enough time to shower and make my hair worthy of the navy blue cashmere dress I'd found on clearance in New York last summer before I'd left. I'd never worn it, and I marveled at how barely-there wool felt as warm as wrapping myself in my childhood blanket. The dress ended mid-thigh, and I paired it with charcoal tights and knee-high, tan leather boots. I dried my hair straight and tamed its horsetail texture with a large-barreled curling iron. I hadn't cut it since long before my return, and it was now long enough for me to wrap in a loose bun at the nape of my neck. I pulled out a few wisps here and there, knowing more would fly free throughout the day. No makeup and no jewelry, and I felt pretty.

I tiptoed back downstairs. Grandma had asked me to set the table, and as expected, she'd double-checked my settings. A month ago, I'd commissioned Virginia Stanley to make napkins for Grandma, and she'd outdone herself by reverse appliqueing big, bold orange roosters under white cotton. I caught Grandma as she unfolded one and leaned in to inspect the stitching. She reformed the fold and returned the napkin to its plate so gently I knew she was pleased.

"So you like them?" I asked.

She looked up, tears in her eyes, and walked toward me to wrap me in a tight hug. "Aren't you just the thing," she said, before stepping back. "Now help me get this food on the table."

I swallowed back the lump in my throat and did her bidding.

The table barely fit it all: turkey, mashed potatoes, cornbread sausage stuffing, macaroni and cheese, sweet potato casserole, roasted green beans with toasted hazelnuts, a spinach salad, and yeast roles. Cranberry ginger ale for the kids and wine mulled with cranberries and oranges for the adults. And of course there were three pies—pecan, apple, and pumpkin—that we wouldn't put on the table for a while yet, but passing them on the way to the front door was the reason I was wiping saliva from my mouth when Jackson knocked.

As always, he came bearing gifts—a glass bowl of cranberry relish, a bouquet of flowers, and a brown paper bag I leaned over to peek into, but he put behind him, smiling.

"Can I help you carry something?" I asked, dying to know what was in the bag.

"Yes, this," he said, plucking a yellow rose from his bouquet and handing it to me. I buried my nose into its infinite cluster of delicate petals and breathed in the sweetness. I looked up at Jackson. The man was smooth, but from a place of genuine thoughtfulness and kindness. I was getting wound up in it.

"Happy Thanksgiving," I said.

"Happy Thanksgiving." He seemed in no more of a rush to leave our position by the front door than I. But then Gracie's family slammed through the back door. I took his coat while he greeted my family, and I joined them after retreating to my room to put the rose next to my cactus on my nightstand. It was becoming quite the interesting botanical garden.

Our dining room table was big enough to fit everyone, as long as you didn't mind cutting your turkey with your elbows digging into your sides and playing footsie every time you crossed your legs. It was a loud affair of three little girls, dueling Grandmas, and Mom popping in and out for reasons I stopped keeping track of. But somehow, we all hushed down as my dad took his position at the head of the table to say grace.

"Lord, we thank you for blessings large and small, for the blessings we can count and the many more we can't see. Thank you for your provision of a table filled with food and family. I pray today we would experience the contentment and joy and peace that come from you alone. Amen."

I hadn't spent a Thanksgiving with my family since I'd graduated from college, but I remembered we accompanied the passing of the plates with a round robin of thankfulness. My nieces jumped right in; Caroline had a list of ten items, ranging from all things pink to princesses and sugar. She ended with Thanksgiving s'mores.

"And what makes a s'more a Thanksgiving s'more?" Ted asked her.

She shrugged. "Eating it on Thanksgiving, I suppose."

He rubbed her head, smiling at her in such a gentle way I forgot he was my pesky older brother.

"I'm thankful for my girls, in particular that one right there," he said pointing to Gracie and smiling at her in a different way, "who I'm pretty sure is carrying another little girl right now."

The news exploded like a bomb on our Thanksgiving table, with the little girls shrieking, "A baby!" on repeat while we adults somehow extricated ourselves from our Jenga dinner formation to give the requisite back slaps and hugs. I hadn't been in town for any of Gracie's other pregnancies. Every other announcement had come over the phone, so I gripped her now.

"Careful," she said.

"The baby?" I asked, nervous I'd jostled the little squirt.

"My stomach. I'm puking all the time."

I hugged her again. She could puke all over my new dress and me.

"Are you going to stick around for this one, Lu?" she whispered.

I nodded, wiping a tear from my eye. "And who knows?" I asked, loud enough for Ted to hear before crossing our small dining room to squeeze his shoulder. "Maybe it will be a boy this time, and you can name him after me."

"Boys are overrated," Grandma Pat said.

"I don't know about that, Mother," Dad responded. "But I appreciate my daughter. I'm thankful you're back with us for Thanksgiving, Lu."

It was a good thing I'd forgone eyeliner and mascara because for the third time that day, I started crying.

"Okay, enough!" I said, waving my hand about. "Can't we think about what we're thankful for so we can stop crying and start eating?"

At which point Caroline started whining about how her turkey was touching her mashed potatoes and Abbey declared she was eating only rolls and Nana asked Grandma what was this white goo on top of her sweet potatoes. Dinner proceeded as normal, and my appetite was back with a vengeance. I refilled my plate three times, plus sneaking leftover mac and cheese off the girls' plates after they ditched the table to play Thanksgiving fairies in the living room.

"Is everyone ready for dessert?" Grandma asked, to which I groaned both a "yes" and "no." I looked across the table at Gracie, who looked the same as me but with the better excuse of a baby in her belly. I intended to help clear the table, but Jackson offered first.

I reclined as best as I could in my dining room chair, tossing around nursery decorating ideas with Gracie.

"Only the first baby gets a nursery, Lu," she pointed out. "This one will get a dresser drawer, especially if Ted doesn't build the addition he's been promising me for the last eight years."

"If it's a boy, I'm going to build the *Field of Dreams* in our backyards," he called out from the living room, where he'd been enlisted as chief villain in the girls' game.

Gracie rolled her eyes, and I closed mine, slipping into a turkey nap and waking up awhile later to the smell of coffee. I opened my eyes to two shots of liquid heaven in a small mug in front of me. It looked like espresso. I picked up the mug and inhaled. It smelled like espresso. I sipped. It was espresso. I closed my eyes again, savoring how the bold notes of the beans played on my tongue— so strong it was hard to swallow. Just the way I liked it. I didn't know the genius who'd invented coffee, but I knew the man who'd brewed this, and I cradled my hands around my mug and got up to find him.

In the time I'd been napping, fairy princess had moved outdoors and turned into a game of monkey in the middle with Gracie and Ted at opposing ends. Jackson was standing at the top of the deck steps, watching. I walked to his side.

"What's easier?" I asked. "Learning Greek or making espresso?"

"Greek, hands down. At least I have the memory for that. I'm all thumbs with the stove-top espresso."

"That you brought in your brown paper bag," I finished, smiling. "I'd offer a sip as evidence to your newfound skill, but you don't like coffee."

"I don't."

"But you learned to make some for me."

He nodded, and we stood there, looking at each other. "Don't think you're getting out of it," Jackson said after a while.

"Getting out of what?"

"Saying what you're thankful for."

I fortified myself with a sip of espresso before returning my eyes to his. "I'm thankful for you, Jackson."

That one surprised him. Not that I felt it—I think it was obvious by now—but that I admitted it. Before he could form a reply, Ted recruited him. "Gracie can't throw or catch a football for anything. Help me out, Jackson."

"Go get 'em, J," I said, slapping him on the back, the unexpected warmth of his skin under his shirt keeping my hand there a second longer than I'd intended. "Try not to make the little girls cry."

He looked like he had something to say, but then he smiled, staring his green eyes straight into mine before he turned to join Ted. I exhaled, not sure at what point I'd stopped breathing. I sat down and leaned into my right hand, trying to rub away the heat from my face.

"Is your face so red because Jackson's so hot?" Gracie asked, out of breath and taking a seat next to me.

I almost snorted coffee out my nose. "Are you allowed to say that about the pastor?"

"I'm not the one getting red about it."

"Plus, you're married to my brother."

"And look at him. All that baseball this summer took off his married man gut, and I can't get enough of him."

"Please stop."

"Plus," she said—because this conversation needed to continue? "There's nothing sexier than a man throwing a football. And I don't like football."

That caught me, and my eyes followed her train of thought back to Jackson. He was smiling and shouting something to Ted I'm sure I could have tuned into, but I was content to hone all my senses into looking at him. His brown hair was longer than in the summer, with a slight wave at the edges, and he'd come back from Arizona a bit tanner and with a beard. That, combined with a flannel shirt rolled at the sleeves and unbuttoned at the top, sent my face straight back into my hands. I groaned while Gracie sat back on her elbows.

"You gonna do anything about what you're thinking?" she asked.

"What? Ask him to go steady?"

She wiggled her eyebrows. "Or not."

When did she get so saucy? I chalked it up to pregnancy hormones. "Ogle away, married lady. This old maid is going to help set out the dessert, unless you all ate it on the sly while I napped," I said, retreating to the house.

I opened the storm door, but before going in, I looked back at Jackson, who was standing with his hands in his front pockets, looking at me. I leaned into the door, and smiled at him, which he returned at the same moment. And there we stood, until Ted threw the football to him and my brazen nieces tackled him to the ground. They made it look so easy.

CHAPTER 21

I popped into the office the Friday after Thanksgiving to prove to RJ I was still alive, but it turns out he never knew I was out of commission. That's how seamlessly my family stepped in to take care of things while I was sick. I planned to stay a full day, but only a half was required, allowing me a siesta plus a bedtime of eight o'clock on Fest Eve.

I set my alarm for six on Saturday, but a gaggle of magpies woke me three minutes before the beep. I wondered, and not for the first time, the point of a third-floor bedroom when I could hear everything happening on the first floor.

There were too many people in the kitchen for a Saturday morning—one dad, one mom, two grandmas, Ted and Gracie, and three little girls. Plus, one Jackson. I'd assigned jobs for the big day, but I assumed they'd meet me at the church long after the caffeine took its effect. Yet here was the whole clan, all talking at the same time.

I closed my eyes and held up my hand. They shut up. A little Saturday morning miracle.

"What are you doing here?" I whispered.

The words sounded fuzzy to me, but they must have resonated because everyone started talking again. I couldn't understand their answers other than they'd decided I needed their help starting five minutes ago. The only way to deal with their kindness was to ignore them and move through my morning routine per usual.

First, coffee. I grabbed the filtered water from the fridge to fill the hot pot, but stopped midpour when I felt Jackson step behind me. I channeled what little consciousness I could muster not to lean against him.

"I made you some coffee," he said, his breath warm on my ear.

I turned toward him. He looked good all the time, but there was something particularly compelling about his Saturday morning self. I knew he'd done nothing more than roll out of bed, throw on some clothes and a ball cap, and brush his teeth. My right hand itched to touch the bristles on his face. I took his cup of coffee instead.

"Thanks." I smiled.

I surveyed my family as I sipped. My grandmas and mom were sitting at the table, combing through the vendor layout one more time to make sure we hadn't missed anyone. Ted and Dad were standing by the back deck door, probably chatting about anything other than Fest. Gracie was kneeling in front of the girls, straightening pigtails and tightening their wayward, matching bows.

"I don't ever want to forget this," I whispered.

"You don't have to," Jackson responded before shouting to the rest of the room. "Guys! Get around the kitchen table so Louisa can get a picture."

That startled everyone. None of us were used to Jackson ordering us around, and we did his bidding for a family picture with all the trimmings.

"You'd better not give me bunny ears," I said to Ted.

"Girls, if you smile at the camera, I'll give you all suckers," Gracie bribed.

"Right now?" Caroline asked.

"No," Ted and Gracie responded in unison.

"Oh, let the girls have a sucker right now. It's a special day," Grandma Pat said, setting all three girls to a jumping frenzy.

"I agree. It would give Lu time to get dressed and put on some makeup before we take this picture. Her cheeks could use a touch of rouge," Nana reasoned from the chair in front of me.

I rolled my eyes. Leave it to my family to ruin the family moment.

"Jackson, please take the picture before my family implodes."

He counted, we shut up—presumably to smile—and then resumed our bickering. Ted cuffed me on the back of the head, the girls chirped for lollipops like hungry little birds, and my outfit

159

choice was now the main topic of conversation between my grandmas.

I raised my voice above the fray to move us along.

"Ted, Dad, and Jackson! Take the truck to church now and start the grunt work. Mom, drive the grandmas over and please run our spreadsheet against the table layout one last time. Gracie, I'll be over in an hour to collect you and the girls."

Everyone dispersed, and I scraped together what would be my last quiet hour of the day. I used it well: I read the rest of Ecclesiastes 12, took a shower, left my hair wet to spring to its natural curl, and of course dressed in my wedding skirt. I'm not sure why that was ever up for debate.

Around seven-thirty, I crossed the yard and entered Gracie's house. She was still arguing with the girls about lollipops on Saturday mornings.

"We're bringing them all!" I announced, grabbing the bag before I ushered the girls to the minivan. Thanks to my fall of babysitting, I was an expert in getting them saddled up in one minute flat. I gave them each two seconds to decide which lollipop flavor best accompanied our drive, handed Gracie an orange and popped a blue raspberry in my mouth, forgetting too late about how it turns the mouth blue.

It was eight o'clock when we stepped out of the car: the sun was shining, the air was warm, and the birds were singing. It was going to be a good day.

The vendors followed my arrival, and as Mom and Nana directed them to their booths, Grandma and I circulated to make sure they had everything they needed. If they didn't, we enlisted the menfolk to retrieve it.

By noon, the vendors were in place, the first round of musicians were tuning their instruments onstage, and by one o'clock, people started to arrive. I knew it'd be a full crowd, but it was startling how quickly the place morphed from quiet anticipation to crazy. By two o'clock, the noise of music, conversation, and laughter reaching the cathedral ceiling felt like the new normal, and I gave myself over to the reality that this big thing was happening.

I could never have done it by myself. A prayer of thanks burst from my heart—I didn't conjure it and I didn't try to stifle it. My professional smile turned real, and my polite small talk became earnest. I exhaled and threw myself into the busy crowd to enjoy

Fest.

By five o'clock, it seemed everyone in Dunlap's Creek had come, and I'd talked with them all. My cheeks hurt from smiling almost as much as my feet from trotting around in wedges all day. Sheer adrenaline carried me as I walked barefoot to break down tables, rewind extension cords, sweep, and remove all signs that this pretty little church Dad and Ted had built was ever used for another purpose.

"Pizza on me?" Dad offered as we bound up the last of the trash bags.

Jackson requested we order in, despite Gracie, Ted, and I shouting otherwise in the background. We finished our night with several large double pepperonis on paper plates on my parents' deck. The older and younger folk called it a night, but Gracie, Ted, Jackson, and I stayed and celebrated Fest with paper cups of old champagne I rummaged from the back of my parents' ill-used but well-stocked liquor cabinet. The Cook's Champagne had long since turned vinegary, but we grimaced it down anyway to toast the day and muse over the next.

"What are you going to do now, Lu?" Gracie asked.

"Not an expo," I said. I had no desire to repeat today, but the idea of returning to beat writing didn't feel right, either. "What about you guys?" I asked.

"Install pews on Monday," Ted said.

"Grow a baby," Gracie responded.

"Write a sermon. Tonight." Jackson ran his hands through his hair and stood. Gracie and Ted crossed the yard to home, and I walked Jackson to his car.

"I read Ecclesiastes 12 this morning," I informed him.

"And?" Jackson asked, leaning back against his car with his arms across his chest.

"And the 'conclusion of the matter is …'" I began, using the subtitle for the last verses of the book, "it ends as morbid as it started. I would steer clear of it."

"There's a happy ending to be had, but you have to take it." Then he pushed himself off the car and opened the door. "But I'll see what I can do for you in the meantime."

CHAPTER 22

"Ecclesiastes, Ecclesiastes," Jackson mused from pulpit the next morning. "Why are you here? The Bible has sixty-six books. Why not make it sixty-five and let this strange little one go? Then we can study a more straightforward, happy book, like Philippians, which uses the word, 'joy,' around eighty-two times. Who wants me to preach from that next?"

I raised my hand on the inside, but at least half the congregation raised theirs for all to see. Jackson laughed, and I sat back and smiled. It took chutzpah to come here every week and preach from something that ran us through the mud, and yet he did it with humor and humility. It belied the intensity of how this book had changed his life. How these sharp words had healed him, I might never know, but from my angle, I couldn't deny it had. I was hoping he would bring it home today, to make me see what he saw.

"Philippians it is, then. But first we need to wrap up Solomon, so please turn with me to Ecclesiastes 12, the conclusion of the matter:

Now all has been heard; here is the conclusion of the matter: Fear God and keep his commandments, for this is the whole duty of man. For God will bring every deed into judgment, including every hidden thing, whether it is good or evil.

"We began with meaninglessness, and we end with judgment. It seems like we're no better than where we started, at least as regards mood.

"But we're a world away because the first part of Ecclesiastes describes a world without God. It counters the atheistic argument by saying: 'All right, you don't believe in God, then here is what you get. As in, here is all you get.' Too which the nonbeliever might respond: 'Fine. I never wanted more.' Or, 'Eat, drink, and be merry: that's my motto.' But that's too flippant of a view to carry through the reality of life, in its downs as well as its highs. It's convenient, but not sustainable.

"Solomon postures like a man from the grave to get us to acknowledge the things we only acknowledge when life is tough—this world is killing. This world is dying. We're surrounded by death, sickness, failure, disappointment, debt, stress, frustration, and anger. Sometimes they take front and center, but when they don't, they're still there in the background. You can't ignore this reality. But if all you believe in is this world, then you don't have room to say, 'He's in a better place' when your father dies. You don't have room to say, 'Everything will turn out okay,' when you lose your job, or 'What doesn't kill you makes you stronger,' when you're diagnosed with a terminal illness. Your coping mechanisms are inconsistent with your bankruptcy of belief.

"Ecclesiastes calls us out on this. Solomon speaks in dire terms to bring us to a point of honesty. We might say we don't care whether there's anything beyond this world, but we do. We live like we do. Regardless of what our mouths say, we live like we're on a quest toward a greater peace. A job is never just a job, a relationship is never just a relationship, possessions are never just possessions—we invest in them like they'll return a greater wholeness. Solomon is asking us to admit it. And then he's asking us to look at where this quest leads, or more accurately, to whom.

"What if here *isn't* all there is? What if there is a God who created this world? What if he's perfect, and we're not, and so a divide exists between us? What if this separation from God describes the restlessness we always feel? What if this is the real reason why the things of this world satisfy us for a time until we're back on the road again? If this world was our true home, we'd rest easier in it. It would satisfy. But it doesn't—we know it doesn't—and Solomon tells us why.

"This world is not our home, but the shadow of it. Our home is with our Creator, and in that home there's no sin, no failure, no death. Just perfection and the utter satisfaction that comes from being where we were created to be and with whom we were created to be.

163

"The conclusion of the matter is this: God exists. And this conclusion does not depend on whether we believe it. God exists because he exists. And the right response to this truth is to fear him. Because this God—who established right and wrong, who will judge according to that standard, and thus is worthy of our fear—is also a God of great love, mercy, and grace. He's a father who doesn't turn away from us when we turn away from him. He stays. He pursues. He pursued to the point of sending his son, Jesus, into the world to live the perfect life and death so we can get back to him.

"He had to do it; we couldn't. Shoot, we can't live up to our own standards. If you were judged by the rules you made up for yourself, how many of you would cross the finish line? And let's move beyond New Year's resolutions to eat better and exercise more. How many of you love perfectly with the generosity and patience it requires? Have you always stood up for what you believe in? Have you consistently put others' needs before your own?

"And where do these standards of love and courage and generosity come from? I'm not talking about cultural standards, but the deeper standards we all seem to abide by. Why, they come from God himself. These are the commands he's hardwired into us and to live by them is our duty. And also our pleasure. It's how we can live life to the fullest. Our relationships and jobs, how we take care of ourselves, how we spend our time—they're not the end game like we make them out to be. They're modes. Opportunities. Blessings.

"We seize them according to God's grace and mercy, knowing we still won't do it with the perfection he requires. We can't. Because God's standard is perfect—much higher, much more unattainable than our own unattainable man-made ones. We can't reach God's standards anymore than Adam and Eve could get back to the Garden of Eden after they first sinned.

"So God made a way, and Jesus lived the perfect life we could not. He died for us. Not because we deserved it. Not because we can pay him back. Not because we asked. He did it because he loves us. God ended our restless search with Jesus. All he asks is you to acknowledge it. Acknowledge who you are, acknowledge who he is. Believe it to be true.

"When we do that, everything changes. The end game changes,

and how we get there changes, too. Our lives cease to be this restless chasing and become a response—a thank-you to God's work on our behalf.

"Because God's work is finished, we can work rightly. I can preach to glorify God. It's an outlet, not something I need to prove. I'm freed up to enjoy it for what it is.

"Because there's a Savior, we can love selflessly. You can love your dad and mom and spouse and best friend without expectation. They don't have to be anymore perfect than you. We're freed up to love them as they are.

"Because our salvation is secure, we can live honestly. We can fail and admit it. We can acknowledge our weaknesses as well as our strengths. We can say when we're confused, sad, insecure, angry, and overwhelmed. We're freed to live without any pretense.

"And because we're still here—and not yet called home—we can really live here, right now. What we confess, God forgives. Our past does not bind us. God also promises to take care of tomorrow's worries. They're not our concern. We're freed up to live in the present—to laugh at the funny joke, enjoy the cup of coffee, delight in the first crocuses of spring, pause as the sun sets on the horizon. We can take risks. We can pull back. We can take on. We can let go. We can dance. We can weep.

"God's work frees us to live life to the fullest measure.

"But you have to accept his work on your behalf. You have to accept he's here—not in some distant, vague way—but here, right now, offering you the way he created through Jesus. It's yours to take. Take it. Just take it. And it will lead you back home, back to that garden where you and God are face-to-face, together again. At rest, at last.

"Jesus is the answer. Jesus is the conclusion of the matter."

And then he was done. I sat, mesmerized by his demeanor. I'd tried to disconnect Jackson from his Sunday, preacher self, but now I could see the Jackson at the pulpit was the same Jackson who sold pierogies at Grandma Pat's stand, learned how to make me coffee, and knew everyone's name. I'd been raised in the church and never heard the Bible presented so plainly, and yet he seemed as relaxed here as at cornhole. Jackson could have done many things, but seeing him now was like seeing him for the first time. What he'd just done was what he was made to do.

It was a short sermon, and not because helping me had

occupied most of Jackson's week. It was a short sermon because he'd said all that needed saying. He'd laid it down, and in a way I couldn't ignore. I couldn't explain it away. I couldn't move around it.

But when I joined with everyone to stand and sing, I also knew I couldn't accept it. I looked at my family. They'd all picked up what Jackson laid down—in their own time and in their own way. Grandma in her ditch, Gracie at the same youth retreat that had turned me off. I wasn't sure about Mom, Dad, Ted, and Nana—I'd never thought to ask—but I didn't need to know the details to know their end game, as Jackson had put it.

I was surrounded by my family, but I was alone. Belief stood between my path and theirs, and I now saw the choice to either walk their way or turn away. Walking alongside wasn't an option because it didn't exist. I didn't want to turn away; I wanted on. I could acknowledge that. But to do that required a greater acknowledgment than I was ready to make.

The singing stopped, and everyone dispersed to their Sunday activities. I told my family I'd be along later and resumed my seat. A crowd larger than normal surrounded Jackson. It was going to be awhile. That was fine. I had nowhere else I wanted to be.

Thirty minutes passed with my attention fixed on Jackson the whole time, but it wasn't until the last of the well-wishers left that he noticed me. Not much I did ever seemed to faze him, but he looked surprised now. He smiled. I smiled right back and stood as he walked toward me.

"Well done, Jackson," I said. There was a lot more to say, but my admiration took center.

"Are we talking in church now?"

I nodded.

"Do you want to take it to fellowship hall? I hear they have some stale ginger snaps and lukewarm lemonade."

"Baby steps, J." I laughed.

"Should we get out of here?" he asked.

My heart clenched and burst at the thought. I'd go anywhere with him; I saw that now. But I also knew what I wanted and what was possible didn't match. We couldn't seem to keep out of each other's orbits, but that didn't change the fact that we were on different orbits. I think he knew it, too. But he offered anyway, and I said yes.

166

CHAPTER 23

Jackson turned his car north to a road I hadn't driven since my return from New York. Country drives are a part of small-town living, but I'd stuck mostly to the mile square of Dunlap's Creek since I'd come back. The spontaneity of this outing felt as freeing as the drive itself, and it wasn't until we were twenty minutes in that I thought to ask.

"Do we have a destination?"

"You'll see," Jackson said.

"How long will we be?"

He looked over at me and smiled. "Does it matter?"

It didn't, so I leaned back in my seat, enjoying yet another warm November day, enjoying the company of the man next to me and the prospect of a whole day ahead of us. Just us.

Another twenty minutes, and we arrived at Roy's Tackle & General Store that also advertised "Pizza" in neon in the window.

"Who needs Walmart?" I murmured as we creaked through the front door.

"Why, if it isn't Jackson Cleary!" exclaimed an affable older man sitting behind a gigantic cash register that belonged in a cash register museum. "How's your family? Where have you been? You in here for some bait to try your hand at fishing again?"

Jackson laughed. "Good to see you, Roy. I'm going to leave the fishing be; I'm here for dinner supplies."

I shouldn't be surprised that Jackson knew people in the middle of nowhere, and I was happy for the first time in months to be relegated as his anonymous companion. I slipped away from their catching up to explore the aisles for what might make a dinner around these parts.

I'm no cook, but even I could see this store was heavy on the "tackle" and light on the "general"—presumably because people were using the tackle side of things to catch their own dinners. Still, the Entenmann's section of the shop was impressive, constituting an entire shelf in the store's one nonperishable aisle. I guess fishermen like something to munch on while waiting for something to swim their way.

"You want something to round that out, Louisa, or does the variety box of plain, cinnamon, and chocolate donuts count as a legitimate meal?"

"I can't think of the last time I had a turd donut."

"A what?"

"A turd donut." I pointed to the eight-pack. "It says 'Crumb Donuts,' but it looks way more turd than crumb. Still, pop it in the microwave for twenty-five seconds, and you've got something special. Ted could eat four in one sitting."

"And you?"

"Well, I'm a girl, so ..."

"So..." he prodded.

"Three." I picked up the box. "Jackson," I whispered in astonishment. "This box expired last year."

"I don't think expiration means much here," he said, waving his hand around a section that also hosted Twinkies, beef jerky, Cheez Whiz, and Chef Boyardee. "And are you going to get snobby about something you call a 'turd' donut?"

"Still." I put the box back where I found it. "I hope what you have in your basket is fresh. I'm one week shy of puke fest," I said before mimicking last Sunday's vomit all over his shirtfront.

"You. To the car. Now."

I obeyed and walked around the gravel parking lot, trying to figure out where we were. I knew we were three turns from the main interstate, all roads I'd never driven on. Dunlap's Creek is an hour from the nearest city when you head south, but head north like we did and it's a whole lot of nowhere.

"So where are we again?" I asked as Jackson came out of the store with two brown grocery bags.

"Not there yet," he said before we continued our drive to

nowhere.

After another thirty minutes, he took a sharp left onto a gravel drive surrounded by overhanging trees, and I caught a clue.

"That's why you grew a beard!" I shouted, not seeing the end of the drive, but knowing it ended at his grandparents' camp all the same. "Is a beard a prerequisite because I left mine at home."

"I have a flannel shirt in the back. It should get you past customs."

I rolled down my window and leaned my head out Odie-style, knowing I had all afternoon, but still trying to take in all the sights and smells of the woods at once. The drive took a couple of more bends before ending with a sharp left at the cabin. Beyond stood a still blue lake.

I sensed the seamlessness at play as soon as Jackson stepped out of the car. It was more than that he'd relaxed or that he took in the sight of this place like how a man looks at a woman. He belonged here. I hoped his citizenship radiated to me.

The cabin was a lost art, chinked together with unmanufactured logs I guessed came from the site itself. It was painted dove gray with a red door and red trim along the windows. We crossed the gravel drive and entered the back door, which led straight into a small hallway with a bathroom to the left and a bedroom straight ahead. To the right was the kitchen, and I turned to set a bag of groceries on the counter. I continued through into one large room with a dining table at the left, a woodburning stove in the middle, and a seating area to the far right. Windows surrounded, making the most of the forest and lake view. Off this room were another two small bedrooms, separated by thin wooden walls that stopped several feet below the vaulted ceiling. More tree trunks formed the main support for the ceiling and from these hung gas light fixtures.

"We're off the grid here," Jackson reminded me as he followed me into the main living area. "Though, Grandma made Grandpa add a bath and bedroom in the back when they retired here. I still use the outhouse, though."

"Well, I was never one to jump off the bridge because everyone else was. I'll use the toilet. Is there anything else to bring in from the car?"

"Nope."

"Can I help you cook?"

"Nope."

"So, you're going to do all of the work, while I … do what?"

"Oh, I'm sure you'll figure it out."

He knew me well, and at first, I confined my curiosity to the inside of the cabin. The smaller bedroom off the large room was lined with built-in bookshelves filled with paperbacks so worn their covers felt like soft cotton. I scanned the titles and found nothing of note except for what appeared to be the entire collected works of Zane Grey. I picked one from the shelf and put it in my back pocket in case I found a good reading spot. I opened the screen door off the large room, which led to a large covered porch and down to the dock and lake. I assume we'd head there later, so I veered left to the big red barn that caught my eye when we first drove in. It had a packed dirt floor and housed a fishing boat and shelves of old canned goods I hoped wouldn't make their way to the dinner table. I spied a ladder to the second story loft, and climbed it without considering safety first.

"Jackpot," I whispered.

The loft held boxes and chests and trunks filled with stuff so old it didn't seem nosy to search through it, including old journals penned in precise calligraphy. They read more like a farmer's almanac than a repository of deep, dark thoughts. But what would one expect of the ancestors in these photo albums? No smiles but looking straight on at the camera in their black dresses and three-piece suits.

I spent enough time in the loft to start sneezing. I busted back into the house, setting down a box of finds before I searched for a tissue.

"Need help?" I yelled to Jackson in between nose blows.

"Nope," he responded, clanging around the kitchen.

I headed back out—this time to explore the woods. I have a decent internal compass and didn't worry much about getting lost as I wandered farther afield. I stumbled into a grove of pine trees, and its green stood in stark contrast to the bare branches of the rest of the forest. I breathed deeply. It smelled like a scented candle, or maybe it was the other way around. I settled against the base of one of the larger trees and pulled out the Zane Grey to pass the remaining time until dinner.

Three chapters in, and I wondered when I should head back, knowing nothing about what Jackson had bought for dinner or how long it would take to cook. But then he rang the dinner bell, and I followed its clang back to the cabin. On the table were two large steaks, two baked potatoes, a bowl of salad, and a serving platter stacked with seven turd donuts. The sight of those warmed me like a vase of roses might for another girl.

"Couldn't help yourself?" I asked, referring to the missing eighth donut instead of my feelings.

"It was sacrificed to some trial and error with the oven since I don't have a microwave."

I put the expiration date out of my mind, plucked the top donut from the stack, and took a large bite. Oh. My. This is the kind of heaven that comes from mixing a bit of flour with a lot of sugar and oil and then drenching it in glaze.

"This donut pile renders the rest of your dinner unnecessary," I said.

"Maybe for you." He laughed. "I'm starving."

We took a seat across from each other. Jackson said grace and divvied up the food as I munched on another donut. He shook his head.

"You don't eat like other girls."

"Oh, I tried. I went through the same phase as every other teenage girl and thought I was fat. But diets never flew with Grandma Pat. To mess with the natural properties of food and turn something fatty into something less fatty is nothing short of an abomination. I'm not saying she's right, though," I said, licking glaze off my fingers before picking up my fork and knife to cut into the steak.

"I'm telling."

"And I have something to tell you."

"What's that?"

"I used the outhouse while I was exploring."

"And?"

"I fastened my pants before exiting."

The artifacts and tales of my attic adventures carried us through the rest of dinner. Turns out, he didn't know anyone's identity, including the anonymous calligrapher, but it made for some fun guess work.

"That's Great Aunt Fanny," he said as soon as he turned the first page of an old photo album.

"Did you have a great aunt?"

"Possibly."

"Is there anyone in your family named Fanny?"

"I feel like there should be," he said before taking the last bite of his steak and then pushing his plate away. "Only you can make digging through boxes sound interesting," he concluded before standing to clear the plates. I reached for his hand, and he sat back down.

"A lady always does dishes for the meals a gentleman cooks for her," I said like I was quoting from an etiquette book I'd found in the loft. "You relax."

There was no dishwasher, but Jackson was an efficient cook, leaving me with a cast iron skillet and sheet pan to clean in addition to our dishes. We were quiet, his head leaning against the window behind the table and my eyes transfixed on the scene outside my own window above the sink. An empty clothesline dipped between the house and two trees. I imagined how the sheets would flap in the summer breeze.

We'd eaten early, and the winter sun was now setting across the lake. I pulled the plug from the sink and laid the kitchen towel over the drying dishes before returning to the dining table.

Jackson opened his eyes as I entered the main room. "Did your exploring take you to the dock?"

I shook my head, and we headed out the screen door and down the uneven steps. Large pieces of slate pockmarked a path to the pond, or at least they used to until they'd sunk into the earth and the crab grass overtook their boundaries. I did my best to tiptoe across them anyway. The level yard gave way to a short, steep slope and a rocky shore. Jackson took my hand to guide me up the two steps to the dock and steady me until I'd adjusted my balance.

"Got it?" he asked.

I nodded, and he placed his other hand on the small of my back to lead me forward to the best view, which I planned to look at in a second. But for now, I closed my eyes at the steadiness of his hand. I wanted him to keep it there past the point of an excuse, but he didn't, and I opened my eyes to the scene.

Clouds always make for the best sunsets, and tonight's was no exception, with each cloud taking on a golden or purple or pink radiance that shone different than the rest. And then there was the sun, sinking behind the trees on the opposite shore, but not without a fight. It took advantage of chinks in the clouds and trees to beam through wherever it could. The view, combined with the sound of the lake lapping against the dock, was hypnotic. I would have dived right in if not for the chill of the November air.

"I can see why you holed up here for six months," I said.

"God healed me here."

"Tell me about it." Not that he hadn't before, but I turned to him, hoping he would say something—anything—to help me cross over to his side.

"You remember the old me. I thought I had it all sewn up, and at some point, I guess I forgot how I needed God. My divorce took me by surprise. My sin took me by surprise. And it was here God reminded me none of it took him by surprise. And he wasn't going to give up on me like Kate gave up on me, and I gave up on her."

He stepped forward, his eyes catching mine. "He's here for you in the same way, Louisa. What you've been through, you don't have to fix, and you can't fix. But God can. And He's here for you like he was for me. Do you believe that?"

We were standing a breath apart, and in that moment, I felt like I could have reached out and grabbed that faith like I could take Jackson's hand. It was that close and that real. But I left the dock without doing either, and by the next day it was too late.

CHAPTER 24

The demands of the expo had set my internal clock to early rising. I jumped out of bed, ready to greet a day that would have been better to sleep through—or at least push off for another hour. I didn't know what to expect in my first week after Fest and the day after my wilderness field trip with Jackson, but I was expectant.

I expected the quiet office. I expected RJ. But I didn't expect him to cross the small office and take a seat across from my desk at eight-thirty, clear his throat, and say nothing.

I assumed it was because he didn't know how to say, "Good job," to Saturday's success. I was happy to prompt him.

"Did you enjoy Fest on Saturday, RJ?" I asked.

"I did, Lu. You did an excellent job. Please thank your family for me, too."

Something in his tone and word choice fell too heavy, and I stopped unpacking my bag to take a seat and look at him.

"What's going on?"

"We've been bought by a larger conglomerate, and there will be some changes."

The office phone started ringing. We ignored it.

"What things?"

"We'll publish once a week for one. Which means we'll need less staff."

"How much less staff?"

"I'll stay on, and we'll keep a part-time admin to manage the office and local advertisers. We'll also keep one staff writer."

I stared at RJ waiting for him to say what he needed to say.

"I need to let you go, Lu."

The phone started ringing again. I wanted to close my eyes and rub my temples. But I didn't want RJ to misconstrue my actions as weakness and result in his pity. I wanted nothing from him, except the answer to one more question.

"How long have you known about this?"

He hesitated, but I stared him down.

"Since the beginning of November."

He looked down at his hands like maybe they could offer a gift to take the edge off the truth.

"And instead of telling me, you let me work like crazy to buoy a paper you'd already sold."

"Don't look at it like that ..." he began.

"But that's the truth."

I hoped this conclusion felt like a slap across his face because it's how I intended it.

"Lu, you've done excellent work for the paper, but ..." he trailed off. The phone started ringing for the third time, and I decided if he didn't start speaking plainly, I was going to chuck it at him.

He must have read the evil intent in my eyes because he picked up his train of thought. "They already have a wedding writer."

And there it was. It's not that the news was a shocker—of course I wasn't the only wedding writer in the whole wide world—it's that no girl likes to be told she's superfluous, especially when it robs her of gainful employment. Especially when she'd started to take pride in her work, only to be told her work is unnecessary.

I closed my eyes, wondering if I could get out of the office before I started crying. The phone started ringing again, and I picked it up to buy myself time to plan my exit strategy. I'd been told I had a strong will, and I willed it now to gird my throat so I could address the person on the other line without my voice shaking.

"This is *The Daily*, Lu Sokolowski speaking. How may I help you?"

"Lu, it's Mom. Grandma Pat fell down the basement stairs of Penny Thrift. She didn't want me to interrupt your work day, but I thought you'd want to know."

Since my work was finished for today—and the near future—I

told Mom I'd leave for the hospital now. I started packing up before I realized there was no point. The notes were for stories I'd never write, and if I wasn't going to write, I had no use for a laptop. It wasn't mine anyway. And it was ancient. I'm sure the conglomerate would recycle it for a tax break.

I stood and my eyes fell on the picture of the tire swing—the only personal possession I'd ever brought to work. That image, more than anything else in the last ten minutes, hit like a sucker punch. A tear escaped from my eye.

"Lu, I'm sorry …"

Maybe RJ had more to say, but I left before he could say it. And I left the picture, too.

I'm not sure anyone likes hospitals—not even the people who work in them. I didn't like stepping into the hospital that day. The immensity of the space made my grandma seem small when I needed her to seem big—if not big enough to take on the world, at least big enough to take on a broken hip. But her bed with its rails and surrounding beeping machines rendered her tiny.

Who knows how long I would have stood in the doorway if she hadn't shouted at me.

"Lu! What are you doing here when you should be at work?"

Shouting was good. Shouting was strong. I smiled like she'd hugged me and stepped into her room. I didn't have the heart to answer her question, though I suspected the fury she'd feel over it might put some color in her pale cheeks. Mom stood up from the side of the bed and said something about grabbing a cup of coffee from the cafeteria before she left the room. Nana Bea, whom I'd just noticed, sat in the corner of the room with her hands folded on her lap. She was in it for the long haul.

As was I. I crossed the room with its polyester linens and sanitary smell and robotic beeps and took Mom's vacated seat next to Grandma on the bed and looked at her. If I stared too long I'd cry. So I transferred all my angst from RJ and rickety basement stairs to her flimsy hospital gown. I understood its practicality, with its open back, but I hated it all the same.

"Now tell me what you need to make this place livable," I said to her, rummaging in the drawer of the table next to her bed for a pad and pen.

Her list of clothes, bedding, pictures, knickknacks, books, and sewing baskets was extensive. I'm not sure we'd get away with hauling it all in, but the brainstorming kept our three minds occupied for the rest of the morning when the nurses weren't coming in every fifteen minutes to poke at Grandma. Revolving visits from the rest of the family filled the afternoon, but I didn't leave until the hospital kicked me out.

I arrived home after dinner and headed to the fridge. I stared at its contents a few seconds before I realized I didn't have the energy to forage for leftovers. I wasn't hungry. Then I remembered the list in my back pocket. I was grateful for a task to propel me from bad-day inertia. I crossed the kitchen to open the door to Grandma's room, but paused.

Grandma's move to our home predated my birth. Her presence is here. I don't see the kitchen table without thinking about her heckling me to eat more. I don't glance into the family room without seeing her in the chair by the bay window, her hands busy at some task or other. I can't imagine someone else cooking at the stove. But my memories of her space—the trio of rooms Dad built for her off the back of the kitchen—are few. She'd always kept the door closed, not in a keep-out sense, but more for privacy, which would have been precious in a house with two other adults and two precocious kids. I hadn't thought about it in this way until now—about how much she'd sacrificed to serve our family. She'd never mentioned it; martyrdom wasn't her mode.

My hand hovered above the door handle. She wasn't around to give me permission to enter, but I suppose the list of items on hospital stationery in my back pocket was a form of it. I turned the knob and stepped into her suite—a small sitting room with a bedroom and bathroom at the back.

I hadn't entered since graduating college, but my younger self wouldn't have seen what my eyes took in now. If Penny Thrift was Grandma Pat on display, this suite was its antithesis. It was sparse and plain, down to the pale cream walls. I assume Grandma kept her best furniture when she downsized, and the pieces were few, but each was unique with some special fabric or shape or finish that caught my eye. One might expect a marble coffee table with its gilded bamboo legs to hold a showy centerpiece, but hers contained an oval wooden bowl stuffed with well-thumbed paperbacks. And of course she'd hung Ted's old drawings above the most beautiful piece in the room—a refinished half-moon cherry table. Not to mention how she cut the stuffy edge off her butternut velvet couch with several throw pillows in bold, colorful prints of turquoise and forest green.

Only Grandma could bend such eccentricities to create a seamless whole, and the place was as welcome and vibrant as the woman herself. I'd come in here intent on my job, but I lingered over it. I thumbed through her books before choosing a few to read aloud to her over the next couple of days before her surgery. I picked up every frame on both the half-moon table in the sitting room and the turquoise dresser in her bedroom before gathering what felt like a reasonable timeline to place on her end table at the hospital, beginning with an old black and white of her parents and ending with the most recent picture of Ted and Gracie's family.

Her closet was packed; I doubt she'd ever thrown a stitch of clothing away. I chose enough to last her a week because she'd enjoy seeing them hang in the wardrobe across from her bed. She'd critique my selection, which would give us something to talk about when I visited.

Of course, Grandma Pat came up with other topics, too.

"Guess who came to see me today . . . and with food?" she asked me as I dyed her hair red the Thursday night before her surgery. She insisted on going into surgery looking good, and had persuaded the nurses into letting her wear her earrings on the big day. The dye job was an awkward enterprise, given the smallness of the hospital sink and the height of her wheelchair, but we were making it work.

I didn't respond to her prompt, but she didn't give up.

"Don't you want to guess?" she asked again. The pain meds that made this beauty treatment possible weren't dulling her matchmaking ways.

"I don't have to guess," I said. I knew Jackson's schedule—his work hours, his meetings. I knew he'd come to see Grandma Pat, I knew when he'd do it, and I avoided being at the hospital at those times, like I'd hid away the three times he'd stopped by the house.

"Now, you know I want to mind my own business ..." she started.

I laughed out loud—the first time I'd laughed all week.

"Since when?" I asked.

She reached up and grabbed my hands, which were busy getting at her roots with the plastic dye bottle. She looked at me, and I had nothing to do but look at her.

"What are you doing, honey?" she asked.

I closed my eyes and swallowed against the truth I'd started to glimpse on Sunday, but realized this Monday. Maybe answering her question would relieve the pressure of it on my chest.

"I can't be with him, Grandma. And I can't go on pretending I'm his friend."

"Why ever not?" she shouted.

"Because I like him too much." There. I'd said it, and I could see the words in the space between us like clothes hung out to dry.

"You're going to give up?" she shouted again.

"What's the point when we don't believe in the same thing? I don't know what drives me, but it's clear what drives him, and I can't keep ignoring it. I can't keep thinking it doesn't divide us when it does. Maybe it wouldn't be a big deal at the start, but it'd turn into one."

"I wasn't talking about giving up on him, Lu! I was talking about giving up on everything you were raised to believe."

I didn't want to yell at Grandma on her surgery eve, but the edge in my voice escalated to a definite shout as I responded to her. "Don't you think I've tried? Don't you think I want to? It would make things so easy! I could be a part of this family. I could be with Jackson. But I can't do this for you, and I can't do it for him. I don't know what's wrong with me, but I can't believe in God. I can't ..."

I collapsed on the toilet and cried the tears I'd wanted to shed all week long but had kept at bay. They wracked my body and ricocheted around the small tiled space. Grandma wheeled herself forward and held out her arms to me.

"You come here, my girl."

I collapsed into her arms. She smelled so good, so familiar. I was much stronger than her, but she held me there, and I knew I was safe in that moment. No way would Grandma ever let me sink.

"There's nothing wrong with you, Lu," she said after the last of the tears hiccupped from my body. "On the day you were born, I thought you were the most beautiful thing. I've never seen anything as perfect since. But you catch God's eye even more than you catch mine, and one day, you'll see that. I know this because I've been praying for it, and God has never, ever let me down."

That set off another round of tears. After those finished, she lifted my chin and her steel gray eyes bore straight into mine.

"You are making the right decision about Jackson."

I nodded, but right decision or no, it hurt. She wiped the last of the tears from my cheeks, and I stood up to finish dyeing her hair.

"Get in real good around the ears, Lu. I can't have gray roots showing when I tuck back my hair to show off my earrings." I was as grateful to her for the topic change as I was for everything she'd said. I rooted around with the tip of the plastic bottle, knowing she'd still find a missing spot. We'd fight about it, and this thought made me smile as I finished the job.

As the dye set, I sat back on the toilet to read her the end of a book she knew by heart. After a half hour, I dried her hair with the roller brush, and then set it in foam rollers for extra lift. I affixed her hair net, changed her into her two-piece paisley pajamas, and lifted her back into bed.

The digital clock with numbers as red as her hair read 7:00 p.m. Mom and Dad would be coming any minute to say good night. But I lingered, tucking the covers around her tiny frame. She'd been in the hospital five days, but she'd lost some weight, which I blamed on pain and bad food. I was thankful Jackson had pitched in where I couldn't and brought her something home-cooked.

"You will be fine," I said with great assurance. There was no other option.

"You will be fine, too." She smiled. "And after God gets ahold of you, you call Jackson straight away."

"How do you know Jackson will still be here for me?" I asked.

"You'll see," she affirmed with a nod of her head. "And then I'll say I told you so."

I laughed and rolled my eyes at her blasphemy before standing to leave the room. But I turned back toward her and pressed a kiss to her forehead. It felt tissue-thin and warm against my lips.

"I love you," I whispered before I left without looking back.

I spent the rest of my night curled up on the couch in Grandma's suite, where I'd come every night after visiting hours. I'd explored and found the rest of the Lu binders, all as meticulously compiled and edited as the first volume. There were three in all, and I poured over them, not for my writing, but for her commentary. She wrote like she talked, holding nothing back.

You should have started differently. The only reason I kept reading is because you're family ...

Who cares about square dancing anymore? You should have told the editor no when he asked you to write this story.

The harsh comments went on and on, but I ran my fingers over her slanted scrawl like they were love letters ... because they were, in her own way.

Around eleven o'clock, I put the last of the binders down, too tired to read, but unsure of how to move myself from her room to mine.

And then I smiled. I knew how she'd want me to end the night. I uncurled my feet, placed my elbows on my knees and folded my hands. I thought about talking to God in my head, but Grandma would appreciate a bolder approach and this was more for her than for me.

"God ... if you exist, then I suppose you know me. You know I can't seem to move past this 'if.' I don't know whether girls with an 'if' can presume to talk to you, let alone ask anything of you. But I know my grandma. There's not an 'if' in her mind about you. So, I'm coming to you for her, asking you to see her through this surgery tomorrow. It's just a hip. Please heal it. Heal her. Because I don't know what I would do without her, and she told me you've never, ever let her down."

CHAPTER 25

Grandma died one week later. I'll always remember it as a cold day. The world remembered it was December and adjusted the temperature.

I'd prayed fervently since my first feeler prayer in Grandma's room—maybe not unceasing, but unceasing for me. The surgery went well, well enough for her to begin physical therapy three days later. But then she caught pneumonia, and we got a call in the middle of the night that she'd passed. Without anyone by her side.

I think it was that detail, more than the unanswered prayer itself, that turned off my communication tap with the almighty. Whether God existed—the question I'd chewed over for the last several months—no longer mattered. I wanted no part.

At a time when I wanted to circle in and shut down, it's like all of Dunlap's Creek tromped through our house with condolences and memories. Grandma's tentacles reached every nook and cranny of our small town, and people couldn't seem to hold off the three days until the funeral to share.

And they all brought more food than we were inclined to eat, even under normal circumstances, but at least cataloging and storing it gave Nana Bea and I something to do other than hover in the background. The evening before the funeral, the food situation had escalated, necessitating us to buy a second freezer, open a co-op, or give it away as a funeral favor.

"Bring a sympathy card, take some pasta," I pitched to Nana as we worked in otherwise companionable silence—her at the table, keeping the master cross-reference of names and dishes for thank-yous. I divvied up yet another lasagna, reserving a third for our freezer, placing the other two-thirds in an aluminum foil casserole for Gracie's family, and setting the original glass casserole in the sink to wash and return. I moved onto the next dish in line.

"Sally Jennings brought gluten-free cupcakes," I announced, thinking this tidbit might cajole Nana into a shared chuckle before I remembered we weren't in a laughing mood nowadays. And she didn't have a sense of humor, anyway.

I moved down the buffet, reading a few more names, and though Nana recorded them, I could tell her mind was elsewhere. I brewed some coffee while I finished the task and placed it between us as I took a seat across from her.

"Something on your mind?" I asked, uncomfortable with probing her emotional depths. Neither of us was one for discussing feelings.

She put down her silver pen and loosened her straight back to lean against her chair. She recrossed her legs and smoothed her skirt before answering.

"I think it's time I moved back home," she said.

Her "thought" landed more like an announcement, and it threw me off. This was the first she'd ever admitted to living here—at least to me.

"But ..." I started, trying to parse her statement so I could counter each part to argue her into staying. Nana didn't keep much here. She could be gone in a moment.

"There's nothing more to say, Lu. I've made up my mind." She left the kitchen without touching her coffee. Was she leaving to pack her bag right now? I pushed my mug away, wondering why I'd made it in the first place. Like anything in that cup could make sense of everything happening right now or hold it together.

At least she has somewhere to go, I thought. What was I going to do? This wasn't the first time I'd thought it, but the closer Grandma's funeral came, the more my predicament loomed. I needed to decide what to do next, but I was fresh out of ideas. When New York went belly up, I'd come home. Now that home had crashed, where was I going to go?

It was a weary question, even without Grandma's funeral tomorrow, but at least her funeral bought me one more day of procrastination. It was six o'clock, and I was crossing the yard in a half hour to watch the girls so Gracie and Ted could accompany Mom and Dad to the church to finalize the funeral arrangements.

I headed to my room to pass the thirty minutes. But the sight of Dad crouching over photos in the family room saved me from that pathetic plan.

"Hey, kiddo," he said as I stepped into the doorway.

"Need help with anything?" I didn't want to look through photos, but I didn't want to leave Dad by himself, either.

"I'm choosing photos for the funeral. Want to make sure I've selected the right ones?"

I crossed the room to sift through the pile—teenage Grandma smiling at the camera, young mom Grandma helping Dad toddle down the sidewalk, Grandma smiling outside Penny Thrift on opening day, Grandma at the pierogie stand, Grandma cuddling little-girl me on the couch. I remembered the day. I had a nasty case of strep, so we'd holed up for three days, alternating between numbing my throat with icy popsicles and warming it with cream of broccoli soup. Instead of making me nap in the afternoons, she'd let me watch *The Young and the Restless* as long as I promised not to tell anyone. I never had. I never would.

"You want me to put these on a poster or something?" I asked. It'd make for a good project with the girls before I put them to bed.

"That would be great." He paused. "There hasn't been a time to say this with everything else going on, but I'm sorry about what happened at the paper ..." he started.

I waved his words away with my hand. "Dad, it doesn't matter."

He put his hand on my shoulder and looked straight into my eyes. "Of course it matters. You've had quite a year, kiddo, and I can see you pulling back. Don't pull back too far. Grandma wouldn't want you to give up, especially not on her account."

I knew that. Failure was another reason to set her guns blazing, but I wasn't like her. And she wasn't around anymore to kick my butt in gear.

I gathered the rest of the pictures and headed next door, arriving in time to hug Gracie and Ted before they left.

"Sure you don't want to come?" Gracie's eyes asked more than that question. She was talking about church and Jackson and my state in general—all things I couldn't deal with right now. I didn't know if I could zip it all up for tomorrow.

I shook my head and ushered them out the door, realizing their house was quiet. The girls were clustered on the couch, each with a favorite toy in her hand, but only in a cursory sort of way. Sadness had taken effect here, too. But I had a plan.

"Girls!" I exclaimed in my most cheerful Aunt Lu voice. "I have a super special project for us to do for tomorrow."

This did little to move their tiny bodies, which otherwise were always on the lookout for excitement. I smiled at them, and they counteracted with sad, wide-eyed stares. After awhile, Caroline said, "We miss Grandma Pat, Aunt Lu."

I nodded, and the lump in my throat burst into tears on my face, and the girls and I held one another while we cried. This was not how I expected the night to go, but I hoped my arms comforted them as much as their hugs did for me.

"I miss Grandma, too," I said, taking the path of honesty over false cheer. "And tonight we have something only we can do for her." I spread Grandma's pictures like a fan in my hands. "These are pictures of her special times, and we need to figure out the best way to show them off so everyone who comes to the funeral tomorrow can see how special she was. Can you help me?"

They delivered like little girls do with poster boards of neon green and pink and puffy paint and glitter and sparkly glue. Grandma Pat would have clapped her hands over it. By the time I hustled the girls off to bed, the kitchen was a total mess, and I was hoping our art ingredients were water-soluble.

I tucked each girl in bed, ending with Caroline.

"Aunt Lu, is Grandma Pat in heaven? Tell it to me straight," she demanded, staring me down. Little Miss had a touch of Grandma Pat in her.

"What do you think?" I deflected.

"I want to know what you think," she dodged.

"I don't know," I responded, and I could tell from how she looked away I'd let her down. I didn't want to do that, so I thought for another minute.

"I do know Grandma Pat believed in heaven and because of that, she wasn't afraid to die. She wasn't sad to die, either—except to leave us," I said.

"But is it real?" Caroline pressed, and the question pierced through my pain and anger and confusion, bringing to light all I didn't know. But it also reminded of one thing I did.

"Grandma wouldn't have staked her life on something she questioned, and she staked her life on this—God, Jesus, heaven—all of it."

My New York wardrobe hadn't been much use since my return, but its monochromatic pieces served me well on funeral day. My black dress over black tights and black heels, all cinched together under my black wool trench and finished with a black wool scarf and black leather gloves—plenty of layers to ward me against the cold and everything else.

I wished I could skip the thing, or sit in the way back where I could sneak out if necessary. These weren't adult options, but I did decide to drive separately so at least I could arrive at the last possible moment. The revolving door of sympathizers in the last three days had sapped my shallow small-talk reservoir, and I was done with crowds. Thankfully, my family had decided against calling hours or a reception. The funeral would last an hour and the burial twenty minutes.

You can do this, I told myself as I took one last look in the hall mirror. My reflection responded that I could use some makeup and sleep and food, but there wasn't time. The funeral was starting in twenty minutes.

I got into my car and turned on the radio, hoping it would crowd out my anxiety. Fifteen minutes of mindless station shuffling later, I pulled into the full parking lot of the new church, taking care to fidget long enough with my gloves, scarf, and coat so I walked to the double front doors with a minute to spare. I stood there for ten seconds too long, but closed my eyes and inhaled the icy air anyway. Time was up. I opened my eyes and reached to push open the door as it opened for me.

Jackson.

I'm sure the church was full behind him. I'm sure they had to bring in extra chairs because the pews couldn't fit everyone who'd come to say goodbye to Grandma. But for me, there was him.

I didn't shrink from his gaze, and I hoped he could read mine. *I'm sorry. I am so sorry.* I couldn't be with him, but I hoped he didn't misconstrue my distance as indifference. I opened my mouth—to say what, I had no idea—but he shook his head and pulled me close, wrapping his arms around my back and laying his head on mine. The smell of him, the feel of him, overpowered me. We'd never really touched. I'd imagined it, but those thoughts in no way captured the sensation of him holding me now, and I closed my eyes and sunk into it.

Eventually, I became aware of where we were. I felt the shift in the crowd, and I didn't need to turn around to see the funeral was about to start. I pulled away, but Jackson seemed in less of a rush. His hands cupped either side of my face, his right thumb caressing my cheek as the tears fell.

"I am here for you," he said, his voice reaching out like a hand to rescue me.

I closed my eyes, willing myself to take it, but then the voice of his father welcoming everyone broke the spell.

I stepped back and wiped my tears with my own hands. And I walked away from him, Grandma's voice resolving me with each step: *You are making the right decision.*

I'd planned to do whatever mental gymnastics necessary to separate myself from the funeral, but the homily Pastor Cleary shared on the woman at the well—Grandma's favorite Bible passage—and the memories people shared brought her close in a way I hadn't anticipated. I listened with such intensity it felt like a shock when my father stood to conclude the proceedings with a brief prayer.

But if the funeral brought me unexpected joy, the burial brought the kind of pain I had to walk away from. There's something about a casket going into the ground. Nothing—no sentiment, story, sympathy—can counteract the finality. As family and friends tossed lone branches of white daisies—Grandma's favorite flower—into the hole, I clutched mine and turned away, unwilling to let the frozen ground claim anything else from me that day.

Of course this was the day John came back into my life. He stood on the porch of my parents' house, his back to the street. I recognized his outline instantly. Six months away hadn't dulled how well I knew his coloring, his shape—how he jingles his change in his right pocket when he's waiting for something. Someone. Me.

I'd taken my shoes off to walk home from the graveyard, welcoming the pain of the frost against my bare feet. He didn't hear me coming.

"Hello, John," I said, startling him, and in the moment after he turned around, I could see him taking me in as I'd done with him. There was pain there and love, but mostly I saw the familiar ice blue of his eyes.

"Lu, I ..."

I stepped forward and put my finger to his lips, shaking my head as tears streamed down my face. I needed explanations—I deserved them. But right now I was struggling to stand.

"I don't know why you're here, and right now, I don't care. We buried Grandma Pat today, so if you could hold me ..."

His arms caught me as I was about to crumble to the ground. How many times had I imagined being with in these past months? They didn't prepare me for the familiarity of him. His touch, his smell, how my body fit to his—it overwhelmed me. After a certain point I wasn't sure what I was crying for or how long it would take to get it all out, but I knew John would stay as long as required.

I raged and sobbed. I spoke more unfinished sentences than I can count, and I have no idea how long we were on the stoop or how we transitioned from him holding me to us sitting side-by-side, not touching. I looked over at him and saw him studying my hands. After awhile, he raised his eyes to mine. He wanted permission.

I nodded, and he moved from my side to face me, leaning on his heels with his warm hands covering my freezing ones.

"Lu, the night you left, you asked me to leave you alone. I've tried, and I know I don't have a right to be here, but I had to try. I came here to ask for your forgiveness and to ask for you back. You don't have to come back to New York. I'll come here, or we'll go wherever you want. I'm not rushing you for an answer, and I'll answer as many questions as many times as you need."

His eyes didn't leave mine.

"Please, Lu. I will wait as long as it takes."

I don't know how long I would have sat there noting the weight of his hands and returning his stare, but the sound of my parents' car turning into the drive snapped my gaze up. John and I stood as the car approached.

I dropped his hands and made my decision.

"Take me back to New York."

CHAPTER 26

A few weeks later, I stepped into John's new apartment. He'd hated our studio, and I assumed he'd move, but I'd never allowed myself to speculate about his new digs. If I had, my imaginings would have matched with the seating, lighting, and art before me now. It was sparse and bachelor, but I wanted to sink my girl self in anyway. I was feeling all eight hours of my drive and the idea of falling onto John's oversized brown leather couch seemed like the right antidote.

I walked around instead. It wasn't a large space, but it was laid out efficiently. The front door opened into the living room, which was separated from the kitchen and dining area by a few pillars. Three large windows lined the back wall, facing the street.

"When did you move here?" I asked as I circled the space, looking from the brick wall on the left to the worn wooden beams on the ceiling. I liked his place.

"Two months after you left."

"Did Avery ever live here?"

"No. We were finished the day she sent back your clothes."

"Because she sent back my clothes?"

"No, but I had no idea Avery would do that. I lasted a month before I called you," he said.

"I hammered my phone into pieces after the clothes came back."

He laughed and then caught himself. "I'm sorry. I shouldn't laugh."

I remembered Jackson leaning against my car and laughing at the same confession. I blocked the memory and smiled at John.

"I was waiting for you to call every day. The only thing worse than not hearing from you was thinking I might break down and call you myself. I smashed my phone instead."

He shook his head. "If I'd known that I would have …"

"You would have what?"

"Come for you six months ago."

"I'm here, aren't I?" Problem was, a lot had happened in those six months. "How many bedrooms does your place have?"

"One, but Lu, I'm planning to sleep on the couch. You can have the bedroom."

I nodded. "If it's okay, I'll head there now. It's been a long day."

And a long few weeks, I added silently. John had left Dunlap's Creek the day after he came. I stayed through the holidays to say goodbyes. Those hadn't been pretty, ranging from the stony silence of Nana Bea, who'd moved out the weekend after Grandma Pat's funeral, to the outright fury of Gracie, who'd reminded me of my promise to stick around for the birth of the baby.

"You promised me, Lu!"

"Please don't hold me to that."

"Why? Why can't I hold you to that? Why can't any of us ever hold you to anything, but we always have to be here to pick up your pieces?"

"Says the woman whose life has worked out according to plan!" I'd shouted, matching my voice to hers.

"In your eyes only, Lu! How about you start really seeing my life?"

"Sure thing, Grace. As soon as you start seeing mine."

I'd slammed out her back door then, and we hadn't talked until the next morning when we'd met halfway across our yards and tripped over each other with apologies.

"I love you; I want to pick up your pieces," she sobbed. *"But how can I if you're not here?"*

"I'm going to patch myself back together this time," I said, wiping my tears away to make room for more.

I hugged each of the girls and Ted, who messed up my hair before taking the girls back inside to finish getting ready for school. I shook my head at Mom's, "Please stay," and ended with a long hug to my dad.

"This will always be your home, kiddo," he said.

I nodded and picked up the two suitcases I'd packed with enough to get me by but keep me light until I figured out where I'd land. I looked up and down the row of clunkers along the driveway, but it was minus my '85 Cutlass.

"Where's my car?" I asked. It's possible I'd taken it to the shop for a once-over before my trip, but I had no memory of it.

"I couldn't let you drive back to New York in the Cutlass. Nana agreed, and she bought you a car," Dad said, nodding toward a gleaming, navy blue Civic.

"Is it new?" I asked in total disbelief. I had no gauge for these things. The car was shiny. I ran my finger along the hood and turned it over. Not one speck of dirt. "I can't take this."

"You can," he said, loading my suitcases into the trunk. "You have enough to figure out. Let Nana Bea figure out this detail for you."

An expensive detail, but I nodded, crying harder. "I don't deserve this."

After one more hug from Dad, and a stop by Nana's place to give her a hug, a thank-you, and an I love you—all of which she waived away—I trekked to where I stood now, in a New York loft, pushing against memories and trying to finish this conversation with John before I could end my day.

"Let's just say no one is thrilled with my choice to move back here," I said.

"Or with me."

I looked at him. "Or with you."

The old John would have crossed the room to hold me. I think the new John would have, too, but after looking at me for a moment, he put his hands in his pockets. "Consider this place yours, Lu. Please. Go to bed when you want, get up when you want. I want you in my life, but I'll give you all the space you need until you decide whether it's what you want."

He gestured toward the bedroom with his left hand, and I walked toward it. The room was painted a pale gray, and the king-sized bed with its down comforter looked incredibly inviting.

"Do you need anything?" John asked, leaning against the door after he'd brought my suitcases. I sat on the bed and looked at him, wondering if I'd ever adjust to this new space. And to him. The John I'd left was so intent, sometimes on me, but mostly on his work. He'd moved about our old apartment with a certain impatience and distraction. This John, in his T-shirt and jeans and bare feet, seemed at my disposal. All I had to do was ask. Instead, I shook my head, and he closed the door.

I opened a suitcase, glad to see I'd packed pajamas on top. I crawled into them and then into bed, grateful to shut my eyes to tears for the day. But the darkness opened them to memories of Jackson.

I'd started packing my suitcases when Jackson came to my room. It was the first time he'd been here, and he looked around before speaking.

"When were you going to tell me you were leaving?"

I thought about making something up—a handful of white lies hovered, and any would sound better than the truth. But he deserved honesty. I stopped folding shirts and sat back on my heels to give him my full attention.

"I wasn't going to tell you, Jackson," I admitted.

His eyes hardened, and a minute passed before he spoke again.

"Why are you doing this?"

"What's for me here? I'm in the exact same place where I started. Still broke, still no job, still not sure what I want. I need to go somewhere, anywhere. I can't stay here."

"That's not true. You've made so much progress ..."

"I'm not a project, Jackson!" I shouted, standing and crossing the room to get as far from him as possible. "I know you want to see my sorry soul saved. I get it; I've entertained it. But I am not buying it."

"Louisa, I didn't mean for it to come out like that. You aren't a project to me, you're ..." he paused, running his hands through his hair. "You're unlike anyone I've ever met. Yes, I want you to believe in God, but not to prove a point. I care about you. Only God can move you forward, and these things you're chasing? They can't. They'll disappoint you."

"Better than the disappointment I've tasted lately. I tried to build a life here, but it's gone now. It's just gone." I shook my head, unable to hold his gaze. "It's time for me to move on."

"Do you want to be with John?" He surprised me, and I think himself, with that question.

I didn't say anything.

"Are you leaving to be with him?" he asked again, stepping toward me.

I looked into his eyes, wanting to ask him to hold me again like he had at Grandma's funeral. If he would do that, then maybe I could find the courage to tell him all the words clogging my throat. But I took one more step back.

"I need to pack, Jackson. I'm leaving tomorrow."

He took one more step toward me.

"Stay," he said. Asked. But it was an offer absent of one important detail. I stepped forward and looked him straight in the eyes.

"Stay with you, Jackson?"

He didn't say anything. He didn't move.

It was time for him to go.

"That's what I thought. Now please leave so I can finish," I said, gesturing to my piles of clothing.

He looked at me for a long time. And then he turned on his heel, walked down the stairs and out the front door. I sat in the doorway, unable to move for the next hour, keenly aware I'd broken my own heart.

CHAPTER 27

John's bedroom window faced east like mine at home so it was a familiar stream of sunlight that woke me. I remembered where I was, but the sound of the coffee grinder shocked me to the present. I was sharing a space again with someone who enjoyed coffee.

I found my gray jersey robe, wrapped the tie around my waist, and headed to the kitchen. John was wearing a white T-shirt, striped pajama bottoms, and leather scuffs—all familiar. The espresso machine behind him was new, though. I pulled out one of the two chairs at the island separating the kitchen from the dining room, and he looked up.

"I'm sorry to wake you. I forgot to grind this before I went to bed last night."

And you get a headache if you don't have coffee within thirty minutes of waking up, I silently added. "As long as that fancy machine puts out something tasty, I don't mind," I said.

He put a demitasse of steaming espresso in front of me before pulling two shots for himself. And then he sort of hovered, shifting his weight from one foot to the other. It took me a sip to realize the problem; he didn't know where to sit.

I gestured toward the empty chair next to me. "John, I don't know what I'm doing here, and I don't know how long I will stay. But I don't want you to be a stranger in your home. Please sit."

He did, and within a few minutes we slipped into conversation. I asked about his family and work, but he seemed eager to move onto me.

"After your voice mail went from full to out of service, I tried to take the hint. You wanted me to leave you alone. But the next few months of not hearing from you and me not doing anything about it were worse. After Thanksgiving, I did an Internet search on your name. It felt like a shot in the dark—I know how much you stay away from all that. So you can imagine how surprised I was when I found everything you'd done. I stayed up all night reading."

He turned toward me. "I'm not sure whether reading it made me miss you less—reading your writing was like hearing you talk after months of silence—or more. Now that I knew where you were, I wanted to call but given everything I'd done and all the time that passed, that wasn't enough. I decided to take some of my stockpiled vacation time to come to you."

"What were you hoping for?" I asked, staring into my empty cup.

"To see you, to apologize, and to tell you I want to be with you."

John put his hand on mine, and I looked at him.

"I failed you long before I cheated on you. You left your career to come here with me, and I gave you no support. There's a lot I'd re-do, and it would start from when we moved here. Lu, I am so sorry. I am so very, very sorry," he pleaded, his eyes filling with tears.

Mine did the same, and we sat there for the next few minutes, crying it out while gripping each other's hands.

"Well, aren't we a pair," I said awhile later, releasing my hand to wipe my tears away. "John, I left you, too. I resented your success. The doors kept opening, and you had more work than time. I had all the time and no work. I hate that you cheated on me, but I was so insufferable, especially in that last year. I can see that now."

And there were other things I could see. Me standing across from Jackson in my bedroom at home. That man could have fought for me with one word—"Yes." Was his turning away any different than what I'd done with John all those months ago? What if, instead of leaving with the Crock-Pot, I'd said, "Stay. With me." I could have refused to leave without a fight, but I was so caught up in what I deserved and what he deserved in return that I lost sight of what we deserved.

I opened my mouth, and then paused, measuring the honesty of what I was about to say. I hadn't returned here with a plan, and John wasn't about to insist. But it was time.

"I forgive you for Avery." John looked surprised. "Don't mistake me. I'm not back with you, but you don't need to keep apologizing for what happened. It's done, though we will need to figure out how to move forward. Can things be different between us? Can I trust you again? I don't know. But John, I'd like to try. We were together for six years, and if it's over, I'd like to know I at least fought for us."

I glanced at the clock: Monday morning, 9:00 a.m.

"Aren't you going to work?" I asked.

John shook his head. "My leave lasts for another week. I'm keeping tabs on a few things from here, but that's it. Not that I'm expecting you to spend all of your time with me." He smiled. "Actually, you might be busy."

"What do you mean?" I asked, standing up to take our espresso cups to the sink.

"I hope I didn't overstep bounds, but after you agreed to come back, I showed some of your work to people I know, who showed it to people they know, and those people want to talk with you about some writing jobs."

I turned around to smile at him. "That was nice, John. Thank you."

He looked so relieved he wasn't in trouble that I laughed and crossed the room to hug him.

"Thank you," I whispered, and then I pulled away.

My first week back in New York assumed its own pattern. John and I bookended our days together, circling with innocuous conversation that caught us up on each other's lives without delving into anything of substance. For his part, I think he wondered what information he was allowed, and so he kept his questions light and few. For mine, I felt like I couldn't share much without sharing about Jackson. If I stayed, I'd tell John. I kept mum, but my thoughts and emotions were filled with Jackson all the same. I didn't mean to, but I was comparing him and John, which were one, if not two too many men in my life.

Around midmorning every day, I'd retreat to the bedroom,

adding a couple items from my suitcase to the drawers and closet space John had cleared for me. It was more of a polite response than a proclamation I was here to stay with him. Then, I showered and dressed and escaped to the city. My interviews wouldn't be for another week, and I spent a couple hours each day at the library getting acquainted with their publications. And then I walked around until dinner.

The noise and crowds of New York felt like a shield when I first came three years ago—behind it, I could realize the anonymity and solitude I'd always wanted growing up in a small town. After a day of wandering John's new neighborhood, I realized I didn't want that anymore. I took to walking a circuit—crossing the same spots at the same times in the hopes of catching familiar faces, but that doesn't happen in New York. And what would have happened if I'd crossed the same face, three, four, or a dozen times? Would I have introduced myself? That doesn't happen in New York, either. But I kept to my routine like I could change the city's stripes or my own.

My cell phone was like an emergency Band-Aid—a Band-Aid with a bite. Every time I took it out, I hoped to see a call or text or voice mail from Jackson. That wasn't going to happen, but I wielded it against my loneliness in other ways, texting evidence of my people watching to Gracie and pics of architectural interest to Ted. The stained glass of a small stone church a few blocks from John's caught my eye on that first afternoon, and I thought nothing of sneaking right up to it for some close-ups. Then I took to sitting on a stone bench inside its wrought iron gates each afternoon before I returned to the apartment for dinner.

It's from here I began calling Nana Bea, not caring that sitting outside on a stone bench isn't the coziest of choices in January in New York. Several rings passed before she picked up on that first day, but by midweek she'd come to expect my call around four o'clock, and she'd pick up on the first ring. I think both of us were concerned about the other's living situation.

"When are you going to move back?" I asked at least once per phone call. I didn't like her living alone, and I suspected I wasn't the only family member calling her every day.

"When you do," she always responded.

So went the cyclical argument that began each day's phone call before we settled into recounting our days.

197

"Where are you calling me from?" she asked me on Friday. "It's noisy on your end."

"From inside the gate of this little church near John's apartment."

"Will you go this Sunday?"

"Why would I do that?"

"For the same reason you went every Sunday at home."

"I went as a courtesy, Nana," I explained.

"Maybe at the beginning, but that's not why you kept going."

I thought she was talking about Jackson, but then she surprised me with, "You were looking for answers."

The shock of her forthrightness shut up any clever responses on my end. "You sound like Grandma Pat," I said.

"There's not a lot of time to mess about, Lu" she said.

"I'm not messing about. I found my answers."

"You think you have. But trust me, you haven't. I once thought the same thing."

We were both silent. I cleared my throat. "Want to talk about it?"

"No."

"Fine. It's Friday. Have a hot date for tonight?" I asked.

"Well, I have to leave in a moment for a meeting with the ladies society."

"Who's driving you there?"

"Me."

I choked on my spit. "In what?"

"The Cadillac. What else?"

"I'd hope anything else. That car has about twenty blind spots. Do you have a license?"

"Don't be impertinent, Lu. I could drive you through the middle of New York City right now."

I rolled my eyes. "How far away is the meeting?"

"In town."

I didn't want to think about the damage she could do behind the wheel of that boat in a mile. I hung up to tattle on her to Mom.

"Nana is about to drive herself to a meeting."

"Of all the ..." Mom began, and then stopped to shout at my dad in the background to go pick up her mother. Then she spoke to me, "If the two of you would quit your weaning dance and come back home, I'd get a lot more sleep at night."

"I'm not the one you need to worry about," I insisted.

"Right. You in New York with your ex-boyfriend. At least I think he's still your ex-boyfriend. I'm not sure which option I prefer. Regardless, I'm your mother, and I'll always worry about you. Where are you calling from, anyway? It's noisy."

"From inside the gates of this little church near John's apartment."

"Make sure you take yourself there this Sunday."

I looked at the freestanding sign advertising service times next to the double wooden doors of the church, but I didn't need to. I'd mentally filed the 10:00 a.m. start time that first day I'd stepped through the gate, and 10:00 a.m. was the first thing to flash through my mind when I woke Sunday morning. I didn't set the alarm the night before, but I told myself if I happened to wake up early enough, I'd consider going to church. These disclaimers were all a head game, though. I'd woken up well before 10:00 a.m. all week.

I did the same on Sunday, but I stared as the clock ticked from 8:10 to 8:22 a.m. before I surrendered. I tiptoed over to the suitcase to unearth the NIV Bible I'd packed and unpacked ad infinitum before tossing it in with a, "What the hell."

But it wasn't a what-the-hell maneuver. I was right when I'd told Nana Bea I'd found my answers, but she was also right about me needing to take another look at what I'd found. I knew this on some level, just as I knew my choice to return to New York and John weren't answers to my questions as much instinctual reactions to do something—anything—with my life. It wasn't only my family wondering what I was doing; I was asking the question, too.

I sat cross-legged on the floor with my back against the mattress and opened to Ecclesiastes 3, which was marked by Jackson's handwritten version.

There is a time for everything, and a season for every activity under heaven ... A time to plant, to uproot ... to tear down, to build ... to weep, to laugh ... to mourn, to dance ...

I traced my finger along his illegible script, intending to read to the end of the chapter, but I paused at verse six—*A time to search and a time to give up, a time to keep and a time to throw away.* I knew where I'd landed in the dichotomies of the previous verses—definitely on the mourning instead of dancing side of things—but verse six stumped me.

Had I given up or was I still searching?

It seemed I'd thrown everything away except John in coming back to New York, but from where I sat now, I could see how maybe my leaving was an effort to keep something close, something I couldn't have kept if I'd remained in Dunlap's Creek. I closed my eyes, trying to make sense of it, but getting nowhere. I wouldn't find my answers sitting on this floor, staring at this paper.

"Okay," I said and rose to shower and get dressed.

John seemed surprised when I stepped out of the bedroom at a quarter till ten, dressed for something other than perusing *The Times*, *The Journal*, and the rest of the papers stacked next to him at the kitchen table.

"Catching up on the world before you head back to it tomorrow?" I asked as I put on my black wool trench coat.

"I'd ask you to join me, but it looks like you're going somewhere," he observed.

"Church." The admission felt a little thick in my throat.

He raised his eyebrows. "You go to church?"

No. I mean, I had. But not really. At least not like I was going to church now. And I wasn't sure why I was going to church now. But I definitely was.

This was all too hard to explain. So I nodded.

"Do … umm …" he coughed, as uncertain of what was kosher as me in this new territory. "Do you want me to come with you?" He asked it like he'd offered to take a punch in the gut for me.

"Do you want to come?"

"Not at all," he exhaled.

"Good because I want to go by myself," I responded, though I hadn't been sure that's what I wanted until I said it. I looked at my watch—9:50 a.m. I rushed out the door, but then popped my head back in with, "Save the crossword for me!" and closed the door at the sound of his laughter. I was miserable at the crossword, but ever hopeful each Sunday would be different. The paper proved me otherwise, leaving me to hit up John for all the answers, who was crossword savvy but ambivalent about his talent. It had often ended in a fight before; I assume it would be the same today. I was looking forward to it.

When I pushed open the heavy wooden doors of the church, I expected the quiet murmurings of people settling into pews for the start of service, but I didn't expect friendliness in the form of a short, rotund, older man in a clerical collar.

"I was wondering whether you'd come inside," he said holding out his hand.

CHAPTER 28

I woke up with a start Monday morning, realizing I forgot to ask John about his work schedule. I assumed it was the same as before—early and late, with twelve hours in between. The clock said five o'clock, and I tiptoed to the shower to make way for his wake-up routine. I left the bedroom as he stumbled in with a grunt. Poor man was less of a morning person than me.

I opened the fridge, thinking I'd assemble John some breakfast. It took a moment of scavenging for pickings—an egg, berries, anything other than the chunk of Parmesan and jar of baby dills staring back at me—before I remembered. John doesn't eat breakfast. I focused on caffeine instead. In the time it took for John to shower and dress, I assumed I could figure how to pull some decent shots from the espresso machine.

But for the next half hour, I cajoled, cursed and employed every other force of language, only to be stonewalled and sacrifice most of John's espresso in the process. I could not make a decent cup from this devil machine.

"I owe you some espresso ..." I confessed as I heard him exit the bedroom. I glanced back a moment later and froze. John stood ready for work, leaning against the other side of the island. If I closed my eyes, I could hone in on the subtle trace of his cologne. A tempting thought if my eyes weren't glued to him.

In the last week, I'd gotten used to the casual John who wore old T-shirts and jeans and barely shaved and never thought to run a comb through his hair. He'd looked good, but like a stranger, and I'd responded to him as such.

But this John, in his fitted navy blue suit and crisp white shirt and shaven face and ... I shook my head against the details. I was rattled by them. By him. And I was overcome by my sudden and unexpected desire to wrap my arms around this familiar man.

We stared at each other, neither of us saying anything for a moment. It wasn't until he quietly but firmly said, "You look beautiful," I realized he was taking me in the same way. I'd made an effort for today's interview—dressing in a fitted, black, capped-sleeve dress, taming my hair against the diffuser instead of letting it air dry, and applying eyeliner. Still, I can't imagine how my appearance affected him as the sight of him did to me. After that first morning, we'd avoided physical contact. But if he reached for me now, I'd go to him like a reflex.

I cleared my throat and gestured to the espresso machine. "Can you help?" I asked.

He stepped to the right, as did I, moving in an opposing revolution around the island.

His eyes told me he knew I was deflecting, and a brief smile flashed before he pulled the espresso and handed me a demitasse. I inhaled and sipped, hoping it would cut the edge off of my uncooperative hormones.

"Nervous?" John asked from the other side of the island.

I looked up.

"About the interview?" he clarified before taking a sip.

Thanks to him, not so much. "No."

"About me, then?" he asked, smiling.

The question put me strangely at ease. "Let's say I'm glad there's an island between us," I said, setting my hand on the thick black granite countertop.

"I'd leap across it in a single bound if you asked."

I had to put my espresso down to laugh. "Been reading a lot of comic books while I've been gone?"

He tossed back the rest of his espresso like a shot and put the empty white cup in the sink. Six o'clock and time to go. John nodded toward his suit jacket, lying on the back of the barstool behind me. I carried it to him, and as he took it, his fingers brushed mine.

"Your espresso machine rejected me," I said.

"Then I'll get rid of the espresso machine."

I watched him put on his jacket and straighten his tie in precise movements. It was routine getting dressed stuff, but the maneuvers fascinated me. I should have stepped back to safety, but I didn't. And when he stepped closer, I looked up into his eyes and saw the lightness of the moment fade into desire. I wanted him to kiss me. And he did, like we had all the time in the world. His hands held my hips as his lips reacquainted themselves with mine. *John*. My mind played his name on repeat as my body responded like it always had to his touch, but with more hunger. It had been a long time. There was a lot about being back with him that would be complicated, but this part? It was a little too easy.

I pulled away, and he looked at me for a second before he stepped back.

"Before I go, can I ask you something?"

I nodded.

"Can I have your phone number?"

Sure. If I could remember it. The ensuing search for my phone broke the spell, though. I retrieved it from the nightstand and texted him my number before saying goodbye. I locked the door behind him and returned to the kitchen.

The man was on his game this morning; he would have no problems jumping back into work. Me? I needed a cold shower.

"Get ahold of yourself, Lu," I whispered, laying my head against the cold granite countertop and wishing I had an excuse to get out of the apartment, but I didn't need to leave for my interview for another hour. I opted for more coffee and searched the cupboards to see if John had kept my old French press. I found it behind some old law school mugs, and set it with a thud next to the espresso machine as a warning.

"You're on probation, buddy," I muttered and then ground the remaining espresso beans and boiled water on a kettle on the stove. After I set the coffee to steep, I retrieved my Bible from the bedroom and flipped past Ecclesiastes 3 to the book of Mark, which Pastor Eddy had preached on yesterday.

After he called me out on my creeping, Eddy had ushered me to the front pew and beelined it to the pulpit, giving me no chance to object and enough time to catch my bearings in the dark hush of the space. During sunrise and sunset, light would illuminate the fractured rainbow of stained glass, but at ten o'clock, the windows served more like a Lite Brite. I could barely make out the faces of the handful of other attenders, let alone the words in the Bible Pastor Eddy instructed us to open without preamble.

"Let's get to it: Mark 1:1-3. If you don't know where that is, use the table of contents."

The man wasn't messing around, and he gave us about five seconds to obey before delivering instruction number two.

"Stand as I read these verses. Just because this book has a table of contents doesn't mean it's ordinary. These are God's words spoken to us through normal men, in this case a man named Mark. But they will hit as God intends, as the light through our church's stained windowpanes refracts as their creator intended. Stand to receive them:

The beginning of the gospel about Jesus Christ, the Son of God. It is written in Isaiah the prophet: 'I will send my messenger ahead of you, who will prepare your way—a voice of one calling in the desert, "Prepare the way for the Lord make straight paths for him."'

"Mark begins his book with a claim. Most people work up to claims, building their case first with evidence, but Mark starts his book with a statement of truth and then uses the rest of the book to prove why it's so.

"What is Mark's claim? If you're not asking this, you should be. It's a three-parter. First, Jesus is the Christ, or Messiah. The deliverer. Second, Jesus is the son of God. Third, Jesus is God.

"It's a lot to take in, and we'll take each in turn. You should take notes."

I did, and it was these I looked at now, flipping back and forth between the books of Mark and Isaiah. Thanks to my church upbringing, I had an operating memory of the big Old Testament stories and characters—Moses and Pharaoh, Daniel and the lions, Jonah and the whale—but Isaiah was a whole other beast, and I couldn't figure out how any of it related to Jesus, let alone me.

I'm sure Jackson could explain it to me, but my decision to leave negated that option, and if negation had degrees, calling him to chat up scripture seemed like less of an option given my primal reaction to John this morning.

I couldn't call Jackson, but I supposed I could write him and never send it. Such a lovelorn action was in keeping with my confusion, and I turned over the back of my note card before I could second-guess myself:

J,

I have another pastor in my life—Pastor Eddy. He's bossy. Grandma Pat would like him, though she'd tower over him, small as she was. The man is built like a hobbit. Anyway, I'm struggling with what he said about what Mark said about what Isaiah said about Jesus. I don't even understand the sentence I just wrote.

And I miss you. I'm struggling with that, too.

—Louisa

I turned the card back over and looked at it one more time before putting it in my Bible. I'd written the word "assent" at the bottom and circled it, and after a sip of coffee, I remembered why.

"These three verses say a lot, but don't get so bogged down in the detail you miss the point," Pastor Eddy had concluded. "Mark is clear about who Jesus is. We tend to turn Jesus into something less—a good guy, a thoughtful teacher, a powerful healer. It's a Jesus who's easier for us to swallow, but not the Jesus who Mark asserts.

"Can you assent there may be some validity to Mark's claim? He's not asking for mindless, brainless acceptance; Mark will present his evidence. But you will never be able to answer the question about who Jesus is unless you open your mind to the idea Jesus might be who Mark claims. Assent to this."

I closed my Bible, so deep in thought that the beep of my cell phone caused me to jump. A text from Gracie flashed across the screen.

Txt a selfie.

I complied, though I wasn't sure why she wanted a pic.

Looking good. Ready for the interview?

Right. The interview. I responded, *Sure*, closed my Bible, and left.

CHAPTER 29

Thousands of twentysomethings flock to New York every year, thinking their homegrown success will translate to the big city. That was me in my first iteration here. In that first year, I trolled the periodicals, publishers, media conglomerates—any entity involved with printing words on a page. If John received a six-figure salary at a top firm upon graduating law school, surely I could land something of note. I'd already been working for three years.

But my search met with mostly silence; rejection was the runner-up. The few offers that did come my way, I disdained. I hadn't left a good job on a features desk for a daily paper to now get coffee as an "editorial assistant"—or so I told myself in those early days. Had I known that within the year, I'd be making the coffee the editorial assistants were carrying back to their editors, I might have made a different decision.

Even in the most hopeful of my early New York days, I never would have considered a job at Condé Nast within my reach. I'd applied, but kind of like how people who aren't really gunning for Harvard still apply to Harvard. Landing any gig here—even as "Assistant Coffee Procurer"—would excuse the Starbucks gap in my journalism resume and put me back in the game.

But as soon as I stepped off the elevator at the 35th floor, I knew this wasn't the place for me. Maybe because the floor was so shiny. I could see my reflection in the tile and in the countless glass panels that partitioned one working space from another.

Everywhere I looked, I saw my startled, squinting self—the squinting courtesy of the fluorescent lights that ricocheted off all the shiny.

I'm not made for shiny spaces, but I followed the receptionist to the conference room anyway. It didn't help that my black patent pumps squeaked with each step. By the time I stepped through the door, I felt plain loud, not the best way to enter the interview mind game.

Regardless, I had the edge over my interviewer, who didn't know my name. At least that's the reason I gave him for not saying anything as he half-stood to greet me. But, I knew his name—Mr. Pat Bronson—and I used it with confidence as I reached across the conference table to shake his hand.

"Thank you for taking time to meet with me, Mr. Bronson."

"Yes, Miss ..." he looked down at my resume again, "Lu? Umm ..." another look down, this time with a wrinkled brow.

"Sokolowski," I finished. No one ever pronounced it correctly on the first try.

He gestured for me to take a seat as he sank into his. He looked again at the resume, which I assume he wasn't any more familiar with than my name. A long time commenced, which I would have passed with a sip of water had Mr. Bronson poured me any from the pitcher on his side of the table. The resume was one-sided, but he kept turning it over as if more data might appear.

"I see you have some journalism experience, but there's a gap ... several years, in fact ... between your last job and the one prior."

I nodded.

"Were you working on other publishing efforts, perhaps some freelancing? Or did you return to school?" he asked, flipping the page—again—to see whether a list of published works or academic degrees beyond my B.A. had presented themselves.

I shook my head, and Mr. Bronson stopped staring at the resume to stare at me instead.

"I've returned to journalism ..." I began.

"Why did you stop?"

"I couldn't get a job when I first came to New York, and I ..."

"You ...?" he prompted after I stalled.

"I quit to work at Starbucks."

He cleared this throat. "I'm confused. You are applying for a job as an assistant editor. At any of our publications that requires a minimum of five years experience, and preferably, a master's degree. You don't have either."

I nodded.

"I think it goes without saying we're looking for someone on a clear career trajectory."

I nodded again. He sighed. He was annoyed. I got it; I was sort of annoyed, too—he's the one who agreed to interview me. Maybe I should have declined an interview for a job I had no shot at. And now we were both stuck with staring at each other from across the conference table, which was also shiny.

The digital clock next to the untouched water tray showed five minutes had passed since I arrived. I didn't want this job, but it seemed rude to leave now. Mr. Bronson was not going to offer me this job, but he wasn't rude enough to throw me out so soon. But as much as I didn't want to write for this shiny place that didn't want me, I didn't want my first interview of the week to leave no survivors.

I continued the conversation.

"I'm sorry, Mr. Bronson. A friend of a friend arranged this interview—maybe a friend of a friend of a friend. I'm not sure how many degrees of separation there are here. You're right; my resume is not the resume of the person you will probably hire."

I'd wielded this honesty as a preamble, but he nodded and stood like it was my closing argument.

I proceeded.

"But just because I don't meet the minimum requirements doesn't mean I can't do this job well. You're hiring for an assistant editor for *Brides* and that's been my writing focus for the last six months."

That seemed like news to him, and he looked back down to scan the wedding beat portion of my resume.

"I see you established a social media presence and gained a bit of a following, but the numbers aren't significant," he pointed out.

"They are if you scale it to my platform: small paper, small town. Also, I wasn't at it for long before I moved back here. I know you're busy, but we still have thirty-five minutes left in this interview. Would you read some of what I wrote instead?"

Mr. Bronson stared at me, and breathless moment on my end passed before he nodded and said, "I'll give you ten."

He flipped to the articles I'd included in my portfolio, but on a whim I pulled out my cell and opened *Creeking*. The last blog entry was dated November 23, the day before Fest. Two weeks before Grandma Pat died. I dislodged the lump in my throat with a light cough and forged ahead.

"Look at my blog instead. It contains links to my wedding features if you want to read those, but these entries are worth your time."

I handed him my phone and stared at my folded hands, sneaking peeks at Mr. Bronson's face as ten minutes turned to twenty turned to thirty. He looked up after the receptionist returned to the conference room to remind him of his next appointment.

He handed back my phone and stood. "Showing me the blog was the right move. Your features are fine, but your blog writing makes me consider your application … but not for this position. Let me check a couple of things, and I'll get back to you."

And before I could parse that information, I was down the elevator and back into the cold, left with the rest of the day to obsess.

"How did the interview go?" Nana asked when I called her from the stone bench later that afternoon.

"Strange," I said and relayed to her the proceedings.

"What do you have scheduled for the rest of the week?" Nana's not one for external processing.

"One interview each day, all less prestigious, which is good because I don't have enough interview clothes. I'll wear jeans to the last couple."

Grandma Pat would have laughed, but Nana met my lame joke with silence, and we hung up. It was a little before four-thirty. John had texted earlier to say he wouldn't be home until eight o'clock. I'd already gone to the library and walked my circuit, but I didn't want to sit here and stare at my interview shoes for the next two hours.

Most churches aren't open on Mondays, so I was surprised when the front door opened at the push of my hand. The sanctuary was empty, but brighter than yesterday—the setting sun cross-stitching the pews in a rainbow of color.

"Just as their creator intended," I murmured, stepping forward to place my hand in one of the beams and twinkle my fingers to watch the patterns of gold, red, blue, and purple play on my skin.

"Hello, Lu!" Pastor Eddy's voice boomed from behind me.

I jumped. Anyone would have. His voice could carry in a crowd, and the empty stone and wood of this space amplified it.

"I didn't expect you to come in from the bench today," he continued.

"Well, my call ended early, and it was either come in here or …" I stopped, catching myself over what I was about to admit.

"Or?"

"Or stare at my shoes until dinner."

"You made the better choice. Follow me."

He turned down a small dark hallway off the entryway. His office was the last on the left, and it made me smile. It was like Jackson's second home—the stacks of old books bound in faded hardcovers, the loose paper covered in illegible scrawl. Doctors don't have anything on pastors. Plus there was half-eaten food everywhere, a risky maneuver given New York's cockroach population.

Eddy didn't excuse the sty; he made room for me by transplanting a precarious stack from an old chair to the floor with a resounding plop. In the face of such gallantry, how could I not take a seat—though the black vinyl upholstery was split down the middle and the stuffing looked as if it was about to explode like a jack-in-the-box.

Instead of sitting behind the desk, Eddy removed the random assortment of clutter from the chair adjacent to mine and took a seat.

"So why are you here?"

"I told you."

"Yes, the shoes. Why did you come Sunday? Why do you park yourself at our garden bench every day? There are plenty of benches all over the city."

"I first came in to take pictures of the stained glass …"

"There's plenty of that around the city, too."

This man's stamina for asking point-blank questions exceeded mine for answering them.

"You remind me of my grandma."

"You're not the first person to tell me that."

I laughed.

"Tell me about her."

I opened my mouth and then closed it, remembering. I shook my head, looked down, and swallowed. He didn't know, and this was the first time I would have to say it.

"She's dead," I said after a deep breath.

Eddy leaned forward, his elbow on his knees.

"Tell me about her," he repeated.

I don't know why, but I started with how Grandma insisted on dying her hair clown-nose red. I talked about how she observed everything and voiced her observations without reservation—pointing out my pimples at the dinner table, for instance. I realized midway through my stream of consciousness memories that talking about her was what I needed, and the stories tumbled out. I couldn't stop talking. I told Eddy about Grandma's man troubles, and drinking, and ditch, and Jesus. I talked about her work—the pierogies, the shop—and how she used it to help people. I told him about my last conversation with her before her surgery.

"Are you here because of her?" he asked.

Grandma Pat would want me here. She'd love Eddy. She'd love to hear this conversation. She'd make a great excuse, but then I thought about the Bible I'd packed, the pictures of stained glass I'd taken, the bench I'd sat on everyday. I thought about tracing verses from Ecclesiastes with my finger.

"No, I'm here because of me."

And then I told him that backstory, too, taking another hour of his time. I'm sure the man had other things to do, but I couldn't shut up, and he didn't seem to mind. The way he listened made my narration feel more like a conversation, which is the only reasonable explanation I could find for talking about myself for so long. I ended with my unanswered prayer for God to heal Grandma Pat.

A short silence followed, and I wondered what Eddy would say, if anything. But I couldn't leave without feedback.

"God is not a bank account, Lu."

"What do you mean?"

"I mean prayer is not a transaction. It's not a business deal. In exchange for your reluctant prayer, you expected God would do as you asked to prove his existence. In return, you would … what? Consider the idea that maybe God exists? And all because God did as you asked?"

That was enough to make me squirm, but he wasn't finished.

212

"Tell me this: Was Grandma Pat scared to die? Do you think she would have prayed for God to spare her from death?"

"No."

"What did your grandma pray for?"

I wasn't sure of how to answer, but then a memory of Grandma Pat appeared, of the time I'd questioned her about second chances outside of god.

Haven't I told you about the time Jesus found me in a ditch? she'd responded.

I'd doubted about whether she'd seen Jesus.

No one else could have rescued me from that ditch.

I'd argued she could have dragged herself out.

Sure, I could have crawled out of that ditch—once I could tell my head from my behind, that is. But it would only have been a matter of time until I fell into another.

I'd speculated on the nature of the ditch.

A ditch is a ditch.

"She prayed people would get some sense and believe in God," I said. "And she always wanted to help people, so I think she also prayed she could help others."

"Did she pray for you?"

I looked at him. I'd never thought about it before. But now that I did, I knew the answer.

CHAPTER 30

Did your grandma pray for you?

Pastor Eddy's question played on repeat as I stopped by a small deli on my way back to the apartment to pick up a loaf of French bread, a hunk of farmer's cheese, a roll of salami, and a jar of olives for dinner. It played in my mind as I opened the front door to the quiet apartment. I'd forgotten to close the blinds, and I stood for a moment, thinking, taking in the luminous skyline of the city at night.

I shut the door behind me, and leaned my head against it. Of course Grandma had prayed for me and not as a "transaction"—as Pastor Eddy had put it—but as an expression. Grandma prayed for me because she loved me.

My attempts at prayer for her felt cheap in comparison. I'd already known my prayers had little to do with God, but now I could also see my prayers had little to do with Grandma. I wanted to rewind time and pray for her from a simpler place. To pray for her because I loved her.

"I miss you," I whispered.

The loss of her prayers—the prayers I'd never given a thought to until a half hour ago—compounded my loneliness. Who was praying for me now? The answer felt suddenly, intensely important.

But I knew the answer. My family was praying for me. And they always had been. This knowledge didn't feel heavy, like it would have before. I'd always interpreted my family's faith as an expectation of me, and subsequent disappointment. But from my place by the closed door of this dark apartment far away from them, I could see it was their hope for me.

My family prayed for me because they loved me.

I slipped off my heels, not wanting any noise to disrupt my thoughts. I moved about the apartment, enjoying the solitude. I put the bread in the oven and cut salami while sucking the salt from an olive in the back my mouth before biting into the pulp. I threw the pit away and noticed a pad of paper and pen on the counter.

J,

You're praying for me, aren't you? Though I left, you're still praying. I know you are. I know you have been. I don't know why I couldn't see this before, but I see it now. Please don't stop.

I slipped the note in my purse and pulled out my phone. 8:03 p.m. John should be home any minute. I started to put the phone away when it rang.

"Hello?" I answered.

"Yes, Miss Sokolowski? This is Pat Bronson from Condé Nast."

"Oh ... hello."

"I spent a better part of the afternoon reading your blog, and I'd like to offer you a position, though different than what you interviewed for."

"I'm listening."

"I'd like for you to set up shop with us, similar to Creeking, but from the New York angle. Single girl returns to New York, making a living writing about other people's weddings ..."

Bronson's pitch sounded familiar. It was the one I'd described to Jackson on the eve of Creeking. I remember the day: my fear of starting something new, of writing about myself. I'd worked all day and gotten nowhere until Jackson smushed his face against the dirty window of The Daily. He took me home, made my family dinner, and afterwards, I pitched my idea.

Cuckolded single girl consigned to the wedding beat ... That's how I'd put it. But Jackson pushed back; he always did, pushing me to see more.

I don't think you've described the real you.

His response changed the whole nature of what I was about to do, and Creeking had become all about exploration—seeing people and situations from new angles and rediscovering myself as a writer. As a person.

Bronson's pitch was like my original—an angle to sell a story. But it wasn't my story now anymore than it was then. It was my circumstances, not me.

John walked in. I gave him a short wave before pointing to the phone. Turning to face the windows I caught my reflection and straightened my shoulders. I took a deep breath.

"Thank you for the offer, but I can't accept it, Mr. Bronson."

"You're telling me no?" He sounded incredulous. That made two of us.

Still, it was the right decision.

"I am."

"You do understand this is the only offer you will receive from us, Miss Sokolowski," he explained, like a teacher reciting basic arithmetic to a child.

"I do, Mr. Bronson."

"You understand my offer is off the table after this phone call?"

"I understand."

He hung up, and I exhaled and tossed the phone like a dirty rag on the table. I looked at John. He was in reverse mode from this morning: coat off, tie loosened, top button undone. Twelve hours hadn't dulled my reaction to these maneuvers. I moved closer.

"Who was that?" he asked.

"Condé Nast."

He raised his eyebrows. "And?"

"They offered me a job."

John produced a bottle of pinot noir from behind his back.

"I'm not sure whether this is in order."

"That depends on how you look at it. Is it a victory to turn down a good offer that's wrong for me?"

He poured the wine and handed me a glass.

"You're more courageous than me," he toasted before taking a sip.

My refusal had felt more like basic preservation. But if courageous was how John saw it, then ... well. I smiled at the thought and took a sip of wine.

"How was your day?"

"Kind of like you tossing that phone on the table, except for right now."

"The gourmet dinner?" I smiled.

He didn't smile back but looked at me. "You. The part of the day where I came home to you."

In my mind, I could see us putting our glasses down. Then we did. I almost closed my eyes at the nearness of him, but his gaze caught mine. Whatever had passed between us this morning was nothing compared to how John looked at me now, and I'd forgotten this sensation—what it's like to be the sole desire of another. I wanted him in the same measure. And we had nowhere to be.

He touched my shoulders and I moved closer. By the time his fingers trailed their way to my lower back, I was on fire. My hands found his chest, his lips found my neck. He lifted me on the counter and unzipped my dress at the same time I reached under his shirt, the heat of his skin under my fingers undoing me.

One button followed by one word brought me back to myself. My name, whispered by him, in my ear.

I pulled back, releasing my hands with a jolt. He stepped back, and I went to bed alone, knowing I had to get these thoughts out of my head or get myself out of this apartment. Or give in.

CHAPTER 31

"I can't believe you declined that job before you received another offer," Mom lectured me on the phone as I climbed up the subway station stairs on Friday to get to my last interview of the week. And of the foreseeable future.

I shouldn't have told her about it. My first time in New York, I'd barely talked to my family, checking in as an afterthought every few weeks. Now, in addition to talking to Nana Bea every afternoon, I called or texted at least one other family member everyday. I missed them. So I called them. And stuff about my life leaked out.

Dad had responded to my refusal of Condé Nast with a typical, "You can only do what you can do, kiddo." Nana equated "blogs" with "diaries." Why anyone would write down anything personal and publish it was beyond her comprehension. I think hers was a vote against.

Gracie came through, of course. When I'd texted her the news, she'd responded with *Condé Nasty*—a pun so uncharacteristic, so bad, I was still laughing about it on Friday.

And then there was Mom, the pragmatic.

"I'm not saying you should have taken it. I'm saying you need income."

"Isn't that saying the same thing?"

Her logic was almost as confusing as my directions to the interview, and I wasn't doing a good job of following either.

"What I'm trying to say is …" she paused.

Oh, I knew what she was trying to say. But my confusion over whether I should have turned right instead of left stopped me from hanging up before she said it.

"No man buys the cow when he gets the milk for free."

There it was. The 4-H sexual metaphor. She'd been trotting out this age-old goody since John and I'd first moved in together. I hoped she'd interpret my silence as a sign to drop this line of conversation, but she persisted.

"Are you sleeping with John?" she asked in hushed tones. Because all of Dunlap's Creek was listening?

"Not your business, Mom," and I hung up. It wasn't her business. It was mine. It was John's. And it was sort of Gracie's because I'd used her call the other night to excuse myself from watching TV with John on the couch. I had no idea what was on the TV because I'd been consumed with thoughts of making out with the man I'd slept with in my former life.

"I don't know what's wrong with me," I confessed to Gracie from behind the closed door in the bedroom. "I'm acting like a thirteen-year-old girl with her first boyfriend."

"You didn't have a boyfriend when you were thirteen."

"You're missing the point!" I whispered. "What am I going to do?"

"It's simple. You need to shit or get off the pot."

She was right of course, but good advice isn't always easy to follow, and I shoved it, and the conversation with Mom, to the back of my mind to focus on getting to my interview. The other interviews from this week hadn't run as awkwardly as Condé Nasty—not because the publications were any more impressed with my resume, but because I was more prepared for how they saw me. I was grateful to whoever from John's end had opened these doors for me, but by this morning, I'd decided no interview was better than a reluctant one.

Maybe that's why I was wearing my skirt from Virginia Stanley and had wrapped my hair to dry in a loose side braid instead of washing and diffusing it. I left the apartment feeling like myself, and this hadn't dimmed, despite being lost.

Eventually, I spied the right street. One more block, and I saw *NYNY* painted in lime green on a small, white square sign mounted to the blackened brick of a building that once housed a factory but was now home to *Not Your New York*: an ad-free, monthly lifestyle magazine for people living unexpected lives in the big city. People who lived outside the glitz and speed of New York. People who frequented restaurants they could get into on a Friday night. People who came to the city with hopes of a flashy job, but chose instead a job they liked. People who championed causes they cared about and lived lives they could afford. In short, if *The New York Times* or *Wall Street Journal* was publishing it, *NYNY* was not.

Out of all the publications I'd researched, *NYNY* was the most interesting. The pages were printed on thick paper stock with a matte finish. The vibrant photography of the people, places, and events was exquisite and transporting—like I'd been there, like I'd met the people from the photographs and could approach them if we crossed paths. The writing was descriptive. And persuasive: the recipes made me want to cook, and the book reviews always sent me to the library. One article on beekeeping in the city even made me contemplate that as my next career since this journalism thing didn't look promising.

Since *NYNY* didn't rely on advertising revenue, the circulation price for twelve months was no joke. But the magazine was going strong into its third year. Circulation was up, and now that I'd read through all the back issues, I was planning to pony up if I didn't get the job.

I pushed open the nondescript metal door, which led to a concrete and metal stairwell with four flights of steps that ended at another metal door. This opened to one massive, multithousand-square-foot room with open rafters and large windows that were more decorative than utilitarian. Not enough degrees separated this room from the winter outside, and I rubbed my hands along the goosebumps on my arms and looked down.

My eyes followed the holes and black markings where industrial machines used to stand. Dad would love this floor. He'd solve the problem of how to refinish it without erasing its history. And the floor could stand some refinishing. Because the floor wasn't shiny.

Nothing in here was. The desks, tables, and chairs pockmarking the space could have come straight from *The Daily's* office. I felt at ease. My skirt belonged here. Now if I could figure out where to present myself for the interview, I'd find out if I belonged here, too.

"Lu!" shouted a woman from across the room. She waved her arm above her head, and I walked her way, smiling at the people who looked up from their desks. They smiled back. How not Condé Nasty. How not New York.

I reached her desk, and she extended her hand, which was warm. I longed to wrap my other freezing hand around it.

"How are you so warm?" I blurted.

"Space heater." She retrieved it from under her desk and put it beside my chair. I sank next to it, holding my hands over the vents.

"We issue one to every new hire. Our building is quirky fifty-two weeks a year but comfortable for only four. In the summer, you'll exchange this for a fan. I'm Molly Frost, by the way—editor-in-chief of this little rag—and I'm glad to meet you. But honestly? I'm more excited to meet your skirt. The Instagram pictures don't do it justice."

"I'm not much of a photographer."

"Good thing I'm hiring you to write instead."

Thus began my second strange interview of the week—the one in which I interviewed for a job I already had. The one in which I would have said yes without the interview.

Because I didn't care what the job entailed; I felt more at home in this drafty space than since I'd left mine. But the job was great, too. Molly enjoyed my wedding writing, but it was my call on whether to continue in that vein. New York was full of single people who'd like to read about something else. She had a list of story ideas I could start with, but I could pitch my own ideas, too.

I also didn't care what the job paid, which is good because it barely paid anything.

"I'll have to get a second job," I concluded to John as we sat down to dinner later. He'd been unpacking groceries when I got home around seven o'clock, and I was too busy babbling about my new job to be of any help, which is why we were dining at nine o'clock. John, ever the gentleman, handed me first pickings of his homemade marinara and meatballs.

"It sounds great, Lu, and I don't want to start a fight, but you don't need to get a second job."

I'd died on many mountains in our relationship, and paying my way was Everest. It's why we couldn't move from our Harlem studio to a place like this; it's why I never sanctioned an espresso machine like the one on the counter. If I couldn't pay half, we weren't doing it.

I didn't want to revive that Lu, but our living situation was more complicated than before. He was already waiting on me. I didn't want him to pay for everything while I figured out how to make a living on top of figuring out what do about us.

"John, even my parents made me pay rent."

He laughed. "How much?"

"Two hundred a month, which included groceries, but I can help out there. *NYNY* will pay meals whenever I do restaurant reviews. Catch is, you'll have to share what I eat."

"I'm not too proud to share your dinner and let you pay for it. Are you too proud to share my apartment and let me pay for it?"

He didn't mean for it to come out like that, and I should have ignored it, but I didn't. I put my fork down.

"That was smooth."

"What?"

"Your argument."

"I wasn't arguing."

I looked at him. I wasn't going to fight, but I wasn't going to agree. John put his fork down and looked at me.

"I was arguing," he said a few seconds later. "I've been arguing all day and forgot to check it at the door. Sorry."

I saw it then. I'd been so surprised by John's return and then unnerved in being around him again I hadn't noticed the lines around his eyes, the gray in his hair. He'd lost weight, and his fatigue seemed deeper than too many nights sleeping on the couch. Deeper than my leaving.

"What I should have said," he continued, "was I don't want you feeling like you have to pay me for anything. I'm not expecting it. I want you to enjoy this job and have the space to do it well. That will be hard if you're pulling double shifts, right?"

I nodded. I picked up my fork, expecting we'd leave this conversation. But John wasn't done.

"What are you really trying to say, Lu?"

What do you mean? I almost asked, but it was a dumb deflection to a gutsy question. John knew I was independent. It's ridiculous, but him making me coffee every morning was a big deal. For me. But I knew John's question wasn't about my self-sufficiency. It was about us.

John didn't wait for my answer.

"You met someone else."

I looked up.

"How did you know?"

"I just did. People just do," he said with a slight shrug.

"I didn't," I said, alluding to him and Avery.

"That's because you're …"

"Emotionally obtuse?"

"Trusting. Plus, you're doing a good job of not letting me come anywhere near you."

John and I had never not had a physical relationship. Whatever our problems, intimacy had not been one of them until … the few weeks before he'd told me he'd cheated on me. How had I not noticed that? It explained why he saw there was more to my distance now, though.

"It's not like you think, John. We were friends. He's a pastor …"

"Is that why you're going to church now?"

"No." I swallowed. "I am going to church for me."

Neither of us had any follow-up to that admission, so we each turned to the now lukewarm pasta. I wasn't hungry, but I forced three bites down before breaking the silence with a question that risked taking this conversation from bad to worse.

"John, don't you ever wonder if there's something beyond here? If we make too much of who we are and what we do when we could be making much of something else?"

"Like what?"

"Like God."

A pause. A pause where I'm pretty sure John was channeling all his energy into maintaining a poker face.

"Is that what your pastor boyfriend told you?"

"Friend," I said, keeping my voice level. "He's my friend or at least he was until I decided to come back here. I sort of burned that bridge."

"Why would you have to burn a bridge with a friend to come back to New York with me?"

That sealed it. This was my worst interview of the week, though I wasn't sure what we were talking about anymore. I wanted to leave the table, but I looked at John again. He wasn't wrong for wanting to know.

"He was my friend. But I liked him. I like him. I still think about him."

The sentences felt insufficient, even to my ears, but they were all I could say out loud about Jackson. And faith.

CHAPTER 32

"Do you have any books I can read about God?" I asked Pastor Eddy after the congregation dispersed from Sunday's service.

"Other than the book I preached from today?"

"I'd prefer a book I can understand."

His sermon had continued with the first chapter of Mark, a passage about John the Baptist. I'd been so primed to receive something about God, but I didn't find any answers. If someone clothed in camel's hair and eating wild locusts, like John the Baptist, told me to repent and be baptized, I'd run the other way. I didn't want to run away anymore, but I needed something to run toward.

"Wait here," he said.

He came back five minutes later with a teetering stack of books almost as tall as him.

"You live close?"

I nodded, thinking he was offering to carry them for me, but he dumped the stack my way with a grunt.

"One would do," I muttered as I shifted my arms to accommodate the books for my ecclesiastical walk of shame back to the apartment.

"Don't give up," Pastor Eddy called as I headed out the door.

I inclined my head to my armful of evidence to the contrary.

"On the Bible," he clarified. "Those books in your arms contain some smart words. But they aren't God's words."

Having no spare hands, I kicked on the front door of the

apartment with my foot. John greeted me with the look I'd anticipated before he took some books off my hands like one might take a baby with a poopy diaper.

"What are these?"

"Not cockroaches," I said, responding to his disdainful tone. "But they might turn out as insidious, so watch out."

John set the books on an end table and resumed his spot on the couch to read the Sunday paper. He wasn't ignoring me, but doing his best to move past Friday's discussion, which had followed with a very polite, very quiet Saturday. It was our familiar pattern of civilized, unresolved conflict, but I couldn't do it anymore.

"John," I said, sitting on the coffee table. I touched his knee, and he put down his paper. This scene, more than any of our kisses, felt the most intimate, and I put my other hand on his other knee without thinking. He covered my hands with his and leaned toward me.

"I am sorry—about a lot of things—but I should have told you about ..." Jackson's name stuck in my throat. I took another breath and looked again at John. "I should have told you about Jackson. We were friends. Technically. But it feels like a different thing entirely, and it's not over for me."

"This is my fault ..." He started, but I silenced him by putting a finger to his lips.

"No. Whoever that was—that Lu who left here six months ago—isn't me anymore. I don't want her back, but that doesn't mean I know who I am now. I know I'm different. The old me wouldn't have admitted I was looking for anything more than a new situation. I see things differently now."

"And church, those books ..."

"Are part of the search," I finished. "No answers yet."

I moved from the coffee table to sit next to John on the couch, my knee resting against his thigh. Now that I started touching him, I couldn't seem to stop.

"What about you?" I asked.

"What about me?"

He was deflecting, and I understood. John and I operated at the same emotional level, but I wasn't going to let him get away with silence. I touched the evidence behind my question—the gray hair infiltrating the dark brown at his temples.

He captured my hand and leaned back against the couch. "Are

226

you saying I look old?"

I smiled. John was the master of self-control; the man wasn't going to say anything he didn't want to say. I waited as he stared at my hand in his. If he wanted it to stay there, he needed to speak. When he did, I think it was because a conflict within him broke.

"My life was predetermined. You know my background, my parents. It's not that I never had a say in the schools and career chosen for me, it's that I never questioned the plan. I went for it. And I've achieved it all—everything they wanted for me, everything I wanted for myself, everything you and I talked about when we were first together. This city, this firm, this job—none of it was easy, none of it a given—all of it, I've worked for."

"And?"

He looked up from his lap, his blue eyes reading so honest it was almost too painful to hold their gaze "And it's nothing, Lu. But I didn't realize that until you'd left. I chased this, but I lost you. And I think I've lost myself somewhere, too. I'm starting to see how the work I've chosen will demand more of me, and I'm not sure whether I can get the parts I've already lost back. You're not the only one here asking the bigger questions. I'm not looking to the guy who wrote *Narnia* for my answers."

"What are you talking about?"

John took the top book from my stack: *Mere Christianity* by C.S. Lewis.

"This is the guy who wrote The Chronicles of Narnia series, the children's books about the lion. I never read them."

"But you know about them."

"Which is why I'll always dominate you in the crossword," he finished, leaning toward me, smiling.

I rolled my eyes and pushed him back against the couch. "Leave it to you to remind me you're smarter."

"But you like my brain."

He pulled me back with him. I straddled his lap and put my hands on either side of his face, telling myself I was content to just look at him. I didn't have to conjure details like I had in the past six months—the clarity of his blue eyes, the square of his face. I could touch him. I spread my fingers along his jawline and down his neck to his collarbone. The hollow there undid me. John was like a whirlpool for me. Always had been. I needed a new word for starved.

I kissed him and had no intention of stopping. It was John who pulled back. He put his hands on my shoulders and looked at me.

"Do you want to be with me?"

One nod would stop this conversation. I almost did when he asked another.

"Only me?"

I closed my eyes and sighed. "John ..."

He squeezed my shoulders. "Look at me."

I didn't want to. I felt horrible, and John must have felt it because he moved his hands to either side of my face as I'd done with his. I opened my eyes, and my tears slid down my cheeks to his fingers. He wiped them away and didn't say anything for a minute.

"I'm not interested in kissing you if there's a chance you'll see someone else when you close your eyes. Trust me when I tell you it's not worth it."

I tried to pull away, but the longing in his eyes and the steadiness of his hands kept me there.

"But Lu, this one's on me, not you. I intend to use everything I have at my disposal to remind you of how you feel about me."

He kissed me quickly and pointed to the opposite side of the couch. "Now go sit there before I change my mind."

I nodded, touching his cheek before extricating myself as instructed. What to do now, though? John opened his paper, and I opened the C.S. Lewis book. My heart was still racing, and I wondered how long I was going to survive this scenario. John was no harmless roommate, but re-reading the prologue of *Mere Christianity* about a dozen times eventually buffered his effect on me. There's nothing like a complex argument on human nature to kill the urge to do anything other than bang your head against a brick wall.

I picked up the next book, written by an archaeologist, and the next, written by a historian. The stack had fourteen books, written by all types—scholars, pastors and scientists. None of them checked their brains at the door of belief. In fact, they seemed to bring the full force of their professional training to argue for faith. Each took a different angle—the journalists investigated, the rhetoricians argued, the historians researched—but they all landed in the same place. God exists. The Bible is true. Jesus is real.

My mind was full, and I'm not sure how well I slept on the eve of my big-girl job. How long had it been since I'd worked a job I'd proudly claim? *Creeking* didn't count, given its affiliation with RJ and *The Daily*. I started in on the math as I lay in bed, but I stopped when I realized I'd missed the mark in the all the previous journalism work previous. I'd used it, but never appreciated it. I'd worked hard, but always as a stepping stone to a more prestigious gig, as John had viewed law school as a stepping stone to a large firm. How often had we mused over where we'd move next? Where we'd work next?

And here we were: John working the plan, with nothing working out as intended, and me quitting the plan, with nothing working out as intended. John on the couch, me in the bed. It was horrible. I groaned, and then I laughed because what else could I do?

Get to my job, I suppose. I rolled out of bed.

I knew my job at *NYNY* wasn't going to fix my life; no job could. But yesterday's reading had opened my mind to what a job could—specifically, what a person could do with one. A person could do good. Grandma Pat had helped Virginia Stanley through Penny Thrift. A person could create beauty, like Ted with his wood carvings. A person could defend faith, like C.S. Lewis.

Writing about the possibility of work—not as an answer, but as a tool—seemed like the right place to start my job at *NYNY*. Surely New York was filled with people doing this.

"Of course there are," Molly said when I pitched the idea to her before lunch on my first day. "And only the big-timers receive press. If you come up with something good, we'll make it a feature. I'll give you some names to start."

I was about to ask about her plans for lunch when a familiar but forgotten smell turned my head. There was John, standing right behind me. My eyes widened, more at the paper bag in hands, which held the source of the fragrance.

"Is that ..." I was too excited to finish my sentence, and I yanked the bag from his hands to see inside for myself: two Gray's Papaya hot dogs loaded with everything.

"And did you ..."

He nodded, producing a paper cup of one of their papaya drinks, which mysteriously and perfectly pairs with greasy hot dogs.

"John," I whispered.

Where to start? Gray's is on the Upper West Side—nowhere

near his work or mine. He'd taken the better part of the morning to bring this to me, which was also his first visit to me at work. Ever. John was more of a send-the-flowers guy: make the call and pay for someone else to assemble and deliver. He doesn't do legwork. He doesn't take time. And he doesn't like hot dogs. He operates with the natural snobbishness of people raised in money. He'd barely tolerated my penchant for stopping at New York hot dog stands; he'd certainly never partaken.

And yet here he stood with a greasy bag for me. I looked at him with what can only be described as doe eyes. If I were writing about myself, I'd say I looked ridiculous.

He put his arm around me and kissed the top of my head before whispering in my ear. "I can't stay, but I'll be home with dinner by seven, okay?"

I nodded and waited to dig into the bag until after he'd left.

"What was that?" Molly asked as I shoved half a hot dog in my mouth.

"It's Gray's Papaya. You know ..."

She cut me short. "I'm aware of the hot dogs, Lu. They've been covered. What hasn't been written about is that man."

"Oh." I swallowed. "That's . . . that's John."

"That's all you have to say?"

I shrugged.

"Are you together?"

I shook my head.

"I think he wants to be," she said, nodding toward my bag as I sipped my papaya drink.

I nodded.

"But you're ... what? Unsure? Because men who look like him are walking all around New York, right? Men like him lining up to bring you hot dogs?"

I laughed, grateful I'd swallowed my drink so I didn't spit it out all over her desk on my first day of work. I knew how John looked in person and on paper —to everyone but my family. They'd never been fans, and their opinions were the only ones I suffered. I needed to shut down this conversation with Molly.

"It's complicated," I said, turning toward my desk.

"No, honey. It's simple. Unless you've got someone else bringing you hot dogs."

She said it with a laugh, and when I should have kept walking to my desk, I gave myself away by braking for half a second.

"You do have someone else bringing you hot dogs," she said, surprised by her own guesswork.

No. Donuts. Expired ones and piled high on a plate.

I put my half-eaten hot dog back in the bag and shook my head.

"And does he look like that?"

"No," I said like a knee-jerk, but wishing I'd kept my mouth shut because to give voice to Jackson was to give way to thought. He was nothing like John. John fit the definition of good-looking. Jackson fell outside those lines, but the effect on me was the same. More. To be in a room with Jackson was to note my proximity and close the gap at the earliest opportunity.

"Do I get to meet the other one?"

No.

"It's complicated," I repeated and headed back to my desk to get to work.

CHAPTER 33

As far as I was from Jackson and my pile of turd donuts, the next Sunday's sermon transported me back to summer. We were still in the first chapter of Mark, but how Pastor Eddy preached reminded me of Ecclesiastes, just with a different metaphor.

"Jesus came to us with the message that the kingdom of God is near, and his death and resurrection brought that kingdom to us. Within its gates lay your answers, your satisfaction, your identity ... all of it. Your search ends here because God is here.

"And the gate is open. But it's the only one, which means you have to stop trying to get here through any other way. You just have to walk through it. But you do have to walk through it."

From start to end, it was so familiar. I turned over the note card on which I'd underlined and circled all the parallels to write Jackson.

J,

In your last sermon in Dunlap's Creek, you said Jesus was the conclusion of the matter. But of every sermon? Pastor Eddy preached on the kingdom of God. Swap out some imagery, and it's your message on escape routes. I guess all my Sunday school answers of "Jesus" weren't far off the mark ...

"Still taking notes?" Eddy asked as I signed my name to yet another note I wouldn't send. I stood and put it in my purse.

"Your sermon reminded me of some sermons I listened to over the summer on Ecclesiastes."

"I didn't know anyone preached on Ecclesiastes."

I laughed. "That's what I kept telling the pastor. But your

sermon had similar themes. He argued there's a chase, and we're helpless to stop. You're saying there are kingdoms, and we're helpless to rule. Your conclusions are the same, too. He called Jesus the way out; you call him the open gate."

"The Bible is sixty-six books in one. Many stories to tell the bigger story that there's a way back to the God who loves us. This is why you see shadows of Ecclesiastes in Mark, and the conclusion is the same."

"Jesus," I answered.

He nodded.

"And what do the people here think about your message?" I asked, knowing how uncomfortable I'd felt about it back in Dunlap's Creek. New York City was another world, and when I'd first come, I felt like the answers it offered for my life were far more intelligent and sophisticated than the dogma I'd been raised in.

"For some New Yorkers, it's as you'd expect, but other people here are advancing the kingdom of God by using all the city has to offer."

That brought to mind my story for *NYNY*, and when I asked Eddy if he had any names, he looked over my shoulder. After a quick scan of the sanctuary, he led me by the elbow toward a blond woman with a bright smile and firm handshake.

"Lu, this is Emily James. She's a grad student at NYU and founded a company that funds college scholarships for women in Eastern Europe by distributing stationary featuring original artwork of those women. Emily, Lu is writing a story for *NYNY* about social entrepreneurship."

Eddy turned to other parishioners after this, but Emily was more than capable of leveraging his brief introduction to talk about her company, Flora. I was not as prepared to take notes, but improvised and helped myself to a mini-pencil and note cards from the pew pockets as if the church provided them for my journalistic endeavors.

I left church with an official interview schedule for the next morning, plus a handful of Flora stationary. Notecards, envelopes, and journals—all designed in different flowers of different watercolors. I sifted through them on my walk back to the apartment.

"Are you always going to come home from church with

233

goodies?" John asked, as he opened the door at the sound of my keys fumbling in the lock because my hands were balancing stationary too pretty to stow in my purse.

"So the books are growing on you?"

"This is a definite improvement, though I don't mind the books."

I looked at him.

"I'm trying not to mind, but it'd be better if you'd keep them in one pile instead of little piles all over the apartment," he amended.

"What would you do if I started leaving toothpaste marks on the sink?" I asked, referring to another fighting ground from former days.

He lifted my chin with his thumb, his forefinger caressing below my lip. "Then I'd know you were here to stay. So be careful where you leave that goop, or I might misinterpret your intentions."

I smiled, tempted to kiss him, but instead I took his hand, squeezing it before I let it go. "How about I tell you about church while you make me espresso?"

I followed him into the kitchen and settled into a barstool. John pulled shots like he'd been the one who worked at Starbucks, and I watched him from the island with my chin in my hand. He placed the small white cup in front of me.

"The pastor argued there's a deeper pursuit driving our life choices. A work under the work, so to speak. I assume you don't agree with his conclusion."

John leaned his weight against his folded arms. White T-shirt, morning shadow, and blue eyes looking straight into mine from across the island. "I think things are what they are, and it's our choice to make something of it. Or not. You?"

"It's been a good week; it's hard for me to admit there's something deeper at play when everything is going well. I would have been more prone to agree after I left New York or after Grandma Pat died."

"And now ..."

"Now the good circumstances feel like a camouflage. It feels like things are on the right track, but why do I think that? Because I got a job? Because I'm with you? I appreciate that life is good, but I don't trust it."

"Because you don't trust me?"

"It's not that. I don't trust I won't make too big a deal of it and set myself up for failure. When I returned to Dunlap's Creek, I made an effort to make a life, and for awhile ..."

I paused and looked down at my folded hands on the counter, remembering the fall. Fest. My grandmas and Gracie and the girls. *Creeking.* Jackson.

I'd built a life.

"It's more than I was happy," I said to John. "I was content, and in a way I've never been. And just when that feeling was becoming my normal, it fell apart."

"But that's life, Lu. That's going to happen."

"But what if that isn't the whole explanation?" I took my Bible and notes from the sermon out of my purse. "This book says my life is more than the sum of my circumstances. It says there's a hope independent of them, and it's a hope I can have."

I took a deep breath, not believing I was talking like this—and to John of all people. He was the one person in my life who wouldn't be thrilled with my turn of thought.

"What if Jesus is the answer?"

John stood up and leaned back against the fridge with his arms crossed over his chest.

"Do you think that?"

"I don't know. Until now, I've discounted it. But I think I've done this out of turn. There's a reasonableness here, John."

"And why does this matter so much to you?"

I closed my eyes and pressed my forehead against my fingertips, thinking. I'd asked a lot of questions and had a lot of conversations about God in Dunlap's Creek. But it hadn't mattered. Not really. I cared about what the people in my life cared about. I was curious to see things from their perspective, but I didn't buy it.

I was back to that platform again. Behind me, the circumstances were aligning—the job, the man, the place. Combined, they even validated my running away from Dunlap's Creek. But what if I still found myself chasing?

There's a way out of the chase, Jackson would say, but you have to take it. The gate is open for you, Eddy would say, but you have to walk through it. The narrowness of the answer didn't chafe, but it seemed too easy. Not simplistic, but too light, too unsteady—to hold all of me. My baggage. My failings. My emotions, which now brimmed to the surface.

I wiped the tears from my eyes, pulling my mind from this deeper wrestling back to John's question. Why did this matter to me? I looked at John from across the bar.

"It matters because if there's an answer out of the hurt like last time, or an answer that makes sense of it, I'll take it."

John came around to my side of the bar and leaned down to where I was sitting, holding my face with his hands. I thought he was going to kiss me, but he said, "Like when I cheated on you."

It's amazing what eyes tell you. His were heavy, filled with regret over his part in what had happened to us. But difficult as that had been, it paled to the pain I'd been referring to.

"No, John. Like when I left Dunlap's Creek to come back here with you."

CHAPTER 34

My admission, which seemed to draw me closer to the root of my search, distanced me from John. He'd released my face as gently as he'd taken it, and we'd quietly gone about the rest of our day, not in the Cold War silence of the past weekend, but in a cautious two-step.

Of course, John was an old dance partner. So much of him was familiar—the disparity of our height as I stepped up to him, the match of his stare against mine, the certainty with which his right hand grasped mine while his left wrapped around my waist. But where did we step now?

My sudden return to New York hadn't meant a sudden return to us. I think John assumed our dance would look like a lot of apologies and reparations on his end. But, I'd forgiven him, and there was a part of me that wanted to be with him, no reparations required.

But I was about ten questions from the question of us. Now that we both realized it, we each took a step back. But just a step. For the first time on my end, there was plenty of work to allow this to happen naturally over the next several weeks. We both left the apartment early, put in long days, and ended most evenings working next to each other at the dining room table.

It reminded me of our early days—me at the paper, him in law school. Working side-by-side with someone gives a sense of mutual purpose, and this proximity also helped me see I wasn't the only one who'd changed. John had always been focused, working so intently his surroundings faded away, including me. The work now took over John in a new way, and he became irritable in moments, like he couldn't control what the job demanded of him.

My work had the opposite effect on me. It energized me so much that my short nights and long days felt more like a preference than an assignment. And it grounded me in this place independent of John. As introverts, we'd had slim needs for social interaction outside of each other before, but my time in Dunlap's Creek had changed me. I would never be the girl to throw myself in the thick of it, but I missed people, which I think is why I interviewed every person Molly and Eddy recommended for my story. Talking with these people about something that was of great meaning to them felt like an unexpected gift.

And their stories of why and how carried the same effect as when I'd shadowed Virginia Stanley or traced my fingers along Ted's engravings. It was both motivating and humbling. I marveled at each entrepreneur's ability to build an idea into a platform benefitting other people. I didn't have that quality. How had I put it to RJ when he asked me to organize Fest? I'm not the type of girl to do big things.

But I am the type of girl to write, and I was happy to use my gift to shine a light on the work of other people's hands. When it was finished, I could see my story was a found thing. The entrepreneurs had created it—the characters, the plot, the resolution. I was the girl who got to write about it, which I tried to do as sparely as possible. I approached it like a field journal, careful to offer the elements in their truest form with as little Lu in the way as possible.

I wasn't surprised the piece ranked as a feature, but when Molly pushed it back to April so it could run as the cover feature? I might have jumped and clapped my hands. In front of Molly. I might have spent my lunch hour calling each member of my family and not letting them hang up until they expressed the right degree of enthusiasm. I might have left work early that afternoon to go to John's office and ask him to dinner.

I hadn't visited his office since my return, but I should have remembered a costume change. It was a rainy spring day, inviting my light yellow rain jacket, unbelted and open over a loose white blouse and cropped, fitted jeans with holes—the type Grandma Pat would have stolen from my closet and Nana Bea would burn. It suited my work home better than the hushed expanse of John's lobby with its row of gilded elevators that led to quieter hallways with carpet so plush it made for walking around in my heeled gray booties a bit tricky. I had the foresight to check with the receptionist before tracking the halls. Sure enough, John had moved up in the world.

"Two windows," I whistled from outside his larger digs.

I hadn't paused long enough in my victory adrenaline to wonder how John would feel about my midday interruption, but the smile he gave me from his side of the desk put me at ease. It was one of unguarded pleasure. Or maybe that's how it made me feel. "I'd have changed into something fancier if I'd known."

He leaned back in his chair and pressed his fingertips together as he took his time looking me up, looking me down. His eyes returned to my face, and he smiled again. "You look great."

I returned his smile and leaned my shoulder against the doorframe. "I've always felt a little out of place in your world," I confessed.

"Really? I had no idea."

We laughed, and I took a seat on the other side of his desk.

"What brings you in, Lu?" he asked.

"Just the fact that I'm all big-time now," I pronounced before gushing to him all the details of the feature—publish date, page count, pictures. The excitement on his face matched my tone, and by the time I wrapped my little tale, John came around to lift me out of the chair and hold me against him in some uncharacteristic lawyer behavior.

After he set me back down, his hands stayed on my waist, mine on his shoulders.

"Can I take you to dinner?" I asked.

He smiled in what I assumed was a precursor to an affirmative, but then his whole body tensed like we were balanced on a wire. I followed the direction of his focus, and there in the doorway stood the loveliest woman I've ever seen outside of a magazine. Brown hair, like mine, but the shinier, straighter, longer version. Tall, like me, but with additional inches that added a glamorous edge. Shoulders back, eyes steady: the woman had poise. She was standing still, but I could tell she was the type to turn heads when she walked. And I could see in her blue eyes that she knew it.

I knew who she was before John acknowledged her.

"Avery."

I intended to introduce myself to the woman John had cheated on me with. I tried to step forward, but his hands tightened around my waist like a safety belt. All I could do was stand there, mute, as they talked lawyer. Avery handed him a manila envelope and left without acknowledging me.

Only then did John release me. He threw the folder on his desk and turned toward his two windows, running his hands through his hair before looking back to me.

"I'm sorry."

I knew he was apologizing for cheating all over again, but we'd covered that ground, and I wanted to let it lie. I picked up where we left off.

"Dinner?"

He looked baffled at my response. "So I can feel like a complete heel?"

"That's sort of the idea."

I didn't get a smile. I continued, thinking what I couldn't address head-on right now, I could make light of. "We don't have to talk about her, but I will say you could have cheated on me with someone a little less perfect."

He looked at me before crossing the room to close the door. He turned toward me, his hands in his pockets.

"You look perfect to me. As you are now, or barefoot like on the day you returned from your grandma's funeral, or in a red dress like the night I first met you. I'm sorry I've never told you how these details affect me, but I notice all of them. I respect that you don't want to talk about Avery—I don't want to, either—but please know I have no words to describe the joy I felt at your standing in the doorway and how Avery standing here was the opposite. I am sorry you had to see her. I'm sorry I ever cheated on you."

I walked to him.

"People mess up, John."

"Not me. Not like this."

"Yes, you. And yes, like this." I put my hand on his arm. "At some point, you are going to have to forgive yourself."

He nodded and opened the door. "You seem to be handling this well."

In the midst of his own turmoil, John observed the one thing I wish he hadn't—the one thing that nagged me about it all. Seeing Avery was too surreal to understand in the moment, but after the shock left by midafternoon, I expected reality to land like pain or jealousy. I walked the streets around our apartment like I'd done when I first returned to New York, combing through every detail. But by five o'clock, objectivity still reigned.

So I did what any girl sitting on her stone bench outside of a church would do. I called my girlfriend.

"Do you remember the Sunday Kate came to church?"

"Who's Kate?" Gracie asked before something that sounded like a bomb exploded on her end.

"What was that?"

"I don't know, and I'm going to hide in my closet so I don't have to find out."

I heard her footsteps gallop up the stairs, the sound of her bedroom door open and close, followed by the closet door.

"Okay, I'm ready," she whispered.

"Kate is Jackson's ex-wife," I whispered back.

"I don't remember her coming to church. Why are you asking?"

I relayed the nitty-gritty of my Avery encounter.

"She can't be that pretty," Gracie said after I finished.

"Trust me."

"It's not like you to compare yourself to other girls."

"That's the thing. I'm not. When Kate came back, I not only noted every detail, I felt every detail. Even the shade of her pink lip gloss seemed like an affront to mine. It's been months, and I still remember every detail and how it felt to sit in the same space with her."

"It seems like you've done the same with Avery."

"Noted every detail? Of course. It's not everyday you get to meet the supermodel your ex-boyfriend cheated on you with."

"So what's your point?"

I'd called Gracie so she could get me to this—to force me to label what was simmering. But now I wanted to avoid it. I stood up, walked around the bench, and sat back down. I wished Gracie was here instead of on the other side of this blasted phone. I needed to say this to her as we huddled in the same closet, hiding from whatever experiments her girls were concocting to blow up the house.

I looked up from my shoes and imagined Gracie in my line of

vision instead of the worn limestone of the church.

"My point is I don't care. I'm not saying I don't care that John cheated on me or that he could change his mind now and walk off into the sunset with Avery, but I don't ... I don't care."

"And Kate?" she asked after a minute.

"I still very much care."

We sat on that, me staring at the imaginary Gracie while the real one plotted a gracious response that wouldn't feel like a slap in my face.

"You've got yourself in a pickle, Lu."

I laughed at the Grandma Pat expression. "Am I also up a crick without a paddle?"

"That goes without saying, but you're not the only one."

"Why? What's going on?"

"I pee every time I sneeze, and we're about to enter the spring allergy season and my third trimester, so it's going to get worse."

I laughed again, wishing I could wrap my arms around Gracie and lay my head on her shoulder. Instead, I said, "Tell me about it," and I slipped off my booties to sit cross-legged on my stone bench and listen to my friend's tales of girls, Ted, and Dunlap's Creek.

CHAPTER 35

I'm not sure whether the Sunday in late March when my story hit the stands dawned bright because I rose before the sun, but I heard the melody of birds—or its New York equivalent, the cluck of pigeons. I took it as a good sign.

I pulled a sweatshirt over my pajamas and slipped out of the apartment to the newsstand a block away from our apartment. *NYNY* wasn't prominent in the cluster, but since I had an idea of what I was looking for, I spotted it from a distance and exerted every ounce of self-control to walk slowly and calmly like a normal person and hand over my $15. Since I wasn't far from church, I waited until I was settled on my cold stone bench before turning the copy around.

The cover photo was so sharp, the colors so vivid—they put me back in the moment. I ran my hand along the title, *The Work of Their Hands* and turned straight to page sixty-two. There it was: a beautiful spread featuring a panorama of Flora stationary with the two founders blurred in the background.

Big ideas don't always begin in big spaces. Sometimes they're founded in a brainstorm between two girls sitting on a dorm-room floor. Or in woman's mind as she stirs pasta in a boiling stockpot in the galley kitchen of her one-bedroom apartment.

"This is too much for me," she thinks. And then she thinks about the people in her neighborhood who have no concept of "too much." Her thought moves to action, and she removes two plates from the cupboard.

That's how an empty belly is filled.

I'd written it, but I felt like I was reading it for the first time. I had no words for how it felt to turn the pages of this story—like both a long time coming and completely undeserved.

"Thank you," I whispered. Then I thought about Grandma Pat and smiled as I tried to guess the Post-Its of feedback she'd generate.

"You're early," said Pastor Eddy from behind me.

I showed him the magazine, and though I'm sure Eddy's prechurch preliminaries didn't involve reading periodicals, he took it and sat next to me. He looked up five minutes later—not because he skimmed, surely.

"I was thinking how great a subject Grandma Pat would make for this article," I said. "She'd like this trend of people's work reflecting their beliefs, though not everyone I interviewed believes in God."

"The help looks the same on the outside, but it's not. Your grandma used what God gave her to answer surface needs, but not without sharing the news that answers the deeper need we all have for salvation."

I closed the magazine and laid it on my lap, looking at Eddy. I knew he needed to be on his way. So did I, unless I wanted to go to church in my jammies. But I wanted to put words to something that had been nagging me the two months I'd been here.

"I've read and re-read all the books you've given me. I feel like I've taken enough notes to write my own book. I've come here every Sunday, and ..."

"And what?"

"And I get it." I pointed to my head. "I can acknowledge it to the point I'm willing to argue for it. Sometimes I feel like this is the only way, and other times it seems like one of many."

"You see the point but not the need?"

I nodded.

"Remember what I said in that first sermon—not to make Jesus into less than what He was. He came here to do one thing: become the way back to God by dying for us. You can't acknowledge he did that and still argue it wasn't necessary."

"Why?"

"Because the gospel is only a rescue for those who take it. To everyone else, it's a death knell. Stop reading the books. You've gotten all you need there. Look at yourself."

CHAPTER 36

By the beginning of April, trees were blooming, and my time was up.

John hadn't set a deadline for my decision, and the encounter with Avery and my questions about faith and feelings for Jackson extended it, if it had ever existed. All that stopped me from being his girlfriend opened my eyes to John in another way. We were friends and helped each other in ways we'd never done as a couple. He used to stumble into the shower at the last possible minute every morning and leave for work without a word. Now, he'd follow his alarm each morning by setting out coffee and a banana for me. It was small, big thing. I used to shove my nose in a book as soon as I returned home from work, barely looking up when he came through the door. Now, we assembled dinner together and talked long after about everything. I could appreciate his nearness without being overwhelmed by it. I could admire the focus he gave his work instead of being jealous it wasn't directed on me.

He wanted to direct his focus to me, though—at least more than I was allowing. The opening was there, but every time I wanted to return the look and reach out for him or turn the conversation, I remembered ours. *I'm not interested in kissing you if there's still a chance you'll see someone else when you close your eyes. Trust me when I tell you it's not worth it.*

If only the visions behind my closed eyes were consistent. I willed them to be. I lectured them to be—Jackson doesn't want to be with you; John does, and you want to be with him. I did. My body hummed when he was in the room, and as the days went on, that room was getting smaller, cornering me to a decision.

Even my mom felt badly for the guy.

"You need to move on with John or move out," she told me after work one evening.

I nodded but didn't answer. I was sitting on my bench, appreciating how sitting here no longer felt like a punishment, but more like the best way to cap a good day. The pleasant weather had something to do with this, and I appreciated how the longer days and warmer weather were waking the garden to life. Arching over the entryway was a thin tree with delicate intertwining branches spotted in red buds. It reminded me of a tree next to my parents' deck, which reminded me of the large maple in the backyard. And my tire swing.

"Hey, kiddo," Dad said. I guess Mom had handed the phone to him since she was making no headway with me.

"Is my tire swing still up?" I asked.

"Sure is. And you're welcome to it anytime. You're welcome home anytime."

I sighed.

"New York is my home, Dad. And it's a good home. I have a good job, a good church. John's great..." I stopped listing the evidence, wondering whom I was trying to convince.

"I understand, but you're welcome home anytime," he repeated.

"What's for me there?"

"I don't know, but I want you to know you can come back. Mom wants you to come back. Nana wants you to come back."

"She's one to talk."

He laughed. "You're both stubborn. I love you, kiddo, and I want you to come back, too."

I sat on the bench awhile longer, measuring what he'd said against all that anchored me in New York. I'd always assumed if everything lined up, my restlessness would quit. I had a good job and a good man, but I was still a flight risk. I could feel it.

I think this was why I agreed to go with John to a firm party that Friday night. He'd gone solo to several engagements since I'd been back, but for some reason he asked me to this one.

I took Friday off and bought a new dress—black, since it was a firm party, simple, since it's me, but fitted in places John would appreciate. I hadn't cut my hair for over a year, and I scheduled an appointment to shape that, too.

I was finishing my makeup when I heard John come home. *Make this work*, I pleaded with my reflection. *You will make this work.*

John was heading to the kitchen counter to drop his wallet and keys, but stopped when he saw me. We looked at each other for a long time, neither of us moving. I'd walked a tense wire the last couple months, wanting to do right by the man who was working so hard to do right by me. I couldn't think of what he looked like under that shirt without taking it off, and I didn't want to take it off unless I was certain.

I took it off with my eyes now. Then, I stepped toward him. An invitation. He crossed the room and didn't stop until my back was against the wall. He didn't put his hands on me, but on either side of me, leaning in. Waiting.

It was my move. I looked into his eyes and kept them there. My hands didn't need help to navigate his shirt off, one button at a time. After I undid the last one, I pulled him to me, and John took over from there, as he had so many times in the past. But those times were nothing like this. We never made it to the bed because we never made it to the bedroom.

And it worked. The intensity, the passion was there.

But his wasn't the reflection I'd been pleading with.

"We need to go," I said, bracing my forearms on his chest to get up.

"Do we?"

John rolled me onto my back, burying his face in my neck. The weight of him, the smell of him. Everything about this situation was perfect except the girl in it. Thankfully, the firm party wasn't the kind of thing John could miss. I showered first, and just finished reapplying my makeup when I heard my cell ring on the kitchen counter.

Gracie.

"You have a sixth sense," I said.

"What do you mean?"

I wasn't going to tell her the whole truth, not now at any rate. "I mean I'm heading out on my first official date with John since I've been back."

"That's great, Lu."

Her response wiped the smile from my face. I'd intended to tell her how this first date would be our only, and I'd be moving out.

But her tone was all wrong. Too cheerful, even for Gracie.

"What's going on?" I asked. "Why did you call me?"

"I debated on whether to call you, but it doesn't matter now."

"Tell me."

"It might ruin your date."

"Tell me anyway."

"Tomorrow."

"Tell me now."

"Why?"

She knew I knew. I knew I knew. But I needed to hear it anyway.

"Because I need to hear the words, and I wouldn't want to hear them from anyone else."

"Jackson's dating someone," she said.

I closed my eyes at the sound of his name. Gracie went on to say more, but I couldn't move past his name. I kept breathing it in my mind. Aside from my one conversation with Gracie about Kate, the topic had been off limits with my family. I would not bring him up, and they'd never broached it. Obviously, they saw him at church, and I assumed they talked to him and maybe still had him over to dinner. But no one said his name, and I never asked. Hearing it now was enough to set me reeling, reeling with the thought of him being with someone else, looking at someone else, smiling at someone else. Laughing.

"I have to go, Gracie."

She was still talking, but I hung up and turned the phone over in my hand. I wanted to smash it, but it wasn't the phone's fault. If this reality landed like a sucker punch, it was my own doing. I'd made the decision to leave and every decision since.

I turned from the window, looking where John and I had been a half hour ago. I loved that man. I could sleep with him a thousand times, and it could be great a thousand times, and it wouldn't change that I wanted him to be someone else. All it took was hearing Jackson's name one time for me to admit that. And what if ... what if when Jackson had asked me to stay I hadn't responded with a stupid question? What if I'd responded with myself? My eyes locked into his, my hands on him ...

I could redo the lot of it—John and I on this floor, Jackson and I in my room, and it wouldn't change a thing because neither of these men could fix me. It was more a question of how much I'd break them in the process.

At least I'd let Jackson go without too much residual harm. Three months, and he'd moved on.

I had no idea how I was going to leave John.

I spied my Bible on the island. I opened my Bible like it mattered. My marker was in the same place from last Sunday— Mark 5 and yet another story of yet another demon-possessed person. That was not going to help. My eyes flashed ahead, hoping, maybe praying, it would be the right one. It was about a dead girl Jesus raised to life. I flicked to the next page—about a bleeding woman who touches Jesus's cloak and is healed.

I skimmed them both. Again and again, my eyes circuited around the stories of the resurrected girl and the bleeding woman like a racetrack, but I felt nothing. Not one thing. I took the Bible to the bedroom, tossing it on the bed as John came out of the bathroom.

Can men be breathtaking? He dominated the room in his charcoal suit and light blue collared shirt, no tie. We looked the part. Now, I had to be the part. I smiled at John, walked over to him, and kissed him softly on the lips.

"Let's go."

CHAPTER 37

One firm party is like all the rest. They correspond each to the current holiday or season—this one probably had "spring" and maybe even "fling" somewhere in the title—but everyone still shows up in black with the same purpose: to drink and schmooze.

By the time John and I walked through the glittering entryway, people were well into the former, which made them believe they were accomplishing the latter. But really, it was just men leering and women laughing too loudly. Everyone talking; no one listening.

I don't like these events. Never had, and I'd stopped coming with John years ago. The parties hadn't changed—though I appreciated how the firm's massive flower budget camouflaged this one in bright cheer and with a fresh smell to counteract the abundance of cologne. I wanted to check out the arrangements and sneak a few stems for John's dining room table.

"At what point can we politely merge toward the flowers?" I asked as we checked our coats.

"To hide?"

His question was an assumption based on my past behavior. To enter a party was to plot a hiding strategy and remind him of my time limit—*Two hours, tops, or I'm walking home by myself.*

"I'm sorry," I blurted, taking his hand and turning toward him.

"For what?" he asked, brushing my hair off my cheek with his other hand.

"For being so ... I don't know. How would you describe my

250

attitude about these before?"

"Stubborn, snobby. No fun at all."

He started laughing. I joined him.

"How long have you been waiting to say that?"

John shook his head. "I'm not answering anymore questions."

"Yes, but is there anything else you want to say?"

"You look beautiful. And I love you."

The laughter left his eyes, and my smile faded. How long had he wanted to say this and how often had I sidestepped it? I could move past this one, too, with a smile or a quick kiss. But that was one-too-many wrongs.

"I am sorry," I said, my eyes searching his. "For how I was, for making everything a fight. For wasting our time when I could have …"

"When you could have what?"

"When I could have loved you without fighting."

"And now?"

I meant to say … something. But I ended up just giving a slight shake of my head and looking down. I took a deep breath and returned my eyes to his. Understanding had replaced the lightness of the moment, and he knew. John knew I didn't love him. Not like how he loved me.

If I were on the receiving end, I'd have turned around and left me standing there. Like I'd left Jackson. Like I'd left John before. But John's not me. He flashed me a smile before looking away and squeezed my hand before letting it go.

"You don't have to stay," he said.

"Will you let me?"

He nodded and put his hand on my back to lead me into the party. John reintroduced me to the lawyer standing nearest the door, his boss, Liam. I smiled as if a smile could redeem the past five minutes. I intended to play my part, and thanks to all the weddings, Fest—Jackson—I was capable enough to do it.

"It's so nice to see you again, Liam," I said, taking his hand. I didn't know him well. He was all business, and I wasn't his target audience for these gatherings. But he was respectful. And direct. I'd forgotten that part.

"We haven't seen you for awhile, Lu," he said.

I'm such a wallflower; it never occurred to me anyone would notice I wasn't around.

"I've just come back to New York. Is your wife with you? I'd like to say hello to her."

The words slipped out faster than my recall. I sure hoped the man had a wife.

He smiled and pointed to a small group of women standing with drinks across the room. "But before you go, let me just tell you what great work John is doing for the firm. We weren't sure where he'd go after his leave of absence this December, but we're glad he stayed. And glad you came back."

The rest of the party ran much the same—people I barely remembered welcoming me back, people praising John's work—and we left after a couple of hours and walked home in silence. When he didn't say anything after opening the front door and started to head to the bathroom to get ready for bed, I was afraid the night would end in silence.

"What are you going to do, John?" I asked.

My question landed like a weight between us. He walked toward me until he was a breath away.

"Are you sure?" he asked.

Sure? Sure of what? And when? When had I ever been sure? And if I had, when had it ever worked out? These were strange questions of relativity to be clanging around my mind, but John's question forced them to the forefront. I'd made a whole life of trying and failing, starting and quitting. Leaving. Even now, when everything was going well, when a man who loved me was asking me to be with him, I was about to start the cycle all over again. I wasn't sure.

But I was sure I couldn't stay with him. I nodded.

"Because if New York is the problem, we can leave. I know you miss your family. We can go back to Dunlap's Creek. Because for me ..."

He faltered, closing his eyes. And when he opened them, there were tears. He took my hands.

"For me, there's you. I want you. I don't care about the rest of this. I'd give it all up for you."

I dropped his hands and stepped back, finding it hard to breathe.

"I don't want you to give it all up for me."

"But I would."

"I couldn't make up for it. I can't be your everything. Don't you see?"

And that's when I saw.

"I can't save you, John."

We looked at each other from across the room. There was so much to say, but nothing that could be said right now. I went into the bedroom, closing the door behind me. I leaned my head against it.

"I can't even save myself," I whispered.

And that's when I knew.

CHAPTER 38

I am the bleeding woman.

I sank to the floor as I opened to the chapter in my Bible: Mark 5:24. *A large crowd followed and pressed around him. And a woman was there who had been subject to bleeding for twelve years ...*

I read. Into the night, I read, and at some point, I saw. I saw the crowds, and I saw myself, a woman with a lifetime of bleeding. I hadn't seen it that way before because I'd called the blood something else. But that night I saw Jesus. I saw that he was here; I saw that he was real. And all that he is brought the piercing red into sharp relief. My blood. Me. I was the problem. I always had been and always would be.

There are no words to describe the despair of this reality. Strength leaves, breathing stops. The only sound is weeping, the only sensation a free-fall into eternal nothing. It's why we see the blood as anything but, and trick ourselves into thinking this world offers permanent healing. It's the vanity of vanities. It's meaningless. But better to chase the wind because to stop and take account—to see we need salvation—is to look at our grave and feel the heavy hand of life pushing us there.

I felt the hand, steady and firm. I was helpless to stop it. I saw the black void of the grave. But then I looked up, and I saw him.

"Wait," I told the hand, and it stopped, but not by my command. I was in command of nothing. It stopped because of where I headed as I said it. Six feet of air separated me from my grave, but I walked on it like it was firm ground. My feet didn't sink because my focus was fixed on him. The crowds were thick, but I kept him in sight.

The walk was impossibly long, crushingly heavy and by the time I reached the edge of the crowd, I was crawling. With a hand followed by a knee, I worked my way through the gaps.

If I can touch his cloak. If I can get to him, I'll be healed.

I broke through the crowd, bleeding and broken. His back was to me, and I wanted to go round, but I couldn't go any farther. So I reached out my arm and stretched my hand to touch his hem with my finger. Just my finger. Just his hem. That was all I needed.

I'll never forget the moment Jesus turned. Seeing him see me is to know he'd been me ... bleeding and broken for me. Because he loved me. That love gathered me, embraced me. I would have happily given over to it carrying me off, but instead found myself facing the man I'd been prostate in front of a moment before. Back on my feet and fully healed.

It was a miracle ... a miracle I had no rights to. I didn't deserve it; I didn't earn it. I fell again at Jesus' feet, trembling, telling him everything. The whole truth of it all. Repenting.

Daughter ...

His voice brought me back to standing like a hand to rescue. He was being more than kind. He was telling me I had a new status. One I could stand in. A daughter of God.

Your faith has healed you. Go in peace and be freed from your suffering.

My chase was done.

And I could go home.

CHAPTER 39

I packed at dawn.

I'd spent the night on the floor next to John's bed reading my Bible. I'd been raised in these words, but I'd never understood them. One night's reading didn't get me much farther along, but I could see how God had always been speaking to me—and not just through the Bible, but also through people and circumstance. Through my quiet moments. *Listen when your grandma talks to you, Louisa. Her words are mine. If you answer your father's question honestly, you'll see me. You don't need that job. You don't need that man. There's a reason you're restless.*

God was everywhere. I reread Ecclesiastes and the first five chapters of Mark, underlining and circling so much it might have been better to underline what wasn't striking me. Then my Bible wouldn't look like my nieces had gotten ahold of it. After I finished those books, I started flipping at random, landing at whatever words struck my fancy. I underlined those, too.

I cried, I laughed, and whispered my thoughts as I filled the margins with notes. I prayed—tentatively at first—but as the night went on, I saw more of God and more of me in this book. There wasn't anything about me he didn't know.

Around six o'clock I realized I'd never changed out of my dress. I thought about showering, but I had a long day ahead. A swipe of deodorant would have to suffice. I put on black knit pants, a gray T-shirt, and sneakers. I pulled my hair into a loose ponytail, washed my face, brushed my teeth and returned my clothes to my suitcases.

It didn't take long. I hadn't brought much, and other than my new dress, I hadn't added anything.

I made the bed. It was early, six thirty. But it was time.

John was asleep when I opened the bedroom door, and I went to him, kneeling close to steal a look. He looked peaceful, like last night hadn't happened.

I reached for John's hand. We'd never been much for holding hands. I wish we had, my hand felt nice in his. I squeezed it, and John woke up, the surprise of my presence lighting up his blue eyes before full consciousness took over and reminded him of the present. Of us.

He sat up and rubbed his face before looking around. His eyes landed on the suitcases.

"You've packed."

I nodded. "Can I make you coffee before I go?"

"You finally learned how to use the espresso machine?"

"No. And that's the real problem with this arrangement," I said, heading into the kitchen and taking out the French press.

"Can I ask you something?" he asked.

I started the water to boil and turned around to give him my full attention.

"You can ask me anything."

He hesitated and didn't speak until I filled the press with coffee and water to steep.

"Are you going home?"

"Yes."

"To be with him?"

"No."

I could have left it there, but that wasn't the whole answer, and maybe John didn't need the whole answer, but I needed to say it.

"He's with someone else."

"But if he wasn't?" John pressed.

If Jackson wasn't with someone else ... what a thought. Why hadn't he waited? The sorrow of it landed and spread; I knew it would be there awhile. I wanted Jackson, but I didn't need him. I shrugged and smiled at John—a genuine smile.

"But he is."

We drank our coffee together in silence. For my part, there was a lot to say, but I didn't know how to say it. And John had said everything.

"I'm going to take this," I said, clutching his law school mug to my chest when I finished.

"Why don't you take the French press, too? I don't use it."

That would make the second time I'd cap a New York departure with a kitchen appliance, which is a lot for a girl who doesn't cook. But I packed both in my suitcase before turning to John. I wanted to hug him but shifted my weight from one foot to the other.

In the end, he made the decision by enfolding me. His embrace took my breath away, not so much from its strength. But from its intensity.

You can't get away from that without crying, and he held me fast while we both sobbed. For what had been. For what couldn't be. Because it was our time to cry. And my time to apologize on repeat.

Eventually I shut up, eventually we stopped, and John released me.

"Are you going to be okay to drive?"

It was also that time. To uproot and drive home. But not by my hand this time.

I smiled and nodded at John. "I'm okay."

And after another hug and kiss on the cheek, I left to make the same return journey to home without a clue as to the next step.

My story ended as it began. Except not at all. It was the beginning.

THAT SUNDAY MORNING

The last time I'd walked into this church was Grandma Pat's funeral. The pain of the day blurred recall, but knowing me, I probably left resolved never to return.

Which is why God was laughing at me right now. I had little time to join in. The music started as I took my seat next to my family. Performance anxiety hit as the congregation started singing. I wanted to sing with everyone, even lift my arms like some, but my desires outpaced my comfort.

So I closed my eyes—a handy, childhood trick. If I couldn't see them, they couldn't see me. The darkness drove away the crowd, and my breathing slowed. I could feel the sweat from my palms receding as I clasped them to anchor me to this space. *Stay here, be here.*

The lyrics from the song overtook my chant. I smiled. I knew this song, an old hymn burnt into memory from Sunday school. Maybe I couldn't sing it now, but I whispered the words as my mind reclaimed them.

My God, my portion, and my love,
My everlasting All,
I've none but thee in heaven above,

The hymn moved to another and another—all unknown—but my mind stayed here; my eyes, closed. God knew. He knew me as I'd been and He knew me now. He also knew what would happen next, and I think that's what gave me courage to open my eyes and take a seat as Jackson took the stage.

My memory hadn't failed me. I hadn't forgotten a single detail of how he looked—his height, the brown of his hair, the green of his eyes—but I'd forgotten how the sight of him made me feel. Caught with no need to turn with the rest of the world unless it somehow brought me closer to him.

Jackson didn't know I was here, so this would be the only time I could look at him without the possibility of my being here in his mind. I took notes from a sermon my mind couldn't focus on because it was more preoccupied with the sound of the man's voice than the truth of what he said.

But all this stopped when his eyes landed on mine. He'd been wrapping up his sermon, but he stopped when he saw me. It was a few seconds of silence, broken by a cough from somewhere to my left, but enough for me to hold my breath.

Jackson finished a minute later, and I stood for the last song like the good little church girl I now was. I kept my eyes open this time and looked over to Gracie as soon as the song ended and church was over.

What do I do now? I silently asked.

She looked toward Jackson and back at me.

I have no idea, the shrug of her shoulders said.

I made myself plain. *There?* I pointed the exit. *Or there?* I pointed to the stage.

She shrugged again, and I grabbed my purse, intending to follow my family out, but Nana Bea put her hand on my arm.

"Retreat now, and you'll keep retreating."

And so I headed forward, wondering if Jackson would meet me halfway.

Dear Reader,

One of my favorite memories about writing this book was hosting the first *Lu*. Book Club. I gave an early draft to a few a friends and bribed them with BLTs and adult beverages on a screened porch. I shared the book to see whether it was something anyone would want to read, but somewhere in the three hours of that summer evening, I realized something else. *Lu*. was a book women could talk about.

I wrote *Lu*. to share a story of one woman's search for God. I hope her story spoke to you, but I also hope that as you read it, another woman – friend, sister, neighbor, coworker – came to mind. If this happened, why not give your copy to her and set up a time in some pretty place with some tasty food to talk about it?

And if several women came to mind, host your own *Lu*. Book Club! Interested but don't know how to go about it? Think of it like making conversation around your dinner table, except the dinner part is optional. Invite all those girls who came to mind, give yourselves plenty of time to finish the book, and tell everyone to come prepared to chat. I've included this Discussion Guide to lead you through Lu's story, but it's only my suggestion. One of the questions is enough to get your group talking, and it'd be difficult to get through it all in an hour. The goal is for your group to discuss this book as naturally and honestly as you'd discuss anything else, so let the conversation flow to where it needs.

And feel free to Skype me in as a bonus at the end! I'm happy to share all the behind-the-scenes writing and inspiration for this story and answer your questions. Just go to the Contact page on my site, www.bethtroy.com, to schedule a time.

Thanks for reading!
Beth Troy

LU. DISCUSSION GUIDE

1. The book opens with Lu quitting everything in her life to head back home. Why did she do this?
   - Have you or do you know of anyone who has had a similar experience?
   - How does this help you to better understand Lu when she says, *All the stories have been written, including mine?*
2. The first several chapters introduce us to Lu's family. How would you describe them in relation to Lu? What motivates their intervention in her life? Do you think their plans for her are ultimately helpful?
   - The interactions between Lu and her family were inspired by my relationship with my grandmothers (which I've blogged about at bethtroy.com). Did any of these characters remind you of people who have impacted your life?
3. In Chapter 4, Lu meets Jackson, and in Chapter 7, Grandma Pat tries to set them up. How would you describe their relationship? How is it different from her relationship with John?
4. In Chapter 6, Lu goes to church at Jackson's request. Why does she agree, given her views on faith at this point? What happens over the next several chapters to make her start thinking differently?
5. Have you ever read Ecclesiastes? Do the ideas the characters have in Chapters 6-10 about Ecclesiastes resonate with disappointment you might have experienced?
6. In Chapters 11-21, Lu begins to slowly settle into her family, work, and life in Dunlap's Creek. But what is keeping her from fully settling into her "second chance?"
7. In Chapter 22, Lu understands faith is a choice and maybe even a choice she wants to make. What stops her?
   - Are you or is there someone in your life who is struggling similarly?
8. Why does Lu return to New York City with John at the end of Chapter 25? Why doesn't Jackson ask her to stay

with him? What do you think about this?

9. In some ways, quitting her life and running to another is Lu's pattern. But from Chapters 26-30, how is the Lu who returns to New York City different than the Lu who left?

10. What do we also learn about John in these chapters and their former relationship? Is there hope for a second chance for them?

11. From Lu's discussions with Pastor Eddy and John in Chapters 31-35, how have her questions about faith changed? What is stopping her from claiming a choice that she now sees as valid?
   - Have you ever experienced a similar disconnect between your mind and heart?

12. Describe the events of Lu's final night in New York in Chapters 36-38. What ultimately led her to admitting that she couldn't save herself? How would you describe the transformation she undergoes as she sees herself as the bleeding woman from Mark 5?

13. If you've experienced something similar, would you share it with the group?

14. What is Lu giving up in leaving New York? What is she gaining? What do you hope for her?

For the fun of it:
- Favorite character?
- Favorite scene?
- What made you laugh?
- What got you thinking?
- How much do you want to eat pierogies right now?
- Team Jackson or Team John?
- Team Dunlap's Creek or Team New York City?
- What would you like to see more of in Lu: Book 2? Tell me about it at www.bethtroy.com!
- Who would you like to give this book to? Do it!

ACKNOWLEDGMENTS

I wasn't too far into writing this book when I realized the insufficiency of my lone name on the front cover. Following is not a mindless list of thank-yous, but the people who inspired and encouraged me to write this book.

First, my grandmas: Virginia Stella Kowalczyk Barovian and Norma Arlene Frost Sawyer. They, more than anyone, served as the inspiration for the main characters. Neither is alive now to read this, but I know how they'd do it. Grandma B would read it in one sitting, and then tell me everything I did wrong. Grandmother Sawyer would flip through it, pronounce it lovely, and never get around to reading it. Their forthrightness, intelligence, and loyalty were my normal growing up, but they were very special women— for their time and for me. I think about them every day.

Next, my parents—Pam and Bernie Barovian. You fed me with books, and you gave me time and space to breathe them in and live them out. So many parents redirect their kid's dreams to the plausible and hireable. Thank you for never limiting my dream to write.

The seeds for writing stories as only I can tell them were planted in 9th Grade English by Jim Michels. You taught me the rules, and you taught me how to break them. You taught me how to set my own bar of satisfaction so that I'd never submit something I wasn't first pleased to read. Thank you for making it about the work and for teaching me how to work well.

This book wouldn't exist without Laura Smith. I was a writing mess when we first met, and over a three-year period, you pieced me back together with constant encouragement. You are my opposite, and I love everything about you that is different from me. It'd take another book to enumerate all you did to make this one happen, but you know. Thank you for all of it … even that time I thought I was finished, and you told me I was five chapters from finished.

My early readers: Pam Barovian, Jeni Panhorst, Gail Troy, Brenda Homan, Joy Becker, Maggie Cooper, Michelle Carr, Anne Lynn Minnick, and Stacy Clayton. I put you in a tough spot, asking you to read my book and give me "honest" feedback. Thank you for reading it! Thank you for affirming it read like a book, and thank you for telling me how it could read like a better one.

A highlight of my week is Thursday night when the women of my small church in my small town get together for Bible study. You girls are where it's at: smart, honest, funny, faithful, compassionate. If a measure of a women is by who she hangs with, well then … Thank you for your support, prayer, and follow-up in the time it took to get this book out of my head and on paper. Knowing you'd ask me about its progress every week ensured I actually made some.

My editor, Stephen Parolini. We've never met, but I really, really, really want to meet you. I kinda, sorta despaired at ever finding an editor, and then I found you, and then you kicked my butt. What a little book-writing boot camp you put me through to turn this book from "fine" to "good." Consider me your evangelist. And my copy editor, Lora Schrock, for removing all those embarrassing errors.

And now for the final lap.

God. You saved me, and you keep at it. You gave me a dream to write and the skills to get it done. When I misappropriated both to go my own way, you shelved them and grew me up until I could handle them rightly. This book is not about me, but it has everything to do with you and me. Thank you for following me when I went away. Thank you for bringing me back, and giving this one back to me. "He who calls you is faithful; he will surely do it" (1 Thessalonians 5:24, ESV). I finally know what it means to work for you. You are my redeemer.

My family—Matt, Jesse, Ezra, and Tommy. Hanging out in imaginary land is a great way to pass the day, but real life with you is my favorite story.

ABOUT THE AUTHOR

I'm Beth Troy, and this is my first book. I live in the Midwest with my husband and three boys, and you can read more about my writing and life on my blog at www.bethtroy.com.